Short story writer and novelist Owen Marshall has written, or edited, twenty-one books to date. Awards for his fiction include the PEN Lillian Ida Smith Award twice, the *Evening Standard* Short Story Prize, the American Express Short Story Award, the New Zealand Literary Fund Scholarship in Letters, Fellowships at the universities of Canterbury and Otago, and the Katherine Mansfield Memorial Fellowship in Menton, France. He received the ONZM for services to Literature in the New Zealand New Year Honours, 2000, and in 2002 the University of Canterbury awarded him the honorary degree of Doctor of Letters. His novel *Harlequin Rex* won the Montana New Zealand Book Awards Deutz Medal for Fiction in 2000, and in 2006 his short-story collection *Watch of Gryphons* was shortlisted for the same prize.

Owen Marshall was born in 1941, has spent almost all his life in South Island towns, and has an affinity with provincial New Zealand.

DRYBREAD

OWEN MARSHALL

VINTAGE

National Library of New Zealand Cataloguing-in-Publication Data

Marshall, Owen, 1941-
Drybread / Owen Marshall.
ISBN 978-186941-919-6
I. Title.
NZ823.2–dc 22

A VINTAGE BOOK
published by
Random House New Zealand
18 Poland Road, Glenfield, Auckland, New Zealand
www.randomhouse.co.nz

Random House International
Random House
20 Vauxhall Bridge Road
London, SW1V 2SA
United Kingdom

Random House Australia (Pty) Ltd
20 Alfred Street, Milsons Point, Sydney,
New South Wales 2061, Australia

Random House South Africa Pty Ltd
Isle of Houghton
Corner Boundary Road and Carse O'Gowrie
Houghton 2198, South Africa

Random House Publishers India Private Ltd
301 World Trade Tower, Hotel Intercontinental Grand Complex,
Barakhamba Lane, New Delhi 110 001, India

First published 2007, reprinted 2007 (twice)

ISBN 978 1 86941 919 6

Design: Elin Bruhn Termannsen
Cover photographs: Matthew Trbuhovic
Cover design: Matthew Trbuhovic, Third Eye Design
Printed in Australia by Griffin Press

For William, Lydia and Sophie

1

The Maniototo is burnt country in summer, and the bare, brown expanse of it has a subdued shimmer. Theo wished he'd brought dark glasses. Even with the air conditioning on, he could feel the sun's heat on his arms. The hills had no bush, and lay like a gargantuan, crumpled blanket, wheat coloured and with the shadows sharply defined, and that shimmer of heat at the base.

Near Drybread are three baches in a gully running back into the Dunstan Range. Not the easiest place to find. A note had been left for Theo at the paper which ended, 'Don't say anything and come alone.' It wasn't as mysterious as it sounded. He was covering a story about a woman from Sacramento, Penny Maine-King, who had fled back to New Zealand with her child in defiance of a Californian court order that awarded custody to her estranged husband. Now she was faced with an arrest and a warrant for the return of the child issued by the Family Court.

Such cases had become quite common, but the editor and chief reporter expected added interest because the couple had been in one of those American television reality shows. They'd been voted out early in the series, but even such C grade celebrity was enough to excite a good many readers. The barrenness of some people's lives is appalling. Theo's friend Nicholas said two-thirds of the paper's readers could be gassed and they'd never be missed.

The chief reporter, Anna, hoped to link the pair's problems with the pressures of the programme. 'See if we can get the two stories to come together,' she said. 'They'll feed off each other: the whole television thing and then the marriage collapsing because of the stress, and she doing a runner back here with the cute kid. And originally she's a Kiwi, you know.'

Theo couldn't see the fascination of it, and in fact the television angle had proved something of a fizzer, but it was the sort of investigative story senior journalists are expected to tackle. It protected him, too, from humdrum rounds of local politics, agriculture or geriatric health. And the husband was rich, at least by New Zealand standards. Anna said people like to read about the rich being in the shit. The greater the fall, the more enjoyable the contemplation of it by those who are lowly themselves.

Penny Maine-King's directions took him into the Manuherikia Valley and finally to that isolated gully: a cottage, the original part of which was sod, and the addition grey, unpainted wood. It was half hidden from the road by an overgrown macrocarpa hedge, the green defiantly incongruous amid the drought. There was no lawn, no garden, no fence to complete the boundary the great hedge pronounced, no gate even, and unseen sheep had grazed to the small concrete front step, and shat in the shade the house made in the everlasting afternoons. A water tank was fed from the roof. The long-drop dunny was twenty metres or so from the house, and a little higher on the slope. A blue hatchback was parked behind the hedge, and a red trike lay on its side in the yellow grass. So dry was the dirt that Theo could see cracks like lightning strikes, as if the ground had given up the ghost.

The other two cottages were hundreds of metres away, equally humble, weathered and pegged into the landscape by a succession of extreme winters and summers. They had no garages, and no other cars were parked beside them. Theo had arrived at the unglamorous part of Central Otago: far from lakes, or ski fields. What could you do here in the gold miners' exhausted gully, except shoot rabbits, wander the bare hills, or shut yourself up in one of the three coffin baches?

Theo could see into the house through the wooden frame window beside the door. In its modest length the room went through the transition from kitchen, dining room to lounge. The bench, sink and woodburning stove at the far end, the wooden table and two chairs in the centre, and then a leather sofa and a single, soft chair in front of a schist stone fireplace. A barefoot boy of two or three lay asleep on the sofa, and a woman sat in the big chair with her head back and eyes closed. The boy had nothing on above the waist: his chest was smooth and pale, and there were bracelets of sunburn on his upper arms. The woman wore yellow shorts, a white top, and her long throat was exposed as she rested, or slept. Penny Maine-King.

For a moment Theo stood there, conscious of the sun's heat on his back, like an iron on the material of his shirt, and aware of the passing intimacy possible with strangers. The boy's nipples were barely more than smudges on his skin, and the mother's thighs were smooth, undimpled. On the worn, uneven carpet beside the sofa was a plate with a rim of crusts. So much exact, external detail, so much vulnerability, yet he knew only the public facts of the experience that had brought them to the place and their predicament. It's what he had become accustomed to in his work: the sudden, close professional focus on people, the establishment of a rapport that enabled the scrutiny of some part of their life, and then the disengagement.

Theo moved so as not to be visible at the window when his knock roused Penny. She came quickly to the door and she seemed not at all drowsy. 'You found the place okay?' she shook hands and led him down the passage, just a few paces, and out of a back door directly aligned with the front one. 'Do you mind sitting out here for a while?' she said, having already decided the matter by her movement. 'My boy's sleeping in the main room. It's cooler there. The sod walls keep the heat out.' A wooden form with a back abutted the side of the house by the door, and a kitchen chair stood close to it in the short, dry grass. The shade on that side of the house reached just a few metres up the slope.

'A good solid seat,' he said.

'It's a pew from the old Anglican church at Dunlathie. The church was sold to make a private house, and my mother bought some of the seats. She took two for the farmhouse verandah and this one ended up here. You can see the edges have polished up from the grease in the wool where the sheep have a good rub against it.'

'So this is where you come from originally?' He sat on the old church pew in the gully, and wondered how Penny Maine-King had got all the way to Sacramento and crap television – and back again.

'My parents farmed not far away, and my father bought this place cheaply for any single worker we had from time to time. It's my inheritance, you might say.' The dry tone, and the slightest grimace of a smile, mocked what she said. 'Anyway, I'll get you a beer and we can get down to business. No fridge here, I'm afraid.'

'That's okay,' Theo said.

So they sat on the shady side of the old place, still hot enough, she on the kitchen chair, he on the church pew with its weathered surfaces and sheep-oiled leading edges, and she told Theo what she hoped for from him. There was a single, desiccated plum tree on the slope, and a pair of paradise duck, each distinct in the plumage of its gender, flew twice up and down the gully, giving their discordant cries. There was the faintest smell of dry sheep shit, gorse and isolation in the drowsy air. Theo remembered the healthier and larger plum tree behind the garage of the place he'd lived in when married. The mind has a predilection for cross-referencing which takes no account of comfort.

Penny said she had liked his first article, thought it fair, and that she was willing to give him more of the personal story as long as her whereabouts remained secret. What she wanted was sympathetic publicity that would help her lawyer get a stay of the warrant for the return of the child. She needed time to work out something with the boy's father. 'I don't give a stuff what happens to me,' she said, 'but Ben's going to have the start he deserves.'

Theo wasn't sure how he felt about her. She was completely open about them making use of each other, and though he understood that, there was a hardness in it too. His response to her appearance was ambivalent as well. There was little indication of her breasts beneath the white top: she wore no make-up and her hair was roughly pulled back into a makeshift stub of a pony-tail. Her face had a determinedly scrubbed, plain look. Only her teeth, even and very white, and her smooth legs, hinted at a Californian concern with glamour. She looked him in the eyes as she talked, with that unsmiling, no bullshit expression direct women have.

'Once the story builds there'll be all sorts of people out to find you, some waving money,' Theo told her. 'And I don't know about the legal situation. Maybe I can be forced to say where you are. I'll have to find out all that before I can make any promises.'

'I can put you in touch with my lawyer,' said Penny. 'Anyway, the sympathy should always be with the mother and child, don't you think?'

'It's the law you've got to deal with, though. If the sympathy is for mother and child, why didn't you get a better shake from the American court on custody, instead of just access?'

She sat forward on the kitchen chair in her urgency to explain the deficiencies of the Californian judiciary, her inability any longer to afford lawyers' fees in the States. There was the slightest sheen of sweat high on her forehead, where her hair was pulled back. She was talking about her husband's use of his money against her when the boy appeared at the doorway, still dulled with sleep. Giving Theo only a glance, he walked over the dry grass to his mother, and she took him onto her lap. Penny didn't stop talking, or make any introduction of the boy, but an arm held him, while her other hand moved fondly and absently over him, smoothing his soft hair, running along his bare shoulder and midriff, flexing his sturdy legs. It seemed a reassurance as much for her as for the child, this establishment by contour of the texture and solidity of her son. This familiarity with his physical presence. 'I'm using my mother's maiden name here,' she said. 'Penny Kayes. People won't make the connection, and I married overseas, but don't include any of that in the paper.'

'You know you can't hide out for long. These things get too messy.'

'Christ, you don't have to tell me that. This has been going on for weeks, here and in California. You think I want to be stuck away in a shack without power and phone? Hello! What I want from you is the right publicity and I'll give you enough stuff to make a good story.'

'Fair enough. I'll do what I can,' he said.

'I'm not even so much interested in money, though I need it,' said Penny. Her son was leaning back on her, wide awake. He looked at Theo steadily, his eyes blue in a face devoid of expression.

'We don't pay, but we reach a hell of a lot of people.'

'Okay then, fair enough,' said Penny. 'Do you want something to eat?'

'No thanks. I better get back to Christchurch asap.'

'I'll give you the lawyer's number, and an email address I can access when I go into Alex. And if you give me your number I can ring you from there if necessary.'

'Haven't you got a cellphone?' asked Theo. 'Wouldn't that be simpler?'

'We're pretty much out of range up here,' Penny said.

He went through some of the questions he'd listed for himself, getting stuff about American life, American marriage and American separation. Something, too, about a Kiwi woman coming back to get a fair deal in her own country, and finding herself on the run. Before leaving he walked up the slope to the wooden long-drop, but although Penny and her son were still sitting outside, he didn't go into the old dunny, just stepped behind it and had a piss into the flattened grass and bare ground where sheep had been resting out of the sun. The ground was so dry that his urine rolled like marbles in the dust. He liked the sense of being in the open, yet with complete privacy. He could see up the slope to a ridgeline that ran back into the steep hills. It reminded him of his boyhood in the hills of North Canterbury, and of going out to the farms with his father, who'd owned stock trucks. Something about quiet land attracted him strongly: something about looking out and seeing natural country with no people there at all. He realised there was vanity in that, an unacknowledged desire for human uniqueness within the landscape.

Afterwards Penny and her son walked from the house to the car with Theo. Penny shook hands for the second time that day, and she said to the little boy, 'Say goodbye to Theo.' It was the first time she'd used his name.

'What's his name?' Theo asked. He should have been able to remember: he'd used it in the article and she'd mentioned it earlier in the day.

'What's your name?' she said, using the boy as intermediary again.

'Ben,' the child replied.

'Well, goodbye, Ben,' Theo said.

He took the Dansey's Pass route on the way home. It was a gravel road stretch, but if you pushed on you saved time by not going through Palmerston and Oamaru. Once he reached the main coast road, which he knew well, he could drive, and think of other things. The Maine-King story was a good one, especially if Penny remained hidden. Theo needed to understand the legal situation though, not just for accurate coverage, but to protect himself. Penny Maine-King could look after herself well enough, it seemed to him: it was the boy he felt for. Poor little bugger bounced from place to place and parent to parent, and having no comprehension of the reasons for it. When Penny had gone inside to get her email address, she'd left Ben sitting on the kitchen chair. No appropriate small talk occurred to Theo. He had no kids. Ben said nothing, and sat with the dunny and the plum tree on the slope behind him, and tried to pretend he was alone and at ease by lifting his arms up and down and making soft, aeroplane noises. Poor little bugger. Penny Maine-King's email address was at paradise.net.nz. 'Yeah, tell me about it,' she said, and they had parted on that irony.

As Theo drove north he had an image of sex with Penny Maine-King on the church pew. It came without conscious inclination. The irreligious incongruity was the attraction perhaps, rather than her yellow shorts, perfect teeth or the untidy pony-tail. His friend Nicholas held that if a woman succumbs in imagination, it's a sign of her inclination. The subconscious is open to such vibes, he said. But then, Nicholas was a divorced man like Theo himself, and wistful in matters of the heart, and groin.

2

Because Penny Maine-King's New Zealand lawyer was American, Theo assumed there was some connection between his origin and the years Penny had spent in California. 'Pure coincidence,' Zack Heywood told him. 'Absolutely. Mrs Maine-King came to me because the firm has experience in custody cases.'

'But it must make it easier to get a handle on what's happened at the American end?'

'Sure, sure. I worked in Richmond, Virginia, however, which is a long way from California. Family law varies dramatically from one state to another. Everything does, in fact. There's not the uniform jurisprudence you have here. It sure makes a difference what state you're in when it comes to what's against the law, and what sort of walloping you get if you're found guilty.'

Theo didn't ask how a Virginian lawyer ended up in

Christchurch, but, accustomed to the curiosity of others, Zack Heywood provided a quick resumé anyway. It was much what you would guess – a Kiwi girl on her big OE had been quite enough to bring Zack to a country he'd barely heard of, and to an income considerably reduced.

Lawyers are unpopular as a breed, and the generalisation suited most of the individuals Theo had met. He'd come to Penny's lawyer expecting to find him greedy, conceited and assured – and found him able, good-natured and assured. He was well groomed and well dressed too, and Theo was conscious of his own scuffed, brown shoes and trousers that pouched a little at the knees. There were sharp creases on Zack's pink shirt, freshly ironed perhaps, or straight from the box.

'I don't want to know where Mrs Maine-King is,' Zack said. 'I don't want to know if you know where she is. She's asked me to work with you and I'll do all I can.' He didn't have that much of an accent and didn't look much like an American, being small, olive-skinned and quite finely built. Maybe there were things of interest in that long Virginian past.

Zack told Theo there were precedents for getting a stay in execution of a warrant, and then a rehearing, if the Family Court felt circumstances had materially changed. There would need to be some sign of compromise from both sides, though, he said; a reasonable chance of the parties working together. What they had to do was provide substantial reason for a rehearing. 'Are you in touch with Penny's husband?' Theo asked.

'Through his attorney, yes,' said Zack.

Theo told him Penny thought she'd have a better chance if she got sympathetic publicity: once she was back overseas, or if the boy were taken away, she reckoned she'd get done. Zack said the husband was pushing things vigorously from the States, and that the courts and police here had become quite active in custody disputes originating overseas. There were international agreements, he said, specifically the Hague Convention, and of course the father's anxiety to be considered.

Theo felt a passing sense of guilt that the lawyer was more aware of the diffuse emotional impact than he was himself. But then again he was in it for the story wasn't he, irrespective of where the rights and wrongs lay. He hadn't warmed especially to Penny, yet it suited him to support her.

'Have you known Penny Maine-King long?' Zack asked.

'No, I've just been covering the story really.'

'Having public opinion on her side is a plus for sure, but I'd go easy on making the Family Court a target if I were you. Doesn't pay to alienate those making the decisions.'

'Fair enough,' Theo said.

'Anything I can help with I will. These cases have so much unhappiness.'

'I've got a few things you could help me with, but we need to clear up who's paying for your time first, I suppose. You know what papers are like. My editor will allow bugger all for legal consultation.'

'I think at this stage we just do what's necessary in the best interest of Mrs Maine-King,' Zack said. It had the ring of sentiments expressed by comfortable, professional people to whom money flows naturally, as if downhill.

'But someone always pays in the end, don't they.' Theo was thinking of his own divorce, but the consequent surge of sadness, guilt, anger even, had little to do with fees.

'If you want me to be mercenary, I can say that Erskine Maine-King is very well set up, and whatever the matrimonial outcome his wife will have a significant share.' Theo was glad for Penny that at least there was money somewhere. 'He's loaded,' said Zack Heywood, with sudden, colloquial indiscretion. 'But of course that, too, becomes a bargaining chip and leverage to get what he wants.'

They talked for another few minutes, and Theo made notes. Zack was easy to like, and they agreed on how best to co-operate for Penny's benefit. Yet Theo felt how close to indecency was discussion by strangers of the relationship of a husband, a wife and a child. He knew the sense of bewildered violation when things most personal were bandied about with routine matter-of-factness by people who understood nothing of the marriage they dissected. Now it was Penny and Erskine Maine-King's turn, and a Kiwi newspaperman and a lawyer from Virginia sat in a Christchurch office with a view of a one-block grass square, Easter bunned with crossed asphalt walking paths, and talked of infidelity, incompatibility and unreasonable expectations; applied their complacent rationality to things so intimate at inception that neither marriage partner ever imagined they could go beyond their own knowledge.

As he returned to work, Theo resolved that not everything would appear in the articles. Enough in his view for a balanced understanding, the arousal of sympathy, but stopping short of the titillation in which the magazines specialised. Both the editor and the chief reporter were keen on the story being kept alive. 'Pump it up, pump it up,' said the editor, shoving clumps of paper about on his desk in a minor agitation of journalistic enthusiasm. 'It's good that she's gone to earth somewhere in the South Island, and that she's talking exclusively to us.' It was always 'us' in such circumstances. 'How does she get in touch? Do you go somewhere?'

'No, she sends a note, or phones,' Theo said. It was a half lie.

'Well, pump it up as long as we don't incur any legal difficulties, or significant expense. She's not asking for money, is she?' Costs were a constant concern. His eyebrows fluctuated in apprehension when he considered any chance of financial liability. 'Is she?' The editor's abilities were almost certainly the equal of Zack Heywood's, but journalism lacks the strong self-regulatory codes that provide lawyers with the confidence of affluence.

Theo reassured his boss, but what was Penny asking for? Theo assumed she wanted to have her child to herself, to protect him, to keep him from a man she was no longer in love with. But what qualities, apart from being unlovable after once being lovable, made Erskine Maine-King unfit to have access to his only child? When Stella and Theo divorced, they had comforted themselves with the thought there were no others close to be hurt. No kids to go through the uncomprehending misery of the break-up, no subtle continuation of warfare waged through the next generation, no complication if either partner found someone else – as Stella had.

Theo knew the editor was still talking – he recognised the rise and fall of heavy, almost ginger eyebrows, the self-affirming nodding, the extension occasionally of his left palm uppermost, as if like a conjuror he wished to show he had nothing to hide – but he heard nothing his superior said. The backdrop of the untidy office was replaced by a view of bare hills in perfect perspective. Where had they come from, those dry hills? Were they the foothills of his North Canterbury boyhood, or were they the steep slopes he'd seen behind Drybread as he drove to the gully where Penny Maine-King was holed up?

'Anyway,' said the editor, breaking through suddenly again, and proffering another palm against trickery, 'you'll know how to go about it in the best way. I'm certain of that.'

'Okay, sure, thanks,' said Theo.

3

A plain clothes detective sought Theo out not long after his second article. He came to the newspaper, and Anna suggested her office for the interview. 'Better than sitting at your desk in the open reporters' room,' she said to Theo. 'And I can stay if you like. I can be your sort of whanau representative.'

'Why not.' The gesture was well meant enough, even if motivated by curiosity, and concern for the paper's interests.

The detective was young, blond and of only middling height. What happened to the old rule of having big guys in the police? Maybe brains were becoming more of a factor in selection; maybe there were just fewer to choose from. Anna stayed at her desk, and Paul Talleon, the detective, and Theo sat together on the other side. The interview was humdrum rather than inquisitorial. The detective retold what they all knew: that there was a court warrant for the child to be sent back to California, and that if journalists, or anybody else, connived in her evasion they could be committing an offence.

'I'm just reporting the story from her point of view,' Theo told him. 'I think she just wants more time to find out what will happen if she goes back.'

'Do you know where she's staying?' asked the detective.

'No,' Theo lied.

'What's the method of contact then?'

'She rings me, or sends a note here.'

'If you know where she is, you're obliged to tell us. You realise that?'

'As a journalist I have to protect my contacts.'

'That's right,' said Anna firmly. 'That's journalistic ethics.'

'Not the law, though,' said the short detective mildly. 'Full co-operation is expected.'

'I'll bear it in mind,' Theo said, 'but actually on the specific matter of this confidentiality the law's ambiguous.' He had done some checking of his own with Zack Heywood.

'We're always aware of our obligations to all parties in such a sensitive and difficult issue,' said Anna.

She was a very tall, rangy woman, and the competitiveness she had shown as a provincial netball player had carried over into her journalistic ambitions. The editor had several times praised her team ethic to Theo, perhaps as a spur to his cultivation of the same virtue. 'We'd like you to feel free to keep in touch, Paul,' she said. 'We'd appreciate word of any developments at your end so that our reporting is balanced.' Her eyebrows were so fair as to be invisible, and her whole face had a peeled look – pale lipstick was her only make-up. She wore flat, black shoes on her competent feet. Rumour among the reporters claimed that she'd had a torrid affair with a city councillor when her round was local bodies, but the humour may well have originated from professional jealousy, and Theo couldn't imagine her inquisitive face buried long in a pillow.

He went down in the lift to street level with the detective. It gave him the chance to ask some questions without Anna's presence. How vigorously were the police looking for Penny? What did he know about her husband in California? What information had been before the court there? 'I don't think there are any real baddies in this case,' was Paul Talleon's final comment, 'but the law's the law, isn't it?'

On his way back to his desk Theo poked his head into Anna's office and thanked her for the help. 'Good story. Stick with it,' she said, having clearly enjoyed the mild joust with the detective.

'You think I should pump it up?' he said. Anna grinned, but was too loyal to make a comment.

As a senior journalist, Theo had one of the two best desks in the large reporters' room – at the window, with a view of a tin can alley and the backs of a beauty parlour and a pet shop. He sat down at the other desk, which belonged to Nicholas, who had the largely nominal title of deputy chief reporter.

'So when do you go to prison?' Nicholas said.

'When Anna ceases to protect me from the police.'

'Have you been to see this Maine-King woman again?'

'No,' Theo said.

'What's she like?'

'Small tits, assertive, preoccupied with herself and the kid as you'd expect.'

'Why would you expect her to have small tits?' said Nicholas.

'Actually she does have bloody nice legs.'

'Just don't end up screwing her,' said Nicholas. 'You screw her and you're done for, drawn into the whole mess – you become some man she can take it all out on. Screwing is how women attach themselves and create obligation.'

'It's wonderful the way you find the romantic element in everything, Nick,' Theo told him.

At his own desk Theo checked emails. Most were spam from such computer-generated creations as Warbles P. Burents, Judith Fhlth, Terrell Sozlly, Tib Uimeuzzc and Guilermo Shinholster. Two messages related to a story he was doing on the possibility of a new wave of boat people from Indonesia and the Philippines, so he settled to do some work on that. The Maine-King custody matter could peter out just as quickly as it had arisen. It didn't pay, he knew, to have any role other than commentator: the real parties would act quite according to their interests.

What disturbed Theo most, of course, about Penny's story was that it reminded him of his own failed marriage, despite almost all the details being quite different: no court drama, no publicity, no ongoing contest or vilification. At the core, though, was surely the same pain that love and commitment had failed, the same bewildered anger, the same barely acknowledged guilt.

Theo worked on the boat people story, avoiding the sensationalism that was its obvious temptation, and exchanged nonsense with Nicholas from time to time. Birds perched, bickered and fouled on the guttering of the building opposite. Nicholas said he was developing a universal theory of incompatibility in life, and that the behaviour of birds was evidence of it: When you painted a house white, they shat dark on it, when you painted it dark, they shat white on it. 'Everything conspires against you,' he said. 'All the forces active in nature are ultimately malicious.'

Theo told him his theory was just a subset of Murphy's Law.

'Murphy's Law is the clockspring of the universe,' said Nicholas, 'and immutable. It proved itself again just this morning.' He pushed his glasses up onto his forehead and turned away from his computer screen, stimulated by the recollection. 'I was trying to pull the hose across to the wall, and it twisted itself so that the metal mount fell and smashed the big, blue ceramic pot that my mother gave us. Hoses are real bastards of things. You can't let them get away with it.'

At the back of Theo's mind a memory was spooling unbidden – Stella and he with their lawyer, in the house they had decided to sell.

The silver birches had been stark, June etchings, but the plum tree behind still had a few caramel leaves at the ends of its most slender branches, and as the wind blew, the remaining leaves were strung out and flipped urgently like lures trolling in swift, cold water. Theo half expected the passing magpie to swoop in flight, to be hooked, to be drawn up through the heavy wind to some surface unknown.

'Well, you'll be satisfied now,' Stella said. 'It's a funny business in many ways.' She wore her observed expression: half humorous, half cautious. I know you're looking at me, her face surely said, but you don't know what I think. True. After twelve years of marriage, true. Theo wondered what her face was like when she was alone; if it was the same as he could observe when she was asleep.

'I'm glad we came. Thanks, I appreciate it.' As he spoke came the immediate conviction that the visit would achieve nothing. It came like a gust from deep within, and passed through chest, neck, face, causing barely a tremor, hissed from his eyes as the clean nothingness that made streamers of the tufted plum leaves. How often could such spirit keep passing away.

'If he mentioned matrimonial home once, he mentioned it a hundred times,' Stella continued. 'I said all along I was willing for the house to be sold. But that's what lawyers are like.'

'I suppose they have to deal with a lot of upset and unreasonable people. They want to make sure there aren't any comebacks.'

'No comebacks?' she said. They were standing on the brick barbecue area that was never used much. It was too shaded, and they weren't a barbecue sort of couple anyway.

'You've made it easier to sort it all out. I want to say that, whatever else happens.'

'Why should we hurt each other any more?' Stella said. 'Why should we be any more hurt or ashamed or angry than we have to be. We don't hate each other, do we?'

'No,' he said.

'We had a nice home. We had some good times,' she said. 'Maybe we were just disappointed.'

'Maybe.'

'We don't hate each other, but we're disappointed,

aren't we. Isn't that it?'

'Everyone has disappointment,' Theo replied.

'Yes, but I'd hoped for less of it,' Stella said with flat finality.

Everything around them spoke of common ground and a mutual past. Even the lawyer just departed had become an acquaintance, almost a friend, over the years of marriage. Theo had noticed his slight embarrassment as he gave advice, as he pointed out he couldn't act for both of them and that if things went ahead, each of them should be independently represented.

The barbecue area was the last of their major do-it-yourself projects: after that they had been able to afford tradespeople. Standing in the cold tide of winter wind, Theo had perfectly recollected the construction over a long summer. They spent hours in weekends and evenings after work, chipping mortar from the stack of used bricks, digging out the lawn to a fastidious level surface, finally laying each brick in the base of sand. How often they discussed the positioning of the barbecue itself – he'd placed tiny home-made pennants to gauge the prevailing wind. The sense of achievement in the construction was greater than the pleasure of subsequent use. Perhaps they weren't informal enough as a couple, perhaps the pennants hadn't been a true augury of smoke drift, maybe they just couldn't be bothered. The lawyer had liked it though, particularly the low brick wall that could be used to sit on.

Neither of them had been to the house for several weeks. They made coffee and Stella took a fan heater into the sunroom, which was small and easiest to heat, even in winter. The house had the bone coldness that came from being unlived in.

'I was in Auckland last week, and it rained every day,' Theo told her.

'Did you see Graham and Yvonne?'

'It didn't work out, but I gave them a ring.' He knew she was wondering how much he was telling their friends. Both of them shied away from a discussion that would result in some agreed new way for friends to view them. 'They send their love,' he said. 'I didn't want to get into any stuff about us on the phone.'

'I've told Melanie how things are now,' Stella said.

'Sure, that's okay.' Melanie was a close friend to both of them.

The indoor plants needed attention. Stella took off some of the dead leaves with her free hand. She didn't sit down as they talked, but roamed the small room with her mug of coffee close to her face for warmth. What do you tell friends? He thought with a pang of their own reaction to the differing separations of various acquaintances: the mixture of concern, curiosity and complacency. The apportioning of responsibility, and that fierce, but unacknowledged, relief that anyone's life but your own is shaken down. But then they were splitting; they were being shaken down.

He sensed that each of them was close to offering support to the other, yet knew that being together wouldn't work any more. And so they talked of offers on the house, and her father's health, as the room grew warmer and the winter day outside grew colder, the wind blowing the magpies past the birches and plum tree, and towing on long clouds with pale bellies, which glided like sharks in the sky.

Theo did a story once about a shark woman: an

Australian of Italian descent who had lost most of her right thigh in an attack while swimming from a launch in Allot Bay. She said it was like being in a washing machine and that she felt the blood draining away from her heart. After that, like women lawyers who fall in love with the murderers they represent, her whole life became devoted to sharks: she wrote a thesis on their migratory patterns, did oceanic field work for a combined universities research team and featured in documentaries that sought to dispel fear and ignorance regarding the shark family. She was damn lucky to be alive. He interviewed her before a talk she gave at the Viaduct Basin, and she lifted her skirt so that the photographers could snap what was left of her thigh. Just bone and the great sunken scar, like the pursed mouth of an old man with no teeth. The shark had teeth all right, though. She must have been in her fifties by the time she came to Auckland, but she flipped her skirt up like a teenager to show the damage. She said the more you learn about the shark, the more you realise what a wonderful creature it is, so perfect in its adaptation to its role. She said there have been sharks for millions of years, long before the first ancestors of man.

The shock of the attack had led to a fixation, Theo reckoned. The trauma must have been so great that the only way she could deal with surviving the shark was to give the rest of her life to it.

4

'You'll end up antisocial,' said Nicholas. 'You need to watch that. You're going to end up a sad, old bore, talking shop endlessly, embellishing your potted stories and not wanting to go home after work.' It was a fear for himself, that he transferred to Theo. 'And you've got too focused on that Penny-farthing woman's court case. It doesn't pay to get emotionally involved with people you interview and write about. Your writing becomes partisan and sentimental, you know that. Cynicism is the whetstone of good journalism. You're not screwing her, are you?'

They were having coffee at their shared office window. The alley below was temporarily blocked by the van of a squat woman who was delivering bags of cat litter to the back of the pet shop. The inside of Theo's mug was stained to a tobacco brown, from having been rinsed only and put back amid the jumble of the draining tray. From farther back in the large reporters' room, where the overhead lights were always on and the hum of computers was a corporate tinnitus, came the snatches of talk among colleagues, and the more pronounced voices of those speaking on the phone, unconsciously compensating for distance.

Theo didn't need Nicholas to point out the narrowness of his life. 'I've invited you to come running with me, haven't I? At least I get a bit of bloody exercise.'

'Exercise doesn't count,' said Nicholas. 'That sort of exercise is mindless and atavistic. We don't have to outrun sabre-toothed tigers any more. Social interaction is the thing, some cultivation of the mind and the spirit.'

'Yeah, sure.'

'That's why I think we should go to that new massage parlour in Cargoe Street,' said Nicholas blithely.

'Ah, a cargo cult,' said Theo.

'I'm serious,' said Nicholas. 'It's the twenty-first century, for Christ's sake, Theo. We're single guys who work bloody hard. We'll be middle-aged soon. Jesus. If we don't watch it, in no time we'll be in carpet slippers and watering a Super Tom daily in a cloche behind the garage. We'll be supervising primary school road crossings, and spilling our self-pitying guts on late-night talkback radio. We'll be watching *Coronation Street*, and doing an extra-mural Massey course on post-colonial literature, or maybe taking minutes for the fucking Society for Sewage Pond Reform.'

'Yeah, but you're older than me,' said Theo.

Maybe Nicholas had a point, though: maybe it was a warning. Theo the sad-sack. Was that how they saw him? Theo looked about the reporters' room and tried to think of the last time he had laughed out loud at anything his colleagues said. So much of his time spent on failed relationships: writing and thinking about Penny with all her problems, and being reminded of Stella and his own marriage. One bag of cat litter had fallen and burst in the alley, and the squat woman drove the van away, leaving the pet shop man in a black apron to scoop up the pellets with a red plastic shovel. 'You know,' said Theo, 'a visit to the parlour sounds a bloody good idea, but don't you dare say anything to Melanie.'

The Cargoe Street premises were in a brick building with tight, orifice windows, above a shop selling photography equipment. 'They take the video footage straight downstairs to be processed,' quipped Nicholas. It was after eight, yet still fully light, and he and Theo stood at the massage parlour entrance. The brazen element to their pause there had more to do with an assumed insouciance than familiarity. 'I've been before. Credit cards are quite okay,' said Nicholas.

'Let's not split it down the middle, though,' said Theo.

The stairs were a straight, narrow ascent, and having reached the top, Theo and Nicholas found themselves facing an elderly man in shirtsleeves behind the desk of the small reception room. His considerable, bald head was in uneasy equilibrium on the thin stalk of neck, but his smile was assured. 'I'm standing in,' he said from his chair, realising that he was somewhat incongruous as the public face of the business. 'My daughter won't be a moment. It's just the change of shift, actually. Some of the girls going off, and a good many more coming on.'

'We'd prefer to be matched with the latter,' said Nicholas.

'Very good,' said the old guy with appreciation, and

his smile widened. 'Reciprocality is important in massage.' The use of such a word, the slight twitch to his smile, were signs that he wasn't as out of touch with the business as he had seemed. 'Look,' he said, 'I'll just take you through, if you like, and then Alison will pop in and introduce one of the girls. The full body massage is ninety dollars.'

Behind the far door, the place opened up surprisingly, with a corridor well lit by recessed strips, and with five doors leading off on each side. Theo was given the second on the right. 'See you at the cars,' said Nicholas, 'but let's neither of us wait for more than fifteen minutes or so.'

Theo's room had an adjustable massage table, two straight-backed chrome chairs, a tiled floor and an ensuite of toilet, basin and shower. Everything was neat. If the padded massage table hadn't been there, the room could well have been a towel showroom. There were shelves of green towels beneath the one high window, more folded on the table, flannels and more towels, all green, padding out the ensuite. Theo sat and waited. He thought for a moment about giving up the idea: he hadn't sought sex in that way for a long time, but he became distracted by the towels, and was counting them when the woman came in.

It wasn't Alison, but Becky. Becky said Alison was still busy, but that it didn't matter, she, Becky, could do the talking as well as the massage, if that was okay with him. Becky was young and attractive enough. Sleek was the word that occurred to Theo. She was well rounded and had dark, shiny hair. Her skin was good, her arms and legs compact and close to her body. She wasn't beautiful at all, but had the sleekness of an otter, and the sleekness of youth. And she was right at home.

'You know the basic full body massage is ninety bucks?' she said. The voice wasn't sleek; rather a retail counter voice, very forward in the mouth.

'What else is there?' said Theo. He had decided to be quite pragmatic about the whole business. Any sensitivity would only lead to awkwardness.

'Well, full sex is another hundred,' said Becky. 'Then there's the other forms of release for less. With me there's nothing anal, or any of that.'

'There's no bed in here,' said Theo. Becky was still standing with the closed door behind her, and Theo was sitting. It didn't feel right, but to stand up would be ridiculous.

'There's rooms on the other side of the corridor for that,' she said.

Theo decided to go with the massage for the time being. Becky told him to have a shower as hot as he could stand, then come out to the massage table with just a towel. 'Wrap it round you like a miniskirt,' she said. 'I'm just going to tell Alison we're underway.' She hadn't returned when Theo came back from his shower. He sat barefoot and bare chested on the massage table. It had a slight springiness. He lay on his back, but that was a strange feeling with no one else in the room, so he sat up again. Becky came back immediately afterwards. 'Sorry about that,' she said. 'Alison's dad needed help with the credit card machine. I don't know, he just doesn't seem to get it. Okay, lie down on your stomach.'

Theo had few sources of comparison, but Becky seemed to be good at massage. She had strong fingers and kneaded the muscles vigorously as well as making firm strokes. There was no obvious concentration on erogenous zones. The massage oil had a pleasant fragrance of the outdoors. She was interested in the profession of journalism, she said. Melanie's community paper came up and Becky said she didn't like it – all second-hand car ads, the miraculous return of pets and people overcoming disease. Theo didn't mention that the editor was a friend and occasional lover. Becky said what she liked was the travel pages. She'd been overseas once already and was saving for a trip to Portugal and Spain. She bent Theo's legs back so far that the cartilage popped. 'You've got a nice bum,' she said.

'I run a bit,' he said.

'The squash players I see almost all have great bums,' Becky said. 'It must be all that sudden change of direction that firms the muscles.' She gave his back a final rub down with yet another green towel, then asked him to turn over. Even though he was then cock up, Theo found it more natural to talk when he could see her face.

Becky wore a short-sleeved blouse, and her breast was close to him as she massaged. Theo was in a state of easy relaxation.

Becky was attractive and he wanted access to that without the hassle of close engagement. 'How about you massage me topless?' he said.

Becky didn't halt, or alter, the rhythm of her massage. She was firmly stroking beneath his ribcage.

'Forty dollars,' she said. She wiped her hands, and took off her top with care: beneath it she wore a black, soft fabric bra. She undid it at the back, shrugged it off and began the massage again, without any inhibition, or pause for conscious display. She had nice tits, with dark areolae. As she massaged Theo, she allowed her nipples to glance his face, her flesh to briefly touch his own, but nothing was exaggerated in her movement; no honky-tonk titillation. 'Anything else?' she asked him.

'Nothing else,' said Theo.

He didn't need anything else, not even to lift his hands the short distance to touch her slanted breasts, or the sleek belly visible above her skirt. He just lay with eyes half closed and enjoyed the play of her hands on his flesh and bones, and movement of her naked torso. She talked about saunas, spa pools and massage. She had formal qualifications, she said, from the Athene Academy in Sydney, which was recognised worldwide.

'Why are there so many towels?' asked Theo, and Becky was for the first time mildly surprised.

'How do you mean?' she said.

'In here. So many towels everywhere.'

'We never use a towel more than once before it gets washed. That's a strict rule here. I reckon our rooms are cleaner than the homes the guys come from. Alison's a real stickler for it,' she said.

Theo made no argument of it.

He saw her once, weeks afterwards, in a mall. She was at a café table half in the thoroughfare with a woman about her own age. Theo paused close by, but Becky's unhurried glance showed no recognition. Sleekness would be replaced by bulk in middle age, he thought. He had a repressed inclination to say hello.

'Is there anything else?' she might have said, but instead she'd asked her friend why a certain Michelle was being such a bitch again.

Nicholas was waiting in his car. 'I was just about to go,' he said.

'You weren't long,' said Theo. 'I expected to be back first. I just had the regular massage, but topless – the woman I mean.'

Nicholas said he'd skipped the massage and gone straight over to one of the other rooms.

'Ah,' said Theo.

'It was both good and bad,' said Nicholas.

'You don't have to give me a blow by blow account,' said Theo, but Nicholas always enjoyed recounting such episodes in his life with a satirical gloss. The woman had continually talked about showtime, which Nicholas had found detrimental to performance. 'She kept saying, "Showtime, Nicholas" as we undressed, and before each manoeuvre, and I half expected her to crack a whip, or introduce a ring of miniature trotting ponies.' Whatever reservations he had about the session, Nicholas would make it work for him as a raconteur. Theo knew the tale would burgeon, and that he would hear it several times and so chart its growth. Experience was only the raw material of life for Nicholas, and subject to processing. 'And what about your woman?' he asked finally.

'Becky was bloody easy on the eye.' Theo felt a slight superiority in mentioning her name: a sign of his awareness of her apart from the transaction between them. Nicholas had not mentioned any name at all throughout his account.

'Maybe I should have just had the massage.' Nicholas's tone was considered, rather than regretful. 'I was thinking before you came about our inability as a society to express ourselves about sex. It's so sought after, so compulsively essential, yet almost all our language concerning it is derogatory. To tell someone to get fucked should be to wish them great pleasure and fulfilment, but we mean the opposite.'

'I feel fine,' said Theo.

'Odd though, isn't it.'

'It's just that you've become meditative after getting a shot away. Blood is slowly getting back to your brain.'

'Language is interesting, that's what I mean. It should be closer to experience.'

'Showtime, Nick,' said Theo. 'That's what you should concentrate on. Keeping all the balls in the air, managing a three ring circus. At your age you're lucky to manage any showtime, I'd say.'

5

Theo liked to run. At the end of the day at the paper, or early, before he began work. He ran down the cycle tracks that parallel the railway line through Papanui, and then into Hagley Park. The park has a changing exercise congregation. In the early mornings many are women with dogs: in the evenings there are more men, some with singlets bearing esoteric lettering. On winter mornings frost encourages a vigorous pace; on summer evenings mood and movement are more languorous. There are cyclists too, on the sealed paths through Hagley, some with leashed dogs which patter, or lope, according to their size and the speed of their owners.

He liked to run. As a young guy he had run to build fitness for other sports, and when he gave them up he continued the running. Journalism is a sedentary, stodgy career. Theo liked the perseverance of jogging, the sense of progress and the evasion it provided. You could concentrate on the physical endeavour for the duration of the run, and so keep at bay those things that gather about you when you're at rest. He ran a lot during the end of his marriage. When he was going through the divorce, Anna, who knew all about fitness, said how slim he was. He felt physically better that he had for years, though his life was crap, though he could laugh only at the misfortune of others, though sometimes at the paper he went into the old photography room and stood alone in the dark there for minutes at a time.

It was after the visit to Drybread, and while Theo was running, that he first noticed the parson. He came later to call him that because he was bald and had an expression of compassionate resignation on his long face. Maybe what Penny had said about the police and her husband wanting to find her had remained with Theo; maybe it was the way the parson didn't look away when Theo became aware of his gaze at the traffic lights. Theo had seen him before, and the polished, maroon Honda Civic which had a bright chrome ball on its tow-bar and was trailing a rubber strap. Something to do with static electricity someone told Theo, which seemed odd, as rubber is a poor conductor. He crossed into the park and ran through the practice fairways of the golfcourse. For a minute or two he wondered where he'd seen the parson; whether he was new to the paper's clerical staff, or worked in a shop that Theo went to regularly. Although the guy looked like a parson, it was highly unlikely he was one – Theo didn't go to church, and wasn't on any ecclesiastical visiting list.

Theo saw him again a few days later as he reached home after work. Well, rather he saw the car, which was parked facing away on the opposite side of the street. The same high polish, same chrome ball on the tow-bar and trailing strap. SJ were the letters on the number plate before the numbers. Saviour Jesus perhaps. Theo couldn't see anyone in the car, and when he'd parked his Audi in the drive, he walked over and past the Honda. He visualised the parson crouched between the seats, ungainly, ignominious, and with a meek and sheepish face, but the car was empty. If he was nearby and watching, he'd realise Theo knew about him. Theo had no substantial debts, no ongoing dispute with Stella, he wasn't writing an expose on some tycoon: the parson was surely connected with the Maine-King custody case.

Theo went through all the rooms of his house and noticed nothing amiss. Two windows were ajar, as he had left them, with no obvious sign of entry. He looked briefly at the phone, but had no idea how to recognise that it had been bugged. In a life as mundane as his, there had been little to fear from surveillance. Penny's whereabouts was the only secret he had which could be of interest to others.

For a moment he saw the place as the parson may have observed it on a quick recce: the newspapers still open on the sofa, the bed clothes pulled up rather than remade, the crumbs and cheese gratings on the tiled floor by the kitchen bench, a piece of cardboard folded and wedged to keep the wardrobe door from gaping, the yellowed sellotape on the fractured edge of his computer keyboard. The soap tray in the bathroom streaked with yellow and blue residue from the precursors of the white oval that lay there. The trivial sordidness of everyday living which you notice in other people's homes, but are oblivious to in your own.

In the spare bedroom, which had become his office, he set a simple test in case the parson came again, or for the first time. Just papers from his case, but with their juxtaposition on the desk exactly measured and recorded. If the parson was dropping in he'd surely be drawn to work documents. After his meal, when dusk was filling in the spaces between houses and drawing down the sky, Theo walked out to the gate. The car had gone. Theo wondered where such a man would go at the end of his working day, and whether he found his occupation more futile than that of other people. Boredom at first hand calls for a form of endurance: to experience it vicariously as a secret observer of the lives of others must be doubly stultifying. Theo hadn't smoked for some years, but standing there in the dusk at the end of the driveway he had a strong desire for one of those thin, dark cheroots. He imagined the texture of it between fingers and thumb, saw the end glow as an ember against the sky, felt the smoke of a deep drag thump into his lungs as if it had a body of its own. Such memory gusts had little to do with addiction: they came as indirect cats' paws of happier times.

A motorbike came past, with a sound like a fat man's rich, bronchial cough, then two cyclists in single file and without lights. Theo could barely make them out, but knew they were both girls because the one behind called out, 'Wait up, Nadine. Nadeeeen,' ending in a sort of angry wail.

A good handful of mail was showing in the box at Theo's gate. Even had there been sufficient light, Theo wouldn't have checked it there: he disliked people who stood at their mailboxes, sometimes in slippers and housecoats, sometimes in gardening clothes and holding a hoe, and read their mail before the passing world. And his eventual perusal when inside showed there was no reason for urgency. All could be winnowed away without leaving solid grain, or gain. The rates demand, the 134th issue of *Behind the News*, a credit card statement, a slip announcing that the milk delivery round was changing hands, with two apostrophes missing and one incorrectly used, a letter from a former colleague saying how much he was enjoying working in Sydney, seven multi-coloured advertising circulars and a donation envelope from the support group for those with clinical flatulence. What more did he expect? But he did, of course – he yearned for something unsolicited and undeserved, a lightning strike that would galvanise his world.

There was no way Theo was going to start smoking again, but he hadn't sworn off a tipple. Whisky was a good friend to him in the evenings: whisky and water, the sports channel, maybe a chat to Nicholas, or Melanie. Whisky and water, and programmes well removed from the present. Maybe just whisky and water. Sometimes just whisky.

While he was sitting with his drink on the sofa, Theo recalled the drifting cry of the girl cyclist in the dusk, and thought of his own Nadine: a woman with whom he'd had a sudden and unfortunate affair that perhaps signalled the failure of his marriage, though the essential causes lay elsewhere. Nadine was a dental assistant, and there was nothing romantic in their relationship there. On his occasional visits she would sit close to his side, but only to expedite the use of the small suction device that removed excess saliva during the pauses in the dentist's use of the drill. Theo hadn't known her name. They exchanged only a few commonplace words, and his main impressions of her appearance were the considerable bosom beneath the white smock and a round face of blameless, schoolgirl innocence, though she must have been in her late twenties. He felt no particular interest in her, and she displayed towards him no more than professional attention.

They met in rather different circumstances at a BP service station in Papanui. Theo was checking tyre pressures, and Nadine was attaching a trailerload of firewood she'd purchased there. He noticed that the trailer was still chained to the fence, and jumped in front of her car just as she was about to drive away. 'The guy's forgotten to unchain the trailer,' he called, when her startled face appeared at the driver's window. 'I'll get him over.'

He knew he'd seen her somewhere before, but didn't know where, and she gave no sign of having recognised him. Perhaps she was accustomed to him only when he was semi-prone and with his mouth stretched open. She thanked him and drove away apprehensively, with the trailer bouncing noisily over the kerb. She drove a Commodore, and Theo imagined it wasn't her choice, but her partner's car.

Theo went to the dentist not long afterwards because a piece had broken off one of his lower left teeth. He and Nadine recognised each other immediately, and entertained the dentist with the story of a small disaster averted. 'I didn't think you looked comfortable in that car at all,' said Theo.

'It's my husband's. By rights he should've been getting the firewood anyway, but he kept putting off ringing up, and then he was away and I needed some right then. My car hasn't got a tow-bar.'

'Always useful, a tow-bar,' said the dentist indulgently.

'So what do you drive?' Theo asked her.

'I've got a Corolla.'

'Bloody good little cars,' said Theo.

'Just keep on keeping on,' said the dentist, who had a Saab.

'I've been pleased with it,' said Nadine, and then all three concentrated on Theo's tooth: in a dental surgery time is money.

It wasn't a conversation that foreshadowed intimacy, but a few days later by one of those small coincidences which litter everyday life, Theo met her again at a private gallery exhibition of lithographs. Stella was to give the speech for the opening, so was in a group closely connected with the show. She and Theo were cooling from an argument in the car on their way to the show: a disagreement concerning Theo's interest in a job in Auckland.

Theo was relieved to move away and look at some of the work. He recognised Nadine close beside him. They were surprised by the meeting, then tried to disguise this lest it be taken as incredulity that the other had any cultural inclination. 'I do mainly screenprinting,' said Nadine, when Theo had explained why he was at the exhibition. 'I'm in a co-operative with several of the people exhibiting here.'

'Dentistry and screenprinting, now there's a combination,' said Theo. He was close to the long table that held ranks of glasses bottom up and carafes of wine, so he filled a glass for Nadine, topped up his own. The availability of reasonable wine was one of the few benefits of attending art functions with his wife. He talked with Nadine of art and the fashion dictates that seemed to rule there.

'Oh, my stuff doesn't sell for big bikkies,' she said. It

was the first time Theo had seen her dressed up, and it was something of a transformation. Freed from her nurse's smock the top of her breasts and smooth shoulders caught the light well. Her dark hair was down, and the effect of that, together with evening make-up, was to make a different woman of her. 'Yes,' she said in answer to him, 'I've had an exhibition of my own stuff here, earlier this year, and most of the prints actually sold.'

'How do you find the time?'

'I only work at the clinic three and half days a week, and we haven't got any kids yet.'

'You'd like to be a full-time artist?' asked Theo.

'I'm not driven enough. Sometimes I go right off it for weeks at a time, and this way I don't have to get uptight about it.'

Theo filled their glasses again, and they went and sat on a black sofa in the small foyer of the gallery. It was the one piece of furniture there, and other people came in and out, but didn't stand about. Theo enjoyed talking with Nadine. She knew a good deal about art, but seemed to enjoy his iconoclastic comments and cheerful slanders of local academics and artists. He didn't bother to ask if her husband was with her, because her manner provided the answer. The night was warm, and from the crowded exhibition room came a hubbub like that from a colony of seabirds. Theo and Nadine noticed when it subsided and stopped their own conversation for a moment. They could hear Stella talking. 'Shouldn't we go in?' said Nadine.

'And lose the only sofa in the place?' said Theo. 'You know, I'd rather go out – go out and have a coffee or something at the Mad Butcher's round the corner.'

'It's the Mad Hatter's.'

'What?'

'The café's called the Mad Hatter's,' said Nadine. She seemed very relaxed, and her lipstick caught the light. 'Through the looking glass and all that. Anyway, what about your wife?'

'She'll be going on somewhere for a meal with the artist and hangers-on. You know how it is at these things. I'll just beg off. She won't mind. I'll say I'm going to have a drink with the best screenprinter in the city.'

He did beg off. He went into the small gallery when Stella finished her speech and pushed his way towards her. The swell of conversation had begun again, and people were on the move about the room as well to view the paintings. Stella didn't mind that he preferred not to go with them for a meal, but she introduced him to the artist, a gaudy young woman with striped hair, and several others. A certain amount of conversation was required for politeness, and Theo half expected Nadine to have left the sofa when he finally got back to the foyer.

She was still there, but had been joined by a tall, loose-jointed old man with a collarless white shirt and Shakespearian eyebrows. 'Walter's one of the co-operative,' Nadine said, 'He's a woodturner and sculptor.' Theo wasn't interested in Walter, woodturning or sculpture.

'Nice to meet you,' he said. 'As a matter of fact Nadine and I are just off. I've been held up in there.' He remained standing until Nadine stood as well, and they said goodbye to Walter, who was still in the process of rising politely as they walked to the door. 'Enough of art speak for one night,' said Theo, and he and Nadine escaped into the coolness of the street.

It was relaxing at the Mad Hatter's. They talked easily

and with an openness that chance meetings sometimes invite. Nadine seemed to find him amusing, whereas Stella often accused him of exaggeration. Theo was able to use some of his best anecdotes on a new audience without any nagging concern that he was repeating himself. They didn't touch, they didn't kiss, when Theo walked with Nadine to her car, but there was just that pleasant charge of awareness between them. Nadine said she was interested in the world of journalism, and Theo said why didn't she come in to the paper and look around with him some time.

She did come. She rang a week later and came in the same afternoon, which was cold, with a southerly on the way. Theo took her on a tour of the building, and she was interested in how much of the paper's production had been computerised, especially the imaging. She said it made her realise how primitive screenprinting was: how physical and tactile. So many of the old handcrafts were giving way, she said. In an annex to the cavenous printing room was a pile of cardboard cylinders. Nadine wondered if there were any spare, and Theo said he'd drop a dozen or so off at her place after work. 'I'm always looking for them to use when I'm sending prints out,' she said.

'You're not screwing her, are you?' asked Nicholas when Nadine had gone, and Theo went back to his desk. To himself, Theo admitted that was exactly his intention, and the thought gave him a sort of eagerness he hadn't felt for a long time. Anticipation of sex, justified or otherwise, rids the world of a paunchy ennui, outlines became more sharply defined, colours more vibrant. He had a shower at work and left a little early, carrying a double armful of cylinders down to the carpark.

Nadine lived in a white, weatherboard home in Hornby:

a house almost in nurse's garb itself. With the cardboard cylinders clutched to him, Theo could barely see his way to the door, and while he was still wondering how he could manage to knock without dropping them, Nadine opened it. Theo went in without invitation, without any query regarding her husband: all the talk at the paper had carried additional communication of which they were both aware. As Nadine began to make coffee at the bench, Theo came behind her and pressed in, feeling the excitement of a new woman's body. They never had the coffee. They went into a very small, white room with a single bed and cartons of domestic surfeit along one wall, they stripped each other without lingering and without much to say, and enjoyed each other without any reserve whatsoever. Theo hadn't been so hard for a long time. 'I don't know what you're doing,' said Nadine, 'but you're really hitting the spot.' Her large, pale breasts trembled with each stroke and the eroticism of that drove him into a sort of delirium.

He went back the next day, and the day after that, as if living in a junkie daze. Each time less was said, though the lovemaking was of almost unbearable intensity, and he left immediately afterwards. On the fourth day, Nadine burst into tears when she came to the door. She felt so guilty, she said, and her husband was coming back from his work trip in two days. 'We don't even know each other, do we,' she said. That was true in a way, but in another sense had little to do with what was happening. 'We've just got to finish it right now,' she said. 'Over, once and for all.' They did finish, and it was rather like waking up, shaken, after a feverish dream.

Theo thought that was it, but such things rarely have a soft landing. Nadine must have felt the need for expiation, because not long after she went round to see Stella and told her everything. She'd told her husband too. 'I actually admire her guts for getting it all out like that,' Stella said, but Theo couldn't understand why you'd do that, unless you wanted to get back at someone. He said it was all his fault, that he wanted the marriage to work out, that he'd try harder, but he felt nevertheless that somehow he'd been done an injustice: that some fraternity of women had been active against him. 'Well, we'll jog along,' Stella said bitterly, 'jog along and see how things go between us.'

He didn't change his dentist, but when he went after that, Nadine was never on duty. She must have worked the roster to avoid him, or perhaps left the job completely and spent her time screenprinting. At exhibitions and art functions afterwards, he at first expected to see her, but she was never there, and the brief affair faded until the only memory that sometimes came, unbidden, with a small jolt, was of the white room with storage cartons, and the trembling of her breasts as he worked over her. Even that seemed a long time ago.

6

Penny Maine-King left a message on Theo's answerphone. She said that if he wanted more for the story, she'd be home all day next Wednesday. She didn't say where home was, and she didn't ask for any confirmation of the visit. Her voice sounded quite offhand. Maybe she was calling from a public booth in Alexandra, and there was a florid man with sandals within earshot, or a sun-baked thin woman with Trade Aid bracelets, maybe a teenage girl with green tints in her hair and a silver ring in her belly button. It was tough for Penny, surely, stuck at Drybread without support, and trying from there to influence the ponderous apparatus of the law.

Theo could have signed for one of the company cars, but didn't want to have to give any reason for going away, so on the Wednesday went south in his Audi. Also, he liked to drive a well-serviced, quiet vehicle that didn't have dockets strewn on the floor, coffee stains on the seats and ash-trays crammed with barley sugar papers and tissues. Communal things are always misused and abused – cinema foyers, public toilets, telephone kiosks, honesty boxes and company cars. No one gives a bugger about anything unless it's a personal belonging: rather there's a strange satisfaction in adding to the dilapidation of things that aren't your own.

For Theo a decent car was a necessity of life. Power in reserve; something there if you had the need, the urge even, to put your foot down. He was impatient with the heavy traffic, especially the milk tankers, which seemed to come out in flotillas at certain times of the day.

He had an early lunch in the Saltwater Creek diner at the south end of Timaru, sitting close to a bikie with fringed black leather and a pale, poet's face. 'So what are you doing?' Theo asked Nicholas on the cellphone.

'Anna's been asking about you,' he said.

'Tell her I'm doing the investigative journalism I'm paid for.'

'You're not going to screw someone, are you?' said Nicholas wistfully.

'Chance would be a fine thing.'

'You are, aren't you,' Nicholas said. 'People all over the world are on their way to get well fucked, and I'm at work looking up the arse of a pet shop. Jesus. We're having a union meeting this afternoon: we'll all get indignant about not being duly recognised and recompensed, determine to stick out for eight per cent and cave in for four as usual.'

'So what are you doing now?'

'I'm cobbling together a quick piece on student loans. Very exciting. I'm pissing myself about it. There's a guy here today from the computer place supposed to be explaining the proposed new set-up, and he's spent the time so far hanging about Angie's desk with a hard on.'

'Would you check my emails for me?' asked Theo. 'Ring me in the next hour or so in case I get out of range if there's anything important.'

'Okay. I can see a kid down here at the back of the pet shop. He's taking dead guinea pigs or whatever out of the bin. Jesus. You know, the more I think about it, the more I'm convinced students shouldn't get any loans at all. Idle, ignorant little pricks. No bastard gave us any loans, did they? They just piss off overseas when they graduate anyway.'

'Hang in there, Nick,' said Theo. As he finished his coffee he wondered why the bikie had no tattoos and the gaze of a poet. Happy baccy maybe, and a middle-class upbringing.

The traffic on the main highway was a bore, but once Theo turned off to go up the Waitaki Valley the congestion eased, and he could set his own pace. It was a warm day with low, even cloud given a pearly luminosity by the sun behind it. Like Penny, he had a country upbringing, unlike her he hadn't come full circle. Yet these trips to Central gave him a certain lift, and he realised that despite all the subsequent years in cities, his natural inclination was still to drive away from them, and that such progress usually gave him a satisfaction quite unconnected with any intention, or destination. And both his Canterbury and her Central were rain shadow regions bleached to wheat colours in summer by drought and sun. The sociologists say people are naturally gregarious, but that doesn't mean you always feel at home in the great rat heaps that develop.

There's a saturation point to fellowship, and after it the spirit aches to be alone.

On the second visit he seemed to come more quickly to Penny's old house in the Dunstan Range gully, dust from the gravel road a drifting plume behind him, and again no sign of life in either of the other two baches. A scatter of tattered willows followed the creek, and the flats were patched with gorse and broom through which stock forced a few narrow trails. Penny's blue hatchback was parked behind the overgrown macrocarpa hedge, but Ben's trike had gone. Absent also was the blazing sun of his first visit, though the temperature was high enough. 'It's supposed to blow,' said Penny at the door, 'and that'll soon get rid of the cloud.' He remembered looking through the window on his first visit to see both of them asleep: the absolute relaxation of their bodies, the peacefulness of the boy as he slept.

She looked different – of course she did, but somehow, illogically, the way someone is the first time you see them is a strong image, and only gradually do the subsequent and multiple exposures reconcile you to variation and complexity. She wore jeans, but perhaps the same pale top. Theo was struck again by the whiteness and symmetry of her teeth in a face free of any make-up. The teeth suggested an American emphasis on enhancement of appearance which she couldn't entirely put aside. Ben was beside her at the door, barefoot and clutching a pink plastic and chrome potato masher. 'You remember Theo, don't you?' Penny said, bending to encourage his attention. He said nothing, but he pointed the masher at Theo, who wished he'd thought to get a lolly for him to make the meeting a little easier.

'Theo's an unusual name, isn't it,' said Penny, as if to excuse her son's refusal to respond to it.

They went to the back of the house again, to the church pew and a kitchen chair carried out by Penny. That's where Ben's trike was, though the hillside sloped up so quickly from the house, and the grass was so rough, that he couldn't have pedalled far. Penny told Theo that Zack Heywood hadn't managed to get a stay of the Family Court warrant, but that the sustained publicity was making the case politically sensitive, and also putting pressure on Penny's husband. Theo said that the public interest would move on to someone else soon if nothing in her situation changed, that a certain amount of progression was necessary if a story was to remain newsworthy. Rape, murder, insolent fraud, deceit by the mighty, exaggerated protest by the marginalised, and the cancer scares of the famous, were as common as turnips.

'So you're not interested any more?' said Penny.

'It's not my interest that's driving it. I'm just saying that time does matter and, as Zack says, if you can reach some compromise with your husband, get some agreement to renegotiate, then the sooner the better. And the police could find you any time while the warrant's still in force.'

Penny didn't reply for a time. She sat looking up the slope beyond the stunted plum tree, then allowed her head to flop back in a brief revelation of helplessness. 'I know,' she said, 'and it's awful for Ben cooped up here with just me. Christ, sometimes we hardly know what day it is. We eat crap food and watch the occasional sheep.' The boy was playing on the small patch of ground worn bare of grass beside the back door. He seemed absorbed in squeezing toothpaste into the cab of a small, plastic truck.

'Crap food,' he said.

'Don't say that,' said Penny.

There was something dislocating about the place and the situation, some quality of latent significance that threatened realism despite it being so closely bound to nature. The half sod house with a large front hedge, and little visible boundary besides, the dry hills rising up, the church pew at the door and Penny sitting on a kitchen chair in the rough grass with her head tilted back again. There was a metal plaque on the back of the pew to record its donation by Randall and Elizabeth Nottage 'Of This Parish'.

'Everything gets so mixed up, doesn't it,' Penny said. 'You think you've got a handle on stuff, you're set up nicely in life, and then it all turns to crap.'

'Crap,' said Ben with satisfaction. The toothpaste on his fingers had picked up dirt and tufts of dry grass and thistledown.

'Don't say crap,' said Penny.

'How long were you in the States?' Theo asked.

'Six years.'

'How did you end up in that television thing?'

'Erskine had some business connection with the guy who was producing the show, or co-producing it anyway. It was about ordinary couples hosting a dinner party for celebrities and being judged on how well they handled it.'

'Who did it?'

'Did what?' she asked.

'Did the judging?' Ben came over and wanted him to get the toothpaste out of his toy. It was a messy job, but Theo didn't like to refuse.

'Oh, the live audience did. They were there throughout

the dinner, on tiered seating. The dining table was on a sort of stage. You did all the preparations, and then were on camera for fifteen minutes serving the meal and making conversation with the celebrities and the series host Saul Vries. You wouldn't know him, or any of the celebrities, here. We lasted only two episodes. The audience the second time didn't like the choice of dessert, or our views on Californian politics.'

'Jesus.'

'I think we did it as an attempt to keep the marriage going, but we never admitted that to each other. Erskine hated it. You make decisions which seem sensible at the time, don't you, and then later you wonder what the hell you were thinking. It's so easy to see how other people bugger up their lives, but you're sure you yourself always act for the best.'

Ben wanted to sit on the pew and he watched as Theo worked on the truck with a handkerchief. 'He likes you,' said Penny. Poor little bugger would probably have taken to the devil himself for variety. He had no sense of changed circumstances, of course, of having come down in the world from an expensive home in Sacramento to a gold miner's hut in Central Otago. Probably the only thing he missed was his father. That was something Theo hadn't got into much in the newspaper articles, or with Penny: why she thought her husband wasn't fit to have custody of their son. Even after years of journalism he didn't like asking a woman about the details of a relationship. Going on a television show to help your marriage sounded very American.

'He needs more people, more kids, around him,' Penny said.

'I thought the phone message you left me sounded a bit odd,' Theo said.

'Well there's probably a bug on your phone. I'm hardly likely to say anything that gives this place away, or anything about my intentions.'

'I suppose not.'

'You're making sure you're not followed, I hope?'

'Sure.' Theo had kept a casual lookout because of the parson. Penny could be quite sharp, almost dismissive, but he let it pass. 'Is any cloak and dagger stuff really likely do you think?' he said. Why add to Penny's concern?

'I'd say Erskine's almost certainly got someone looking for us. He'll be pissed off the police here haven't been able to find me. He won't want to rely on just them: he'll be trying to find us.'

'He loves the boy a lot, I suppose.'

Penny just looked at him. She looked at him as if he wasn't on her side, then folded her arms and watched Ben go up the slope a bit through the rough, cropped grass.

'The thing is,' Theo said, 'I'd like to be able to give some better reasons in my articles why you're so determined to have Ben with you – why the little guy should live with you, and why you've done all this to evade the decision of the Californian court. People will be sympathetic if they think the boy's in some sort of jeopardy, and that it's not just you being bloody-minded to punish your husband. Does that make sense?'

'You've been married. Could you make any sense of it to a few thousand strangers?'

It wasn't the same, though, was it? Once you decide to use publicity to strengthen your case, there's a sort of contract formed by which you provide a confessional feast, and hope to receive sympathy and support in return. Nicholas had a saying – publicity is the bear: sometimes you eat the bear, and sometimes the bear eats you. Theo could see that Penny wasn't going to say any more about her marriage than she had to, and he could understand that. Maybe, too, she didn't want to tell him, didn't feel easy enough.

'My life must seem a mess,' she said. 'It is a fucking mess,' she continued more emphatically, 'and I can hardly believe it myself. I wake up some mornings feeling okay, and then I look around this place, realise what's happened and start crying. Christ, I've gone from corporate cocktail parties, shopping trips to Europe, to this dump in just a few crap months. I used to come here sometimes as a kid, and I didn't much like it then either.'

'What's actually at Drybread? It's even marked on the map.'

'Nothing,' said Penny.

'Nothing at all?'

'Well, there's a graveyard sitting in the paddocks, with a few huge macrocarpa, or pines. That's about it. All vanished with the gold. I feel like some bloody relic myself.'

'How did the name come about?'

'They say a disappointed miner cursed it as a place of dry bread only.'

Theo told her she was at the bottom of the swing, and things would improve, that transitions in life were often especially painful and yet essential. Such stuff is true, but very little consolation when the ground is breaking up around you. They should go for one more hard-hitting article and then sound out the court, and her husband. He asked her why she wouldn't share custody and let Ben live mainly with his father.

'Because he'll gradually take Ben away from me,' Penny said.

'He'll grow up to be his own man anyway. That's what you want for him, don't you? Someone who's strong.'

'I want him to love me. I want him to be happy as a kid, and not have the sort of time I did.'

The little boy was almost to the plum tree and still holding the truck in one hand. He stood looking up at the tree, wide-eyed because the cloud kept the dazzle of the sun from him. Maybe he knew they were talking about him, but it didn't matter. He was so young that he would never remember any of it – not the bach in the gully, not his mother talking to the journalist at the back step or crying in the morning, not even that he was the reason for a good deal of sadness and anger and bewilderment, and the object of much love from two people who now had little for each other.

Penny brought out some of her lukewarm cans of beer and she and Theo drank as they talked. She showed him recent articles from American publications concerning custody issues, particularly what was termed father backlash. One singled out the Californian judge who had decided her case as a known supporter of non-sexist rulings. 'You become part of a larger agenda,' Penny said. 'They're not necessarily on about individual justice.' Theo would make that the angle for his next article.

He felt a sexual curiosity about her for the second time. Her jeans were nipped in at the waist and tight on her thighs; her hair was more free than on his first visit. Because she was animated, she lost for the moment the expression of unhappiness that drew her face down. Naked, she would have an agile, loose-limbed body, good to look at even if her breasts were small. He imagined that, even as he nodded in agreement with her views on parental custody: he imagined her hair fallen back from her face, her mouth open to show those Californian teeth, the arch of her taut throat as he had seen it on his first visit while she slept.

Ben had grown tired of the plum tree's uncommunicative company so he came back and stood between Penny and Theo, between the pew of this parish and the kitchen chair. The truck remained in one hand; in the other he clasped a few pellets of sheep dung.

'Yuck, dirty. Throw it away,' Penny said.

'Yuck, dirty,' he said, and knew to retain his toy while dropping the dry shit away.

'He loves to repeat things, doesn't he,' Theo said.

'It's a natural stage,' she said sharply.

Theo had written about him as a three-year-old kid, but not from any personal experience of children. He was black and white – dark, soft hair, pale skin, though the Central Otago summer was beginning to tan him. Theo's car keys were beside him on the pew, and Ben picked them up and rattled them, turning round and round as he did so. Not only had Theo no children, but he retained little memory of infancy apart from the bright, open spaces of the North Canterbury downs, and the occasional family incident rendered dramatic at the time because of trivial eccentricity: a visiting minister fainting in the hallway and the glint of his clerical collar like a tusk as he lay there, the gorse fire by his father's truck yard, the soft thrush that broke its neck in sudden impact with the glass of the French doors as Theo stood watching his mother put the washing out.

'I've got something to ask you,' said Penny when they

had been quiet a while. 'I feel a bit silly about it.'

'Ask away,' Theo said.

'I wonder if you'd visit my mother – she's in the retirement home in Alex. I can't go, because that's sure to be one of the places the police will be keeping an eye on. I don't mean they'll be standing in the corridors or anything, but I suppose the staff will have been asked to look out for me.'

'You haven't seen her at all since you've been back?'

'No.'

'Won't they wonder about me? Your mother won't have a clue who I am.'

'She hasn't got a clue who anybody is,' said Penny. 'Well no one who's alive anyway. She's got dementia. She's in full care. She's not seventy-five yet, but seems like ninety.'

What else could be fucked up for Penny? All the marriage and custody worries, on the run from the court order, and then her mother close at hand, but out of reach in more ways than one. At some time in our lives each of us seems to be singled out as the whipping boy, and the reasons beyond comprehension.

Penny suggested that Theo say he was a cousin from the North Island if anyone bothered to ask. She said there were cousins called Booth there. She told him she just wanted to be sure that her mother was okay, to know how she was looking: whether the people at the home were doing her hair and bothering to get her out of bed. Maybe the ones without visitors were neglected.

'So what's her name?' Theo asked.

'Oh Jesus, yes. You're right. She's Mrs Bell. You expect everyone to know the things you know yourself, don't you.'

'I'll go today,' said Theo. 'I'll go now, and send an email when I'm home to let you know how she is.'

'I feel bad about asking, but it would be one less thing eating away. You know? Here I am living reasonably close, and I can't even visit my own mother. Jesus, it's a fucking mess.'

'Ben's very lucky you care about him so much,' said Theo.

'You haven't got any children?'

'No,' said Theo.

'It's a special thing,' Penny said. She had one hand over her son's fist as she gently took Theo's car keys from him. Neither spoke, but the boy gave them up with little resistance.

'It's the only love I know that doesn't need anything at all in return, but then, Christ, I've gotten pretty cynical about love, I guess.' Penny seemed to think she had disclosed too much. 'And of course, kids can be a right pain in the bum at times. Can't they, Ben, eh?' The boy just smiled, responding to the tone, rather than the words.

'You really don't mind checking on Mum?' she said when it was time for Theo to leave. 'It's going to make a hell of a long trip for you. I feel bad about that.'

'That's okay.'

'That's great. Thank you. I've been worried about her. I feel so useless sometimes, but maybe I can hold on a bit longer. You don't think I'm just some crazy, off-the-wall bitch, do you?'

The cloud was breaking up, and Penny and her son came out to the macrocarpa hedge to see Theo go. In the bare crucible of the hills they made a lonely pair.

7

His earliest recollection was of sitting on a large post in the stockyards of a Canterbury farm, aware of dry hills twitching in the distance and cattle immediately before him. A black steer had thrust its warm, snot-flowing nose onto his leg, and he'd been too afraid to move or call out. He began to cry only afterwards, and his father came and lifted him down, asking what the matter was, but he'd said nothing. It was the unsought surprise of it, rather than threat, which had unnerved him, and when he thought of it he had again the exact animal smell of the dusty stockyard, the great dark head looming, the folded, dun hills beyond.

It was an anomaly of childhood: its experiences had a vividness never afterwards attained, yet the very early years were resistant to memory, with just a few tableaux of surreal and lasting power in the time before a continuous recall.

The Malahide Eventide Home was close to one of the

schist outcrops typical of the higher part of Alexandra. A modern, sprawling sort of place with long-run steel roofing, covered walkways and wide, wheelchair-friendly doors. There were a lot of reflections from the strong evening sun and the woman at reception wore a loose, green T-shirt and black shorts. 'Mrs Bell?' she said. 'Mrs Bell is in the full care unit, but she may be having her meal. Have you visited before?' Theo explained that he hadn't, that he was just passing through, calling on the off chance. 'It's not always convenient for full care people,' the receptionist said, but not unkindly. She spoke on the phone to a colleague, then turned to ask him if he could possibly come another time. Theo told her probably not. 'Probably not. He's a cousin from the North Island,' she said. She was a solid, middle-aged woman with brown knees like steamed puddings and fair hair glinting on her bare arms. 'I'll let him come on down then,' she said, after a pause.

She got off her swivel office chair, yet barely increased in height: one of those wide-bodied, short-legged women with a spreading bosom that guaranteed a certain amount of personal distance. She came into the corridor and gave Theo cheerful directions, pointing through a large window into the sunlit grounds. 'You're very welcome,' she said when he thanked her. There was something childlike about her, not a lack of maturity, or understanding, perhaps just the way she had to lift her face up to him. Theo couldn't imagine her vigilantly keeping a record of Mrs Bell's visitors for the law, but rather saw her involved in neighbourly domesticity – at a barbecue with home-made chutneys and stocky kids bouncing on a trampoline.

Despite her guidance Theo lost his way and hoped she didn't see him consult a lugubrious man in a walking frame.

The population of the Malahide Home moved with caution, with difficulty, or both. Theo found himself repressing his own agility in case it became a superiority too apparent. In the small-town summer the staff didn't bother with uniforms, but there was a man about Theo's age at the entrance to full care, so he assumed him to be an employee. He was talking with three women whom old age had reduced to a sisterly uniformity of stick limbs, forward curvature, anemone mouths and hair as lifeless as that of dolls. They stood, absolutely silent, while the carer gave Theo final directions to Mrs Bell's room. 'I'm afraid you can't expect a great deal of recognition,' the man said. He wasn't to know that aspect of her affliction was a comfort for Theo.

The room was more a cubicle, though with bright colours and a window view of a pebble garden courtyard with lots of empty seats, and frogs and lizards petrified among the cacti. One high, narrow bed and one chair. One bedside table and one silver-framed photograph of a young woman in a dress no longer in fashion. Mrs Bell on the rise, Theo assumed. It had the emotional ambiguity that all such photographs have – on one hand the proof of vivacious youth, on the other the sadness of embalmment. We are gone, silent, dispossessed, is the message seen on all the faces. The more permanent the photographic record, the greater the sense of life's transience.

Penny's mother hadn't answered his tap on the door, or his false and cousinly introduction as he sat down in the one chair. She was a sister to the women clustered at the unit entrance: He could see nothing of Penny in her appearance whatsoever. She half sat, half lay back, clasped within the bulky fabric arms of one of those convalescent pillows.

'So how have you been keeping, Mrs Bell?' Her eyes

slid past him almost with disdain. 'Penny sends love,' he said conspiratorially, but there was no catch in her even breathing. 'She'd like to come herself and bring Ben, but you know what the circumstances are.' He realised she didn't, of course: she had no idea what the circumstances were. 'Well anyway,' he said, 'they seem to look after you well here. It's a bigger place than I thought.' He tried to think of the information Penny would find most comforting from the visit. Her mother's doll-like hair looked tidy, the bedjacket was clean, the room also. No outward signs of neglect, or distress; no access to the inner world. There were no flowers, and Theo wished he'd brought some.

Mrs Bell gave a sigh from time to time, not of any heartfelt sorrow, but as if expressing some slight exasperation. 'I'd better be on my way,' Theo said. 'I'll be able to tell Penny you're fine. That old church pew is still there at the back door of the bach, you know.' He could think of no reason for giving such trivial information, except that it was something they both knew. 'Is there anything you want me to pass on to her?' No reply, and although her eyes met his, there was only a mild enquiry there. She had some longish hairs on her lower face, like the whiskers on the soft lip of a horse, and her loosely knuckled hands showed a deep, multi-hued pattern of veins and arteries in semi-translucent tissue.

How little distinction there seemed between the internal and outside scene, both bright, hot, immobile, with Penny's mother almost as generic and indifferent as the lizards and frogs of the courtyard. Theo half expected the arrival of a nurse, or a gardener, to check up on him, but he exaggerated the interest in his petty espionage. No one came, no one challenged him as he walked back through the corridors and then the grounds of the Malahide Home, and the sweat that stuck his shirt to his back was induced by heat alone, not suspense. The temperature inside the car was even greater, though he hadn't quite wound up the windows. He opened two of the doors and stood there in the carpark for a while, flexing his muscles. Despite the heat he wished he had his running gear, so that he could set off and prove his body still a willing mule for the mind within. Isn't it our secret belief that senility is a form of contagion: that its sufferers are best kept in quarantine? Old age never comes alone, his grandfather Esler used to say. What could he tell Penny in his email except that her mother was kept clean, the room had therapeutic blue and yellow on its walls, there was that one photograph of her as a young woman: that she was alive. But of course you haven't completely grown up until you realise that death is not the worst thing that can happen.

It was late before Theo reached home. The email he sent to Penny in paradise read – 'Your mother is well cared for so put your mind at rest about that. I had no trouble getting in to see her, and wasn't quizzed in any way. Enjoyed the time with you today and I'll keep in touch.'

It was fundamentally inadequate. But even to her face, especially to her face, Theo couldn't have said that he wished he was still at Drybread in her direct gaze, still seeing her slim hand stroking the hair forward on her son's head, aware of her full thigh beneath the denim.

There was a strength and resilience to her, but also a contained hurt and bewilderment. Theo had only platitudes and a knowledge of print media to offer her when he wished for a consolation which would be swiftly practical, but also have some nobility of compassionate understanding.

8

Theo had nothing to do with art history before he met Stella. Afterwards it still seemed to him a rather peculiar field. He had tried to get interested, but found it a disembodied discipline. Stella didn't practise art of any kind: there were no studios, kilns, canvases, brushes, cutting tools, chemically vivid concoctions, beaten copper, strung looms or closely grained timber, no rich odours of creation and no debris. Just books full of commentary and rumination, with illustrations of the works that inspired them. And the academic journals with articles of intense and lengthy focus on increasingly specialised aspects of other people's work: people spiralling in as if they could not only see the world in a grain of sand, but live there.

Stella contributed articles. During the time they were talking of divorce, she was working on the influence of traditional Aboriginal art on Australian faux primitivism at the end of the twentieth century. Sometimes, as Theo stood at her shoulder by the desk, in the laundry they had converted into her study, he would look at the reproductions of Howellenson and Picoutt as they argued about her refusal to shift when he got the Wellington job offer, or the lack of work he did around the house. 'You think I like cleaning toilets, and coming home to think of a meal every day?' she'd say. They were always civilised, these discussions, carried on without abuse, or raised voices, but with a painful disregard for feelings nevertheless. Maybe there was something of transference of discomfort: those works of art which were Stella's focus, flat in his gaze as they talked in quiet tones of controlled personal disappointment.

Theo knew that some friends, and more acquaintances, thought the marriage failed because they didn't have any children after twelve years. People can't resist a little complacent interpretation at such times, and that must be borne along with all the other bewilderments. But rather than childlessness being the cause, it was more likely a consequence. At first their careers were the given reason for the precautions Stella took, but then came a mutual unease at the prospects a child would have. They never talked about it, never came clean about the sense of separateness that grew between them, when the hope had been a growing closeness and understanding.

It's absurd that you don't discuss something so essential, but common nevertheless, despite the absurdity. The risk is too great: too much turns on the outcome, in the same way that a man with an obscure and certain sense of illness refuses to get any medical opinion. It's better to talk of trivial practicalities, better to discuss other people's lives rather than your own.

Anyway, no children and nothing between them that wasn't divisible. Everything they had made together could be separated: house sold, assets apportioned. Like so much, however, that was only partly true. There remained twelve years of a shared life – ribs which can be split at the front, but remain connected to the backbone.

When Theo thought of Stella, she was at her laundry desk, or eating. Both characteristic recollections. Although quite slim, she was always snacking on something – a piece of toast and lime and orange marmalade, half a muffin, a sliver of carrot, a plain wine biscuit, a nub of cheese, mandarin segments, maybe one of those fruit and bran twist things in foil. She would wander through the house eating, or come out to the car, chewing, with other things on her mind. Yet seated at a table with a meal as the priority, she had little appetite. 'Not as much as that,' she'd say. 'I'm passing on the meat today', or 'I've done just the one for you'. She would sit patiently during the time it took Theo to finish a full meal, talking a little of the trivial politics of the university department, or of the plans for the barbecue area.

No, no children, although occasionally Theo found himself turning over names in his mind. Journalists need to get the name right: they recognise the importance of names and their pedigree. Hector is a name with a grand, sad history. It is one of the names he might have given a son, but perhaps it would have been an imposition. Theo could imagine the boy being disgruntled, and then, after Theo had told the story of the Trojans and Achaeans, becoming enthusiastic about bearing the name of Hector.

For some time after they sold the house, Theo continued

to feel a certain amount of proprietorial responsibility. There was a birch tree that overhung the front bedroom and clogged the spouting there if you didn't get up with the ladder three or four times a year. Driving past, he saw that the new owners had neglected to do that, and the water had backed up and flowed down the wall enough times to encourage a green stain on the roughcast. At first he felt the itch to fix the problem, or go in and instruct the new people, then he became accustomed to it not being part of his responsibility. For Stella too, he experienced a sense of obligation that waned only gradually. He knew she'd struggle with her tax return, but resisted the idea of offering to do it, and rang with the name of an accountant. He sent a card for her first birthday following the divorce, and the first Christmas. He rang when her father became seriously ill, and later warned her of a virulent new computer virus when the IT guy at the paper got wind of it. Each of these contacts was negotiated with civility, but was buffeting all the same, at least for Theo. Afterwards he would be for a time emotionally stunned. It was bewildering that small changes of direction could in the end bring you to an unsought destination. He still had dreams in which his marriage was accepted and familiar fact, and woke to find it was his real life that seemed imagination.

After the divorce, the recollections of good times shared gained in lustre and significance, and the issues that had led to separation became increasingly insubstantial. It was the natural sentimentalism of a parting, Theo told himself, and not proof they'd made the wrong decision, yet how powerful sometimes was the evidence from their shared past. Theo remembered Stella's surprise gift to him when he'd been awarded the Wintermann Journalism Fellowship, which took them to London for six months. She led him to a narrow shop in Kings Cross, and insisted he try on the long coats of Italian leather that were top of the range there. Despite his protests at the cost, she bought for him a shin-length, belted black coat, the leather of which was soft as a flannel and as finely wrinkled as the face of an ageing duchess. Stella called it his French gangster's coat, and Theo would wear it as they went sightseeing in London. They would clasp their hands within the pocket of the coat and squeeze their fingers together in a sign of intimacy and happiness as they walked. The coat ended up at the far end of Theo's wardrobe: too opulent to wear, he might have said, yet knowing its real failing was as witness to a lost time of happiness.

Only once after their divorce did Theo meet Stella with another man, although of course she had male friends. Theo had been to the Coast for yet another story on disputed mining rights, and came back over Arthur's Pass on a hot, Canterbury afternoon, and stopped at the Darfield pub for a drink. Stella and a tall guy with a lot of floppy hair were at an outside table. Theo stood by them briefly and talked. They also had been on the Coast for several days. She introduced him without detail, and the guy said that, as a lawyer, he had a bit to do with forestry and mining issues. He would be interested to read Theo's articles. Theo stood, and they sat, which made a demarcation plain between them. She was eating more substantially than he remembered. How many times he'd sat beside her to constitute a couple, and they had talked to someone outside that partnership, and now he was the one excluded, passing by.

It was almost a physical dislocation, worst when Theo

left them. To walk to his car, to drive away without waving, and see them talking together, caused a mixture of sadness and anger. Logic is powerless against habitual things, and failure is debilitating. Maybe she told the floppy-haired guy a bit more about Theo. He's my ex, she might say. It didn't work out. He's never fully grown up in some ways. Maybe they had more personal things to talk about. Theo and Stella had needed to part; they had agreed to part, but life seeks continuity, and an end to love's endeavour is always painful.

9

Nicholas and Theo went to a Thai restaurant together once a week or so if it suited. Nicholas said Thai cooking had less sodium something or other than Chinese cooking did. The chemistry of the meal didn't interest Theo. What he did like was that the Thai place was BYO, with a moderate corkage charge. Theo knew that journalists have a reputation for meanness, but being ripped off went against his professional pride. At Thai Hai Nicholas and Theo could bring a decent cab merlot, and not have to pay $35.

Nicholas was forty-six. Theo had been to most birthdays he'd had in the last decade or so, several of them in the Thai Hai where they were sitting, a couple of the earlier ones at his home when Nicholas was still with Trish. For some years he taught journalism at the university, but had then come back to the paper. He said he'd given up the varsity work because of the temptation of young women there, the disclosure of the loose tops as they bent over their notes, their willingness to be educated. Too many tar-babies, he'd say: far too much entanglement. The real reason was that he was by disposition a journalist, not a teacher, and couldn't be happy without the investigative challenge. For the same reason, Nicholas had turned down offers of promotion. He was iconoclastic, and reluctant to have any responsibility for other people. His talent and seniority were recognised by the title of deputy chief reporter, but the leadership he gave was by way of his stories, not administration or pastoral care.

Nicholas seemed to wish he was doing the Maine-King story. 'What does she look like?' he said.

'I've told you.'

'You're not screwing her, are you?' he said. 'Keep yourself clear of that while you handle the story. Women are tar-babies, you know that.' The tables were close together in Thai Hai, and at his enquiry a small, overdressed woman stared across at them. It seemed to Theo a warning, rather than embarrassment expressed, but Nicholas lifted his porcelain soup spoon in salute to her and went on. 'You won't be able to handle it, you know, mixing work and your sex life. And anyway, you've got Melanie to consider.'

'We're friends.'

'Yes, but you're screwing her, aren't you?'

'Oh, shut up about it,' Theo said. The small woman looked at him, almost approvingly he thought.

Nicholas was both right and wrong about Melanie, and Theo wasn't going to explain that over a meal at the Thai Hai. Melanie and he were friends, and because they were both journalists, they could unload on each other knowing they would be understood. They did make love, but not often, and although on those occasions she was an active participant, Theo knew it was more for his sake than any great need she felt. It was the quid pro quo of such friendships, though never talked about as such.

'Anyway,' said Nicholas, 'tell me about this new Family Law Act and what difference it's going to make in your Maine-King case.'

'Not a hell of a lot, I imagine. I ploughed through some of it and then gave up. Zack Heywood says the main changes are procedural, making the sittings more open to other parties, that sort of stuff.'

'Heywood's shit hot I'm told.'

'One quite important thing is that the court's been given greater powers to enforce its orders. Maybe that's going to make it more difficult for Penny.'

'I'll have extra steamed rice and some of that sweet and sour,' Nicholas told the waitress. He enjoyed his food. 'Heywood acted for the council when that building assents guy took a personal grievance case for wrongful dismissal.' You could categorise Nicholas as crass and lacking concern for others, but you'd be wrong. His often disconcerting directness was not an entirely true representation. He vacuumed up information, and recalled it, with impressive ease. He took nothing at face value. As they went on to talk more about family law and Zack, Theo knew that long after the conversation Nicholas would retain the useful bones of it. 'Two years ago I interviewed one of the founders of that group set up by men who considered they were discriminated against by the Family Court,' said Nicholas. 'He was an angry, disappointed guy all right. Does the new law address that issue?'

'I'm not sure.'

'Like Dr Johnson he wasn't a fastidious man about his linen. The inside of his shirt collar had a ring of grime like candle smudge.'

'Who's this?'

'The leader of the discriminated men I interviewed. I've just been talking about him. This stuff I'm doing at the moment about the origin of party funds. It's not a very interesting story. I have a feeling there's something more significant going on in our relations with the States. There's been undisclosed meetings right up to ministerial level. I'm going to ask to go to Wellington for a few days, and poke around. If we weren't run by useless tight-arses I'd go to Washington.'

'Won't it just be the old nuclear-free waltz again?' Theo asked.

'Nah, a fresh scent on the breeze, I think,' said Nicholas.

The evening with Nicholas, his projects and opinions, made Theo realise how preoccupied he'd become with Penny and her circumstances: how closely focused on the connection between their lives. Even the small woman at the next table was a reminder that everyone has a life going on, though it seems only shadow play to others. He was half aware of her conversation with her nodding and acquiescent female companion, even as he and Nicholas talked and ate.

She was a dumpy woman, full of unnecessary movement like a clucky hen. She had recently lost a husband named Bruce, and expressed bitterness at his desertion. 'He didn't put his affairs in order,' she said. 'Not at all, despite the diagnosis. He left everything to me. I mean he left everything for me to do, as well as everything to me. He never could make decisions.' Her friend nodded over a plate of noodles and cauliflower stalks.

Nicholas interrupted himself on diplomatic chicanery to lean closer to Theo. 'What ever order his affairs were in, I'd say, by the look of her, that each one was both a necessity and a blessing.'

'People don't realise the pressures of being a carer at the end,' she said. 'Bruce became a sad child, and petulant too. People have no conception, no idea until it happens to them. And they have a misplaced sympathy, don't you think?' Nod, nod was the response at her table, a grimace from Nicholas was the acknowledgement at his.

Theo glanced at his watch. It would be night at last in the Drybread gully. There would be no strong lights in any of the three huts, but if there was a moon the serrations of the Dunstan tops would perhaps be clear on the skyline. The wind would stream down the small valleys, and the rabbits would appear in silence like target pop-ups on a fairground range. Ben would be asleep, and Penny too perhaps, or she might be sitting by herself with a Tilly lamp, wondering just how she had ended up back at Drybread as a fugitive. At night resolution is at its most precarious, and misfortune the more naturally nocturnal creature. Sometimes there was a wind in the dark which came directly north – a drop in temperature as if a great door were opened somewhere and the air moved in from above that long ocean between Antarctica and the South Island.

When Nicholas got up to leave, he paused at the widow's side. 'Our condolences for your loss,' he said, and was rewarded with an affronted, yet impersonal, stare and an agitated rustle of clothing. The woman's companion nodded agreeably. Perhaps her mind was far away. Maybe her body too. They say women of a certain age become invisible to men as they cease to register sexually. A certain agitation of matter particles occasioned by admiration and lust in the regard of others might be necessary to maintain their corporeal existence; otherwise they disappear, slipping beneath the male radar.

As he paid his share of the bill, Nicholas spoke to the slim Thai woman who very much existed. He used a sentence of Thai which Theo knew from other visits meant thank you and good fortune. It wasn't entirely affectation, but also an expression of Nicholas's wide-ranging curiosity. Theo was reminded again of his own limiting and selfish preoccupations. Why didn't he give a rat's arse for the Thai culture, the sorrows of Bruce's bantam widow, the possibility of a change in our relationship with the USA? Nicholas's personal life was as humdrum and as much a failure as Theo's own, yet he was more active in observation of the world. His sons were growing up in Australia with his ex-wife. He sent them presents, visited occasionally, tried not to think of his true obligation towards them. He told Theo they never gave any outward show of missing him, and he was grateful for that. Maybe they didn't miss him, he admitted. No use deceiving yourself.

As they left the restaurant, Nicholas told Theo about the windfarm protest story that Anna had pushed onto him. Stories were his profession, and that's how he managed his life also, packaging his experience as commodity: shaping it from the raw until it was external to himself and so less threatening.

'So how did it go?' asked Theo. 'They get worked up?'

'A bunch of country bigots who reckoned the turbines would drive them all mad with noise not audible to humans. They had a protest march along a goat track in the Seaward Kaikouras. A day of follies really. Linda and I drove ourselves up there. At Amberley we picked up a hitchhiker who had a placard claiming the Americans were building spy stations in the South Island. Linda didn't want to give him a lift because of her cameras in the back, but I said he'd be a useful addition to the protesters and be good for some copy and photos. He never once looked us in the face, and spoke as if he had a treble pipe in his throat. When he wasn't talking about the worldwide conspiracies of American capitalism, there was still this slight whistle when he breathed. We were up by Cheviot when there was this strong smell of plum jam in the car. You know the smell of home-made plum jam?'

'Sure.'

'It's not entirely unpleasant. Anyway there was this strong smell of it, and in the end I said something to Linda, and she said the guy had taken his shoes off a way back. That's just what it was. The guy can't have washed his feet for weeks. We dropped him at Kaikoura, and Linda wouldn't have anything to eat. She was pissed off with me for most of the day, but the smell was exactly like that – like plum jam.'

'You could do a story on that, about hitchhikers who don't wash and smell like plum jam.'

'Exactly like,' said Nicholas. 'It's funny isn't it.'

'It's actually quite nice, plum jam.'

'Did you know that twenty-four wind turbines can provide power for thirty thousand homes?' Nicholas asked. Theo didn't answer: none was expected. Nicholas said such things just to imbed them in his capacious memory.

As they neared the work carpark a tall boy in a tracksuit

loped past. 'Are you still running, Theo?' Nicholas asked.

Theo chose not to take it as a figurative summation of his life. 'A couple of times a week at least.'

'You must be a fit bugger,' Nicholas said. 'I should be doing it, but somehow I can't get into the routine. We should try for a fishing trip soon. Blue cod in the Sounds – what do you reckon?'

'Good idea, if Anna will let us off together. I've got a fair bit on. This Maine-King story is taking up a hell of a lot of time, what with the secrecy and everything.'

'You want to watch it there,' said Nicholas.

'They're not divorced yet.'

'Whatever. Anyway, you watch yourself, Theo. Catch you later.'

Nicholas went into the building that housed the paper; Theo wandered into the darkness of the carpark. The distant artificial light glinted here and there on glass, chrome or a polished bonnet, but wasn't strong enough to cast definite shadows. The carpark was almost entirely walled in by the high buildings around it. Traffic noise was muted, and more insistent over it was retro ballad music from the direction of the beauty shop. There seemed to be plenty of overtime available for beauticians. The smells were not of the cars, but of wood and lino corridors, refuse skips, female potions and, faintly, the penned lesser creatures of the pet shop.

A pace or two from his Audi, Theo used the remote to unlock it, and in the quick flash that the park lights gave in response, he glimpsed a figure standing close by. 'Theo Esler?' the man said pleasantly. He came closer to the side of the car. Even in that dim light Theo recognised the parson, though standing near him he realised that he was a bigger man than he'd appeared while driving.

'Nice car,' the parson said.

'Thanks.'

'Very nice cars these.' He nodded. 'You're the reporter who's been dealing with the Maine-King custody business, aren't you?'

'That's right, and you are?'

'My name's Hugo Doull.' The parson didn't extend a hand. Hugo Doull was a good name for a private detective, the carpark was a suitable place for him to materialise – slightly noir in atmosphere. But Hugo didn't have a trenchcoat, or a felt hat low over his face. He wasn't smoking.

'Ever been in holy orders, Mr Doull?' Theo said. After the wine and meal with Nicholas, he couldn't see that Hugo Doull's appearance was something to be taken seriously.

'I'm a private investigator,' the parson said. 'Maybe we could sit in your comfortable car for a while and talk.'

'I haven't got that much time,' Theo said.

'Okay, just a quick word here then.'

Was that the parson's life: attempting to get reluctant strangers to talk to him, standing on the outside of doors and gates and open friendship? A life of uninvited and reluctant intercourse. A dispassionate professionalism would be needed, otherwise you'd come to believe other people found you personally unattractive. He tilted his head back in the semi-darkness and worked his shoulders a little. Maybe he'd been standing in the carpark a long time, and was disappointed at not being able to sit in the car. He seemed in no hurry to begin. His shirt had a soft collar, and there was a monogram of some sort on his jacket pocket.

'The thing is,' he said. 'The thing is Mrs Maine-King's

in defiance of a legitimate court order. She's in hiding despite that court order and warrant to enforce it, and the authorities and other parties concerned are entitled to know where she and the boy are.' There was nothing threatening in the parson's tone, rather it was one of gentle reproof. 'And your articles, Theo, although perfectly justifiable in themselves, indicate you know where Mrs Maine-King is. You know where to contact her.'

Theo told the parson about journalistic freedoms, about the protection of sources and so on, and the parson nodded slightly in the dark, even worked his shoulders. It was late enough for them both, and the novelty of the encounter was wearing thin for Theo. 'I'd better be off,' he said.

'The thing is,' said the parson, not moving from the car door, 'that my client's willing to pay for information. How to get in touch with Mrs Maine-King, I mean. Her whereabouts in fact.'

'Not interested,' Theo said.

'Willing to pay quite a lot. Remember that Mrs Maine-King's in the wrong here. Breaking the law in fact, Theo.'

Being called Theo by the parson irritated him. It was the talkback host's unjustified assumption of familiarity. And Theo didn't like to have Penny classified as a law breaker when he was aware of her suffering. He told the parson he didn't want to talk any more, and without much thought put the flat of his hand on the parson's chest to move him from the car door. He wasn't thinking all that clearly. The parson took his wrist with a markedly firm grip and suggested they didn't need to get physical. 'Fuck off,' Theo said.

Having had a few wines and feeling morally superior, Theo assumed that dealing with the parson would play out according to their respective just deserts. He was wrong. Theo hit the parson's long face with his free hand, but thereafter it was all parson. He slammed Theo into the side of the car and kneed him in the hip, catching a nerve. He put a hand behind Theo's head and pushed him into the outside mirror. The mirror unit came away from the connection as it was designed to do after such trauma, and bounced on the carpark seal. 'Maybe you need to do more than just the running, Theo,' the parson said, trying to keep his breathing even. 'I don't like to be pushed. Sorry about the mirror. They're excellent cars these – hold their resale value well, I'm told.'

He walked away quickly, already regretting what had happened. There would be no repercussions: he was disappointed in a lapse of professionalism, and Theo was humiliated at being so easily bested one on one. Theo was left alone in the dim carpark and glad of it. He retrieved the plastic mirror unit and sat in the car for a while to calm down. He told myself that if he hadn't been drinking he'd have had the bastard. He decided he wouldn't worry Penny by saying anything about it.

In the morning he noticed a bruise on his cheek, the fractures on the glass of his watch face and the scratches on the door of the car. That pissed him more than anything. The Audi's colour was a metallic blue of deep iridescence, and any touch-up from the bottle was always obvious. He would be on the lookout for the parson in the future, feeling a playground determination to get his own back. Stella used to tell him that he could be very unforgiving. 'You can be so proud, can't you,' she'd say. 'You find it so hard to let things go.' He never understood what she meant by it.

10

Melanie was the editor of the leading local community newspaper. It wasn't cutting-edge journalism by any means, but she didn't care about that any more. She'd been on the main newspaper with Theo, Nicholas and Anna, but the community newspaper gave more regular hours and was less rigorous regarding copy: mainly feel-good Christchurch stories and thinly disguised advertising. She had an acknowledged flair for computers, and her male colleagues were sexist enough to be impressed. She was good at friendship too, without the exclusiveness that marks some women's affection. 'Come round for pasta tomorrow,' she said on the phone, the day after the parson and the carpark.

'What have you done to your face?' she asked Theo on his arrival, and with the misdirection that truth allows he told her that he had hit his head on the outside mirror of the car. 'Looks sore, Theo,' she said. 'You should take better care of yourself.'

More than usual he was aware of her appearance, perhaps because it was Penny who had been on his mind. Melanie was small, and when they lay together her head almost tucked under his chin. Her height was less noticeable when she was upright because of the great, springy fan of her brown hair. The exaggerated, cheerful hair seen in a child's picture book, but quite her own, and although she used the brush often, it remained recalcitrant. Sometimes, when they were quiet together, Theo would rest his hand on that abundance of hair and feel his slight pressure returned by natural resilience.

They ate with trays on their knees and watched the television news. An easy domesticity although Melanie was unmarried, and Theo lived alone. She carried on a sort of derisive interrogation of the newsreaders, reporters and interviewees which required no response from him, and surely would be just the same if she were alone. 'Christ almighty, call that national news,' she would say of an item in which a spaniel was rescued from a sewer after three days, a Lithuanian woman won a newt-eating competition, or a potato looking like the Duomo in Florence was dug up in the Weka Weka. 'How do you think she feels, you cretin,' she would say when a dead boy's mother was invited to elaborate on her state of mind. 'And they call this headline news,' she would say. 'I can't stand to watch it. I just can't.' But the deficiencies, and her vehement criticism of them, kept her before the television.

Only when the news was over and the screen dead did they begin to settle to talk. First she wanted Theo to tell her about the colleagues they both knew, and the trivial yet absorbing politics of the workplace which is so much of life, then she shared her own experience of a personal grievance case arising from the sacking of a journalist, and the commercial resistance to the hike in advertising rates she felt obliged to introduce. The childish mass of her springy hair, her round face, the overall smallness of her person, were all in constant, startling juxtaposition to the shrewd and mature understanding of her conversation.

Later she talked about Stella, and that too was a usual, if passing, topic of their evenings together. Melanie remained a friend to them both, and was one of the few intermediaries equally trusted. She had had no part whatsoever in the collapse of the marriage, and only months later had she agreed to have sex with Theo, who never asked if she later told Stella they were occasional lovers.

'Stella's father isn't well,' Melanie said. 'He's been having blackouts, and now he has to go for a brain scan. Stella thinks he won't be able to live by himself for much longer, and yet he swears he won't go into a home. You know what he's like. She thought you might like to call him.' Theo thought of Mrs Bell in the Malahide Home: the slowing of time there, the lizards and the one-bed rooms, the drift of the past behind the eyes. Norman was right not to go gentle into such a place.

Theo liked Stella's dad. He'd never interfered in their marriage, and never accused Theo of destroying it. He was a quiet man who spent his professional life drilling people's teeth, and his private life absorbed with the geological formations of Banks Peninsula. He published papers on the drowned calderas of the peninsula, and discovered several volcanic dikes. He never asked Theo if he could keep Stella in the manner to which he'd accustomed her, or why there'd been no children. Theo admired the way he could sit still, relaxed, for long periods of time, and his thinning, grey hair immaculately harrowed into lines by the comb. Of course Theo would call, but what annoyed him was being pushed towards it by Stella, and indirectly at that. It was a sort of exemplary manipulation that was difficult to criticise, but which he resented all the same.

'Stella could have told me herself, couldn't she?'

'We happened to meet in Merivale, and I said you were coming round. "Tell Theo about Dad," she said.'

'I like Norman.'

'Why don't you ring from here?' said Melanie.

There it was again, the disposition of other people's lives. Theo waited a bit to let the small irritation subside. 'It's okay,' he said.

'She's going to Melbourne soon for an art historians' conference. The head of department chose her over more senior people, apparently.'

Theo knew the head of the university faculty. He was an intellectual bore who specialised in kinetic sculpture and hung his glasses on his chest by a blue ribbon. Most of Stella's university colleagues had spent too much time, mole-like, in libraries and study cubicles. Each seemed to have cultivated some small but determined idiosyncrasy of appearance – a goatee beard, a Mexican silver medallion, striped winter stockings, or a green corduroy suit – which served as a signal of academic and personal freedom. Stella said his mockery of her work friends arose from insecurity. 'Theo,' she'd say, 'no one cares if you haven't got a doctorate, just be yourself. You're good at what you do. You've had a fellowship in London, for Christ's sake.

You've won awards.' She'd enjoy the Melbourne trip, even if in the company of the intellectual bore.

'She always asks after you,' said Melanie. 'You guys have managed a split as well as anyone I know.'

'What is it they say – We Are Still The Best Of Friends.' The truth was that Theo believed pain a form of anaesthetic, and so you learn to touch and talk with a detached and mutual sympathy, your other feelings reduced.

Later, Melanie and he got onto the Maine-King case and his articles. She thought it was some of his best writing. Nicholas had told her that the pieces were being run even in competing papers and magazines. It was the best exclusive story for Theo since the Flowerday audit fraud, and he'd won a prize for that. Because he was the only one with access to Penny, and because she trusted him, he could shape and develop the story as he wished, with plenty of personal stuff and parallels with other cases. A couple of other journalists had made contact with Erskine's lawyers, but he didn't open up his side of things, and just pushed the line that he wanted the custody orders enforced.

'You get the sympathy vote, don't you,' said Melanie. 'She's a Kiwi, she's a mother come home with her child, she's a victim of foreign judicial processes, she's attractive and she did that trash television thing. It's all there as a magazine package.'

'I've had approaches from other papers – bribes really. And there are people sniffing around to find out where Penny's hiding. A detective came and interviewed me at the paper.' Theo decided not to go into detail about the parson – not to mention him at all.

'What's she like?'

'I think she's quite gutsy really,' he said. 'I didn't like

how self-centred she was at first, but now I realise the pressure she's under: holed up with a kid and everything stacked against you. In a way, I suppose, she's fighting for her life.'

'Nick says you see her quite often.'

'No, I've only met her a couple of times.'

'He says you've hit it off.'

'You know Nick: close a door on any man and woman and they're shagging.'

'And are you?' said Melanie.

'No.'

'But you like her, I can tell.'

'I like her okay now I've got to know her a bit better. She's been in a hell of a situation.'

Theo thought of Penny right then. No phone to ring anybody, no neighbour, and if she went to the curtainless window, or the door, there would be just the country darkness with no lights at all. Just the far removed stars in a plush, shadowed sky, and the massed hills even darker; just the occasional sheep in its stupid sleep; just the wild briar with no sun to show its burnished orange and red rose hips; just the oily flow of the dark creek.

Melanie liked beer, but had no interest in sport, which in some ways was a bit odd. On the other hand she was a very direct person, completely without snobbery, and accustomed to working with men. Theo preferred wine with meals, but brought export lager when he came to Melanie's place. They drank it after the meal too, when the trays and pasta bowls had been taken back to her small kitchen and they sat talking on the sofa facing the blank television. She was having a disagreement with her proprietors about the space given to obituaries. She was opposed to extended eulogistic accounts of locals who achieved nothing of significance except old age, extended service to fatuous organisations and a multitude of children and grandchildren. The owners believed those children were her readership. 'So help me God, Theo, is there anything more crassly commercial than a community newspaper?'

Theo, running his hands over her warm breasts, of course agreed: a flat earth apologist would have had his endorsement at the time. 'Let's go through to the bed,' he said. It was a large bed, the cover of which had Christmas trees of different colours on it. Whenever they lay across it, he could see through the screen of Melanie's springy hair a narrow strip of carpet between bed and wall. The carpet had a haze of pale fluff, and on it, sealed in green and blue foil, was a cough lolly. He had seen it occasionally over the months, but never mentioned it to Melanie. She may not have understood that such conscious observation was no indication he was less than fully involved in lovemaking: she may have taken disclosure as a criticism of her housekeeping.

That night he was to see nothing of Christmas trees, or cough lollies. 'No, I don't think so,' Melanie said. 'I don't think we should shag while there might be something developing between you and Penny Maine-King. It doesn't feel right, Theo. I'm happy enough with our style of friendship, but not while there's someone else in the picture.'

Theo's first response was a purely selfish one: he told himself he was a fool to have said anything about Penny until after Melanie and he had sex. He knew her well enough to have anticipated both her intuitive sense of Penny's significance and her reaction. She was right, of course, but his cock was aggrieved. A cock has ancient wisdom, but little awareness of what is politic in the contemporary world. The cock is an equal opportunity employer, yet has no deeper motivation than mere opportunity. Melanie didn't demand marriage, or any proprietal relationship that involved living together, but she did insist on being the one lover in a man's life. Absolutely right and wholly admirable, but cock thought bugger to all that.

'You understand,' she said.

'Sure,' he said.

She was relaxed on the sofa, leaning on his shoulder. 'Tell me how things work out,' she said. 'We go back a long way, Theo.'

'That's right.' They did go back a long way. She was a good friend, a good person.

'You won't forget about Stella's dad, will you?' she said. A good friend, but not perfect of course: capable of arousing irritation as well as desire.

In the office the next morning Theo was checking Reuters reports when he thought of Stella's father. Maybe Norman came to mind because the editor passed by, with his thin hair combed forward as the weed aligns in the current of a shallow stream. Maybe it was the report of how many people had died at a wedding in Hyderabad because of illicit booze made from refrigeration fluid.

Theo rang Norman, who answered with the courteous professionalism of the dentist he'd once been. 'I heard you haven't been so well,' Theo said. 'I'm sorry about that. Hope they can get to the bottom of what's causing the turns.' Norman told him he was having both brain and chest scans, and a raft of other tests. He said he was finally getting something back for being overcharged by his private health insurers for years. He made a joke of it in his typical, wry way. He'd still be waiting to see a specialist if he'd relied on public health, he said. 'Anyway, you take care of yourself. If there's anything heavy to do around the place don't hesitate to give me a ring,' Theo said.

Norman didn't say anything at all about Stella. Her mother had been dead for a long time, but perhaps Norman still remembered how private a thing a marriage was, and could imagine the complex pain of its deliberate dissolution. Maybe that pain was not so different from the grief Norman had felt at the separation forced upon him. Theo wanted Norman to call him by name, say he shouldn't feel blame for what had happened, that relationships collapse of some subtle and external volition rather than at the instigation of those concerned. Theo wanted Norman to absolve him of some offence to the family. He might say, Theo, don't beat yourself up about such things. He might say, I know there was no cruelty in it all, no intention to hurt. He might say, personal growth is achieved by accepting the inevitable, and that human personality is intractable.

'Well, thanks for calling, Theo,' Norman said calmly, and rang off.

11

Angie was the hottest of the women reporters. Nicholas and Theo agreed on that. So did the entire male editorial staff, though no formal vote was taken. The consensus was apparent in their jocular acceptance of her. No doubt in the end she'd be overweight, but in her mid-twenties the fullness of figure was just contained by the elasticity of youth. She had that confident disregard for her own attractiveness that naturally good-looking women can afford. Allure was second nature to her, as much a part of who she was as the relaxed laugh and the love of innuendo.

She could get anything out of Nicholas, and the others would sometimes use her as emissary to tap his contacts and his expertise. He knew, she knew, they knew, that proximity to such buxom promise cheered him greatly, and he was old enough to understand that simple and healthy pleasure was as far as it went. Since his divorce Theo had sometimes imagined a relationship with Angie might be one of greater and more profitable ambiguity, but she treated him in just the same way. Theo was never quite sure how he had reached the age of thirty-eight, or why. He wasn't conscious of growing older, but Angie obviously placed him in the same category as Nicholas.

'You know the boat people stuff you did,' she said. Standing at Theo's desk she looked out into the alley and back entrances to the beautician and pet shop, as all journalists from the dark side of the reporters' room tended to do when they came over to the window. The reminder of a world external to the baleful flicker of computer screens was intriguing. 'Anna's asked me to do a story on the women – their perspective, motives, how they cope and all that.'

'How predictably inclusive,' said Nicholas.

'I know,' said Angie. She said it in a conspiratorial whisper, and drew out the vowel in an exaggerated way. She really was a good-looking woman. Even her hands were perfectly formed and indefinably suggestive. Do such women ever have feelings of inadequacy, fully realise their power, and how are they reconciled to life when their beauty fades? 'Anyway, I thought you might be able to give me a couple of contacts from the refugee people you spoke to for your piece.'

'He's still in touch with a few Philippine and Indonesian women,' said Nicholas slyly. 'They look to him for succour.'

'Really,' said Angie, and gave Nicholas the eye flash he sought.

'He's offered to go down to the centre and help them

get orientated. I don't know which direction they'll end up facing.'

'Really,' said Angie.

'Knock it off, you two,' said Theo. 'You'll end up mud-wrestling together soon.' Nicholas made as if to take off his shirt, and Angie wriggled slightly and pouted. Nicholas then returned to his work, and Angie pulled a stool to Theo's side. He found his file on the boat people and suggested some contacts, especially an Indonesian woman who spoke good English and whose reasons for getting out seemed to be political rather than economic. And there was a much older woman who had given her life savings to some con man who promised fully authorised and official admittance to the country. Angie was relaxed and professional, flirtation done with at a stroke, unless of course Theo chose to begin it afresh. He admired the ease with which she altered her response so surely from one mood to another, and without apparent calculation. He felt the pleasure of being beside her, yet recognised how instinctive it was, how little concerned with his knowledge that she was intelligent, ambitious and good-natured.

His feelings for Penny were different weren't they? Or rather they included the same response, but more besides. There was something about Penny that discovered in him an emotion he'd not felt before: not for Stella, not for Melanie, not for women important in his life before either of them. Some combination of sympathy and apprehension: a protective concern for some recovery in her life, and a wish to be part of that restitution. The closer he came to her, the more he sensed in her something drawn dangerously tight, something suppressed, which might snap with immense consequence. Even as he talked with

Angie, even with the physical awareness of her presence, in the quieter preserve of his mind he thought of Penny and Ben, hidden and isolated in the Dunstan hills. Penny's hands on the little boy's shoulders: her preoccupation with his happiness, and his careless possession of it.

You could leave a woman, or have a woman leave you, but you could never fully abandon the experience of the relationship, for that isn't amenable to conscious choice. Like the time of childhood, it may seem to have concerned a different person, but it held its own power nevertheless, and had an independent influence on all that followed.

When Angie went back to her desk, Theo returned to his own work, but uppermost in his mind was an incident of over two years before. He had come home early in the afternoon, after saying he would be late. The politician he'd arranged to interview had postponed his flight and was no longer available. Theo didn't realise there was anyone in the house at first. There were no cars in the drive, and he used his key on the door. He left his jacket hung on the back of a dining room chair, and went through to the kitchen to make a corned beef sandwich. As he finished that small task, he heard a man's voice and then Stella's quick, subdued laugh from one of the bedrooms.

He could have left the house then, for everything except the identity of her companion was in that laugh. He didn't, of course. He stood indecisive at the kitchen door with the sandwich on a white plate. The sun through the dining room windows made bright geometrics on the carpet and table; a circle of pale petals lay beneath the roses on the table; Theo's jacket was unmoved. So the jester challenges us to see the subjective and objective as distinct.

Had Theo been an innocent, as well as injured, husband,

he may have burst into the bedroom in the pantomime way. Instead he walked quietly into the passage, glanced into the empty main bedroom and passed on to the guest one, in which Stella lay on her back. There was no movement. Her eyes were closed, her hair spread on the sheeted mattress from which the pillows had been tossed to the floor. Just her head was visible above the pale shield of her lover's back. He was partly bald, well muscled and had a patch of dark hair at the top of his spine. Theo wasn't interested in the man's identity, and surprised himself in that. Before he could leave, however, he needed to have his presence acknowledged by his wife. And so the three were quiet and motionless together there for a moment – Theo at the doorway, Stella and the other man on the bed. Theo had time to recognise that post-coital hiatus of relaxation and achievement; time for the thought that Stella had chosen the spare room, as he had himself in similar circumstances, then she opened her eyes and saw him at the doorway.

Their gaze met. Just for that instant the stark pain registered for both, then she squeezed her eyes shut and turned her head to the side. Nothing was said; nothing external changed. The stranger's back remained relaxed, and only as Theo was taking his jacket from the dining room chair and preparing to leave, did he hear the murmur of voices from the bedroom.

Theo had driven back to the paper and sat at his desk overlooking the service alley. He wrote up a piece about high country runs being bought by overseas buyers, and the possible economic and political implications. He did nearly a thousand words of serviceable copy before he finished work for the day, and during the time it took, one part of his mind was in a quite different, empty space, considering what the afternoon had made inevitable. Sadness it was, rather than indignant surprise, or anger. The man in the spare bed was a consequence of failure between himself and Stella, not the cause of it. Theo knew it, just as he knew the mixture of guilt, remorse and justification that Stella would be feeling.

He was about to leave when Anna asked him to come into her office. She was alarmed at the standard of work coming from Michael, a middle-aged reporter not long over from a newspaper on the Coast. 'The stuff's crap,' she said. 'The subs are really struggling with it. I've talked to him – I've tried him with all sorts of stories, and nothing decent comes in. If he was a kid it would be bad enough, but he's been a journo for years, for Christ's sake.'

Theo made an effort to bring Michael to mind, and gradually assembled the image of a badly dressed guy known in the office mainly for being able to imitate the prime minister's voice and run an office sweepstake on anything from rugby to the hip measurements of the editor's wife. He also had the habit of ridiculing others, then laughing so loudly that no rejoinder was audible. It was a stupid, irritating and effective technique.

Theo saw Michael most working days, talked with him, but didn't give a damn about him at that moment. He felt glassed off from the rest of the world. He sat in Anna's office as she asked him if he would take a mentor's interest in Michael for everybody's sake, but the words seemed to bounce away before they quite reached him. 'He nominated you as someone he was prepared to take advice from,' said Anna. 'He's got some hang-up about being told anything by a woman, I think, though he won't admit that of course. It's funny, isn't it, the less ability some guys have, the greater their conviction they know it all. He doesn't seem to realise his job's on the line here.' A woman less comfortable with her role may have insisted that Michael be instructed by her, but Anna was looking for a sensible solution.

Theo could have said he didn't give a fuck. He could have recounted the story of his afternoon and taken note of the chief reporter's response. He could have said Michael was a useless prick and should be fired as soon as possible. He could have said nothing, and concentrated on Anna's competent netball hands as an anchor in the here and now. 'Yes, okay,' he said. 'I'll give it some thought over the next few days and get back to you. It'll have to be something reasonably formal, or he'll just arse around.' Anna seemed quite happy with that. When Theo stood up to go, he felt for a moment as if that normal propulsion would keep him rising steadily until he was held, checked beneath the ceiling, with unusual view upon Anna and the flat of her desk, the framed awards on the wall behind her. But then he steadied and was able to walk out, though very light on his feet.

He knew that Stella would be there when he went home. It wasn't in her nature to evade a meeting. She was sitting in the sunroom, looking out to the brick barbecue area and the plum tree on the boundary. She had no book, which was unusual. Her face was blotchy, but her voice steady. 'You told me you weren't going to be home during the day,' she said. Was his inability to keep his word the issue between them? It wasn't of course – her comment was meant to indicate she'd been discreet. Theo felt better standing by the French doors: sitting seemed to indicate a complacency, a relationship, neither of them felt. 'It wasn't to hurt you, you know that. You told me that about your women.'

'It does fucking hurt though, doesn't it,' said Theo. Stella had never been avid for sex in their marriage. That had been one of the justifications for his own brief affairs. Theo thought her concern was more to maintain attractiveness than any joy in sex. 'So who is he?' he asked. It didn't really matter. Theo wanted no biography that would provide for his existence in their lives.

'An old friend. You wouldn't know him. We met up again just recently. I haven't seen him much at all.'

'So it's serious?'

'I don't know. It's all just happened so quickly.'

'Well, it's the end of us, you realise,' said Theo.

The direct accusation, the bitterness of it, surprised him, for he disliked any overflow of emotion. It was the end of them. They talked for over an hour, Theo standing all that time as the light gradually faded in the sunroom. They arranged their separation with conscious, reined in reasonableness, as if each were determined to escape the clichés of passionate denunciation. What Theo suppressed wasn't anger so much as the sense of bewildered failure and futility. What was the use of talk, what was the use of it when they realised that they were no longer essential in each other's lives.

Whenever Theo thought of that night, he remembered the brief awkwardness which arose when it was time for bed. Stella came to the study door, her face with the soft sheen of moisturiser she applied when she'd removed her make-up, her eyes bright with tension. 'I'll use the spare room,' she told him. Nothing more was said of it. Both could appreciate there was too great an irony in Theo going to lie in the spare bed alone. He half wished she'd shown less sensitivity. He wished also that she had made more apology, taken greater blame on herself, and so let him escape it. 'I never felt cherished,' she told him before she went away. She said it on the spur of the moment, without much emphasis, as is so often the case with words that matter. 'I never felt cherished.'

12

Theo found no evidence that the parson had entered his home, despite the little placement traps he set. He didn't sight him, or the immaculate Honda Civic, in the days after the carpark confrontation, and thought maybe that was the end of it. He was content to forget him, as we all wish to forget those who are witness to our failings. But the parson wouldn't be forgotten: he was being paid to continue to feature.

There was another windfarm protest at Mount Somers, which had been mooted as a site, and since Nicholas was in Wellington researching his US story, Anna asked Theo to cover it, with Linda along for the photographs. Anna told him that Linda had said she didn't need a companion, that she could cover the story as well as the pics, but Linda said nothing of that to Theo as they set off. Nicholas called Linda the sourpuss in her absence, and SP to her face. It annoyed her, even though she never understood.

She was a lank, competent woman in whom feminist principles had hardened to a habitual competition with, and denigration of, men. Theo wasn't interested in the value or otherwise of windfarms, and found Linda's company a trial in any case. 'Hi, Linda,' he said when she came to his desk.

'I need to be back before five,' she said.

She had a habit of looking away while talking, and a flat weariness of tone that deflated enthusiasm in others.

'Sounds okay by me. Let's head away pronto then. Do you want a hand down with your stuff?'

'It's at the bottom of the stairs,' she said.

'Would you like to drive?' said Theo, when they were standing beside one of the staff Mazdas. Linda talked slightly less when she drove, and Theo also thought his offer demonstrated a non-macho disposition that might ease the relationship for the afternoon.

Theo was never able to ignore the driving habits of others, no matter how much he concentrated on conversation, the passing world or his own thoughts. He had trained himself not to actually watch the various manoeuvres of hand and foot, but was aware of it all, and slight, almost involuntary, movements of his arms and legs betrayed the parallel simulation of driving. With a good driver he would gradually relax; with a poor one his exasperation would express itself in increasingly critical views of politics, acquaintances, sport and the efficacy of the major international aid agencies – whatever. It wasn't that he feared for his life; it was the incompetence that rankled with him: the lack of any feel for the vehicle, or awareness of its susceptibilities. Someone with no appreciation for mechanical function could have no sympathy for the feelings of people either, no comprehension of the synthesis necessary if the world is to turn smoothly.

He would never allow Linda to drive his own car. The thought brought a quick grimace to his face. She drove as if pushing a sofa about the living room: a series of violent lunges and pawings at the carpet. She tended, on the open road, to forget there was a fifth gear, and talked more loudly to be heard above the crescendo of the engine. Theo at these times made a small gesture with his hand to indicate the change required, while trying not to seem obdurate.

Photography has its own skills and secrets, he was sure, and Linda had won awards for it. She had a flair for black and white night scenes – rain falling on silvered puddles, the neon sign with a letter missing, an alley dog with its arse above the rim of the garbage bin. She fancied herself as a journalist also, and insisted on taking part in the occasional editorial staff meetings, at which she complained of a patriarchal bias in the paper's underlying attitudes and choice of stories. Nicholas of course said that she needed a good shagging, which would encourage a mellow and balanced view of the world, but he didn't go as far as offering his own ministrations. He was a stirrer, and professed such simplistic prejudice to make life more interesting for himself.

To Theo he admitted that Linda was the best photographer they had, and a better reporter than most. Talent is not personality, however, and Theo was glum as they drove towards Methven. Stella had curated one of Linda's photographic exhibitions, and Linda, who seemed oblivious to the divorce, often talked admiringly of her when with Theo. It wasn't that Theo wished his ex-wife to be disparaged, but that too many regrets and memories were resurrected. Linda tortured the gearbox, and told Theo of meeting Stella not long before at an Arts Society function. 'She was with a surprisingly nice man. A successful man – a solicitor I think.'

'I know,' said Theo.

'He's completely behind her having her own career. Very supportive. I've been talking with some friends about nominating her for president of the society. They've had that witless old fool with a knighthood for years now. She's highly thought of by her academic colleagues, I'm told.'

Linda was the sort of woman who baulks specific physical description. Even seated beside her, Theo had only a general impression, compounded of height, angularity, wholesomeness and large-featured intensity. He trailed his attention and one arm from the car window, watching the farms of the plains pass by.

He wished to be in far poorer country; in the raddled, sluice-despoiled gully at Drybread with the rabbits, the paradise duck pair, the dun harrier hawk and the few merino, their fleece grey with dust. Penny and her son would be there – in the clay cottage, or on the rough slope around it which was Ben's playground. Her hair would be pulled back from her face and she would be displaying active enthusiasm for her son's benefit, when confusion and apprehension were her true feelings. Penny expected some support from him, some exercise of ability and energy on her behalf, and he was on a journey to a windfarm protest with an opinionated woman who had some small fame for photographing canine arses, and insisted on praising his ex-wife. He could see exactly the absorption on Ben's rather beautiful face as he played. He could see exactly the way Penny's top teeth rested on her lip at the conclusion of a smile, and the smooth base of her throat, yet had nothing in his mind of Linda beside him.

Only when they had left the main south road at Rakaia, and the traffic immediately thinned, did Theo notice the car at a distance behind them. He watched in the side mirror, and soon decided it was the parson's maroon Civic. For a moment he felt some melodrama in it, and thought of telling Linda to speed up, or stop around a blind corner so that the parson would pass close by and realise he'd been recognised. But then it came to Theo that Penny's hiding place wasn't at risk, that nothing in fact was required of him, and that the parson should be allowed his professional perseverance. And Theo didn't want to make any explanation to Linda – didn't want to talk about Penny and Drybread to her at all.

Linda had moved on to a more negative aspect of the sisterhood and was complaining about Anna. The chief reporter was the most highly ranked woman at the paper, but rather than taking satisfaction in that, Linda considered she had become complicit in a male hierarchy. 'She's so blokey,' said Linda, almost tearing the sunshade from its fitting as she tried to lower it. 'She talks sport with the guys, and loves to get into the bar with them on Fridays. She lets Nick and you do what you like virtually – you get away with hell. I can remember when she used to do great stuff, challenging stuff.'

Why did she talk like that, when she knew he and Nicholas were close friends, when she knew he was likely to pass on her criticism to Anna? Was it a source of pleasure for her to put out such challenges? Was defiance of conventional subterfuge in relationships a matter of principle for her? 'I think Anna does a bloody good job,' he said. If Linda wanted something to chew on then he'd oblige, but he wasn't interested except not to appear too faint-hearted. He gave more attention to the parson's car behind them, and to thoughts of Drybread and Penny.

'She should be giving more of a lead,' said Linda, 'should be making sure there's more on women's health and equality in the workplace – even sport. She's supposed to be shit hot on sport.'

'Angie's a damn good journo, I reckon,' said Theo. He made a shifting motion with his hand: Linda hadn't changed up into fifth after crossing a narrow wooden bridge. The comment was such an obvious provocation that Linda didn't reply, and they drove on in silence for a time until she began to tell him of the last time she covered one of the windfarm protests – how Nicholas had insisted on picking up a hitchhiker who stank the car out by taking off his shoes, and that she was sure he would steal some of her expensive equipment.

'What did it smell like?'

'What smell like what?' said Linda.

'The hitchhiker's feet.'

'Like plum jam, actually,' said Linda. 'Just like home-made plum jam.'

It was one of those small synchronicities which life provides. Theo savoured it, then went back to thinking of Penny and Drybread as Linda thrashed the Mazda towards the hills, and the red car presumably driven by the parson trailed after them at a respectful distance.

There was barely a Mount Somers settlement: a bunker-like electricity sub-station, the road lined with pale-leaved eucalyptus trees, high, shaped windbreaks in the paddocks, and a couple of old community buildings stark on their rough lawn. Not far beyond, a hillside had been partly excavated and there were small, semi-abandoned shafts for low-grade coal. On the hill crest the protesters had set up camp, claiming some connection between the minor despoliation caused by the coal mining and the environmental threat of the proposed windfarm in the area. Sixty or seventy people milled about a makeshift wooden and fabric wind turbine replica, and some rather self-consciously held stick placards that read 'Peace Before Power', 'Scenery Before Turbines', 'Natural Skylines'. It was not entirely a homogeneous group: there were representatives of the local iwi, some ill-defined supremacist organisation and several buskers and impromptu players from a polytechnic.

Linda's camera equipment identified her and Theo as the media, and in the absence of the more favoured and glamorous television crews, they became the focus of protest. A furrowed man in a yellow anorak and a cheerful Chinese woman introduced themselves as the spokesperson for opposed local residents and the representative of the Kiwis Against Windfarms organisation, respectively.

'Do you know if the TV is coming?' asked the man, and when given a negative answer the lines on his face deepened, until it resembled one of those historical photographs of defeated Sioux chiefs. How does a twenty-first century New Zealander come to possess a visage of such endemic suffering and exposure?

'Never mind,' said the Chinese woman, whose face was as smooth as a flower bowl. 'We're pleased you're here. We don't plan too much in the way of formalities, the weather isn't that great. I'm going to talk briefly, and then Guthrie will say a few words on behalf of local people opposed to the turbines. Right, Guthrie?'

Guthrie nodded, but with the bitterness appropriate to the receipt of a death sentence.

Linda wanted photographs before the speeches, because she said the light was going, so the Chinese woman used her bull-horn loudspeaker to round up the protesters, and she and Guthrie stood in front of them. The iwi representatives also claimed a central position, and the polytechnic entertainers and leather-clad supremacists formed a rather uneasy margin. Theo could see no sign of the parson. Maybe he had remained close to the gate, where cars were parked on the grass. Perhaps he was a supporter of windfarms, and had no wish to appear within the protest.

The young Chinese woman showed her organisational instinct by beginning her speech immediately after the photographs and before a dispersal could begin. A rising wind tended to buffet and distort her words, but she made her points clearly, briefly and even with humour. It was Theo's practice on such occasions to alleviate boredom by mentally grading each speaker while getting the gist in shorthand. He gave her a B plus, but was more interested in what Guthrie might have to say. His bitter zealot's face held promise of profitable eccentricity.

The promise was fulfilled when Guthrie took the bull-horn and stood in the flurried, shin-high dry grasses to talk. He began with wind turbines, their inherent evils and proximity to his own eighteen-hectare angora goat property, which had fallen on hard times, but he worked back along the timeline of his life, cataloguing injustice, misfortune and betrayal at every point. For each tribulation some external malice or discrimination was proclaimed, and never a personal failing admitted. It was pre-ordained that all the world, both living and inanimate, would conspire against him: his haggard, generic face had been ritually buried in Neolithic bogs, hung in stocks, lampooned in broadsheets and captured in the grainy photographs of soup kitchen queues and the death pits of genocide.

Nothing would deter Guthrie from a recital of injustice: a captive audience was the balm he needed. But that, too, let him down soon enough. People eased away, or began their own conversations and activities. Guthrie stood on the slope in the brown grass and the wind tossed his words away, the polytechnic entertainers began small mimes and gymnastic feats to instrumental music, the Maori group started an action song, a placard bearer fell heavily at the entrance to one of the small mines.

'Jesus,' said Linda, 'let's head back. We've got what we need.'

'I just want a quick look in one of the coal diggings,' said Theo. He was her senior after all, and a weary representative of male autonomy.

'I'll wait in the car. Don't be all day,' she said.

A fine, almost horizontal rain began to come in with the wind. It occurred to Theo that whatever the aesthetic and economic arguments concerning the turbines, the meteorological consultants had got it right about the wind. Rain is always welcome in Canterbury: the treeless brown hills stretching back to Mount Somers were proof of that. He went by himself down one of the rough dozer tracks and into a small shaft at the end of it. Theo expected to see railway lines, perhaps of wood, but there were no tracks, or skips, just a scattering of poor quality brown lignite on the tunnel floor. He wasn't interested in the excavations, or the coal: he wanted to see if the parson would be drawn after him. He stood back from the entrance, protected from the wind and swirling drizzle, and waited. It was possible, of course, that he'd been mistaken about the car behind them earlier in the day, or that the parson had turned back once he saw that the protest was Theo's destination, not a rendezvous with Penny Maine-King.

A protester wandered away at a distance, placard held in front of her body as a shield against the rain, then there were just the gravel excavations, the shafts, the scattered rusting implements of a barely profitable enterprise, and the hills beyond. Linda wasn't a patient woman, and Theo didn't wish to antagonise her unnecessarily when they had a considerable drive back. He was on the point of leaving the shaft when the parson came into view, walking with an assumed casualness, and with a frayed parka as inadequate cover. Theo kept close to the side of the tunnel so that he wasn't easy to see from the track. He enjoyed the feeling of being dry and out of the wind there, while able to see the parson uncomfortable in the elements, and not sure whether to enter the shaft. To watch and yet not be seen produces a powerful, atavistic satisfaction.

The parson seemed concerned for his town shoes, so picked a path to keep him from the worst of the wet clay and the brown, soft coal. He saw Theo, was indecisive for a moment before continuing forward sufficiently to gain shelter from the tunnel overhang. 'I'm afraid Mrs Maine-King doesn't live in a coal mine,' said Theo.

'No.' The parson seemed relieved to be recognised. It meant he didn't have to bother any longer with surveillance techniques, which were inconvenient in the worsening weather. And his meeting with Theo in the carpark had proved he needn't feel apprehensive about a physical contest. 'I don't suppose you've thought any more about the advantages of co-operation,' he said.

'Not at all,' said Theo. It was the first really close-up look he'd had of the parson, and what struck him was the unadulterated physicality of the man: the heavy flesh of his facial features, the creases in his clothes containing that large body, the faintly audible breathing as he pumped in oxygen. 'You enjoy hounding Penny Maine-King and the boy, do you?' Theo asked.

'In this case I'm a sort of sheriff,' said the parson. 'I'm trying to uphold the law.' He set off an even, metronomic laugh, like a wooden clacker deep within, while his expression underwent no change.

'What a bullshitter you are,' said Theo. 'You don't care about them at all. You're taking advantage of a family in trouble to make some money out of it all. You're a sanctimonious prick. Well, you won't find Penny Maine-King here.'

The parson made a small movement as if to leave the shaft entrance, then pulled back, came a step closer to Theo, so that even in the poor light his pale, bald head had a cheese rind gleam because of the raindrops there. His expression was still one of conscious composure. 'You realise there's no personal grudge in anything I do,' he said. 'Nothing unprofessional, or illegal. Quite the contrary. The thing is that I've been engaged to assist in finding Mrs Maine-King. It's just that I represent another party in the matter.'

'You push into people's lives and misfortune, though, don't you?'

'Any more than yourself, Theo? Isn't that what you do often as an investigative journalist – search things out that you think the public should be aware of? The only difference is that you carry your findings to the public and I deliver to a single client.'

'Yeah, well, my loyalty's elsewhere on this one,' said Theo.

'I've read your pieces. I suppose everyone feels sympathy for the mother and the kid, but the thing is there's always the law – what it provides for, its obligations.'

It was incongruous, Theo and the parson sheltering in a coal pit at Mount Somers and discussing ethics, while the people who, for one reason or another, had been drawn to a protest against the establishment of a windfarm gradually dispersed. It had the precarious structure of a dream, but the parson was such a palpable presence, so physically detailed, that he grounded everything. The leather of his brown shoes was darkening with moisture, the tattered parka gave off a faint reminder of past fishing excursions, his arm hung in just that slight arc of assumed relaxation.

'I'll tell you what,' said Theo. 'If I find your car at any place I go to, I'll put some work the panelbeater's way. Okay?'

'No need to take that attitude,' said the parson. 'I can see it's become a personal thing with you.' He walked back out onto the track, glancing up to the grey sky, but not back to Theo. 'Goodbye,' he said to the air ahead, giving dignity to his withdrawal. It had become a personal thing – not so much between Theo and the parson, as between Penny and Theo. Perhaps that's what the parson meant, but he'd become too far away for Theo to make a reply.

Theo followed the parson up the track, then onto the

grass slope that gave access to the road, but they took no notice of each other, and Theo made no effort to catch up. There were no other people in the open because of the rain, and only a few cars were left, some of them nosing away. Linda was behind the wheel of the Mazda, and, since he'd kept her waiting, Theo didn't insist on driving during the return trip. He told her that the coal shafts were pretty small scale and the coal itself low-grade stuff. 'Oh, come on,' she said. Theo watched the parson's car move off. As Linda paused at the gate, Guthrie appeared and tapped on Theo's window. The rain made his hair a goatish forelock above his dismal face. Theo wound down the window a little.

'Have you got all you want?' shouted Guthrie.

'What?'

'All the stuff you need for coverage. Have you got enough?'

'Yes, plenty thanks,' said Theo.

'This bloody weather, eh,' said Guthrie. 'I wondered if you might like an extended interview some time about some of the other issues I mentioned in my speech.'

'I think we'll leave it at what we've got for the moment,' said Theo.

'We can't guarantee a great deal of space, you know,' said Linda. 'It all depends what pressure of news there is.' She gunned the car forward and Guthrie's lugubrious face fell quickly behind. 'Useless, moaning prick,' she said. 'He tried to hijack things from Sue Chen, did you see? A born loser.'

In an attempt to disregard Linda's driving habits, Theo concentrated on the road ahead. He had a last glimpse through the drizzle of the parson's car before it turned a corner in the distance. The parson had wasted a day too, but like Theo he'd get paid for it. Unlike Theo he may have had no other ambition. Theo resented time that wasn't furthering his wish to be with Penny, or to be of use to her.

'You should take off that damp jacket,' said Linda. She began to recount her conversation with Sue Chen in full detail, and said she was going to see Anna about a feature on her.

Theo imagined himself running on the brown hills, with the fine rain on his bare legs and face to cool him, and just the sound of his own breathing. His sweat would mingle with the drizzle on his skin, and the taste would have a saltiness which always surprised him.

13

When Penny rang him from Alexandra to thank him for his latest piece in the paper, she mentioned again his visit to her mother in the Malahide Home. She felt claustrophobic, she told him, if they didn't get away from Drybread from time to time. 'We spend time in the park here,' she said, 'and Ben gets a chance sometimes to play with other kids at the slides and swings. We insinuate ourselves into the family circle of others.' She gave the last sentence a certain acidity.

'Why don't we meet somewhere then and make a day of it?' Theo asked.

'I'd like that,' she said, 'but what about being recognised?'

They'd be less noticeable as an apparent family group though, and she didn't much resemble the photographs taken in California. Theo pointed all that out, but the essential thing was that they wanted to see each other again, and that wish was clear to both of them behind their casual conversation.

'Why not Timaru?' suggested Theo. It had no specific association with either of them, and was about halfway between them. 'Plenty for Ben to do there,' he said.

Just to hear her voice was a pleasure. He was talking from work, and swivelled his chair towards the window, so that his colleagues couldn't see his face. He had spent time with Penny only twice, yet the surge of emotion surprised him.

Theo arrived in Timaru well before eleven that Tuesday, and parked the Audi at Caroline Bay, close to the loop overhead road. He wandered towards the area where the Christmas carnival had been set up. The grass was parched, completely brown in arcs around the trees where the competition for moisture was greatest. The carnival was over, but the merry-go-round and the octopus remained on site, the chairs chained together, grey canvas covers lashed down, in out-of-season mode. The Big Wheel, partly dismembered, was stark against the sky. The circular railway was permanent. The small train, painted in Thomas the Tank Engine colours, and the open carriages, were parked in the corrugated iron tunnel with metal portcullis gates for security. Ben would have got such a kick out of a ride, but the information board showed that once summer holidays were over, Thomas made his circuits only on fine Sundays. It would be best not to bring Ben past the railway, in case he glimpsed Thomas imprisoned, and mourned the lost opportunity.

Closer to the sea was a narrow belt of small dunes and marram grass before the curve of the fine, grey white sand.

Theo walked that way back to the carpark. Despite the clear sky few people were at the shore. Two older women walked dogs, and were less inclined to acknowledge each other than their pets. 'Come here, Cromwell,' one woman commanded her Labrador. Rather than resembling her gambolling dog, she was very thin, with a mass of grey hair loosely pinned above a sharp-featured and austere face. At the water's edge, with its gentle ripple, a man and woman supervised the darting ventures of two small boys, laughing and vainly calling for them not to wet their clothes.

Theo could remember being on Caroline Bay only once before: a summer when he'd still been at university, and even that recollection was hazy, because he'd got very drunk and ended up vomiting from a walk bridge above the railway cutting as the ships sounded their horns together at midnight to welcome the new year and the municipal fireworks festooned the dark sky. In the rough morning that followed he'd hung dolefully on the railing along the clay cliff, watched the breakers overcome by swell from behind so that the white crests were captured beneath the smooth surface like frost within jade.

Now he was back by chance and circumstance, walking the bay when he should have been at his desk in the newspaper office. He was there with the two elderly women, Cromwell and the jubilant nuclear family. He was there because he couldn't put Penny Maine-King out of his mind, or her small son. He was there because he had hopes again that he might find someone with whom he could be relaxed and unreserved, and yet excited by too, in every way. He was searching, without being able to acknowledge to himself the importance of search, or quite what its object was.

When Penny arrived, only a few minutes after eleven, she parked close to Theo's car. She stayed sitting inside for a time, talking to Theo through the wound-down window, as if being so far from Drybread and the bach was something to which she needed to become accustomed. 'There's hardly anyone here,' said Theo. 'It's a weekday, a school day, and people are too busy.' Ben sat quietly too, strapped into his child's carseat. Even after being so long confined, he was silent and watchful, looking at Theo and at the beachfront with its broad, grassed expanse, modest sand dunes and glittering sea. 'This is a good place, isn't it,' Theo said to him. Ben nodded his head, but remained cautious still.

'He's been good,' said Penny. 'Only a couple of stops in all that way.'

'That's a good boy.'

'He's been looking forward to it. Anything for a change from the hut.'

'You said ice cream,' said Ben accusingly.

'If you're a good boy, yes,' said his mother. She got out of the car and went round to the passenger seat to release him. 'I haven't even got a bucket and spade for him,' she told Theo. She had just the semi-transparent container of a Chinese takeaway and a wooden cooking spoon. It wouldn't make any difference to the boy, but Theo knew that for Penny it was yet another sign of how far she had come down in the world. She gave a quick laugh with nothing at all of amusement in it.

They walked across the grassed area, and Theo spread the car rug just before the sand began. The tall blue and white cranes of the container port were clear and noiseless in the distance; an overweight jogger put in her best effort while in their sight. Ben began a collection of marram stalks. The sun was warm to the face.

'You need to get away from Drybread more,' Theo said.

'There's Alex every so often.'

'But you don't have any friends there. No one to visit and talk things over with. No one to make you laugh or cry. You're holed up there in the cottage, getting tighter and tighter.'

'Yeah, well, every place reflects yourself,' said Penny. 'A happy person might find Drybread idyllic.'

'This is a tough patch, but you'll come out of it,' said Theo.

'I hope so. Sometimes I feel lost to myself, if that makes any sense. You and Zack have done a lot, and I'm grateful for that. It mightn't look like it, but I feel more optimistic now. If I'd known, though – known how awful it all was – I don't think I could have gone through with it.'

'Guilt and failure,' said Theo. 'I reckon guilt and failure undermine you so bloody easily.'

'You mean your divorce, don't you.'

'Yeah, I suppose so. It's so common, isn't it? It happens to so many people, yet there's a terrible novelty when it's your turn. Anyway, let's not get into all that today.'

She and Theo lay on the rug: Theo on his back with a hand over his eyes, Penny on her stomach so that she was able to watch her son as he played. They weren't touching, but close enough for Theo to be aware of a faint perfume and the smell released from her clothing by the sun. She wore blue shorts and a blue and white striped top. Her arms and legs were brown from the Central Otago sun, her hair longer than when he first met her, and loosely tied back. A couple and a child: it seemed a very natural and comfortable grouping. Penny talked a bit about Zack and how the judicial stuff was going, responded to her son occasionally, but mostly she and Theo just lay. Theo hadn't felt so relaxed for a long time. He didn't care about the work he should have been doing for the paper, or what might happen long term for Penny and himself. He wanted to lie in the sun, aware of her by his side, and take no initiatives at all.

Ben, though, grew tired of the dunes after a time and began asking to go to the sea. It was mysterious for him, as neither Sacramento, nor Drybread, possessed such a thing. As the three of them went barefoot across the sand towards waves that were not much more than ripples, the little boy had incessant questions concerning the sea: where it came from, why it moved, why he couldn't hold it, whether he could take some home. Theo and Penny took a hand each and swung him above the shallow water and he cried out with the joy of it. The present is everything of life for children, and not shadowed by the past or the future.

He got wet through, of course, and when they went back to the rug on the grass, Penny took off all his clothes except a cotton top and sunhat, and he dried in the sun as he played.

'Do you ever hear from your Californian friends?' asked Theo.

'No one knows where I am.'

'You could write to them under another name, use a post box. You could send an email.'

Penny didn't reply for a while, held up her hand as if to feel the blue of the sky, and then laid her wrist over her eyes to block the sun.

'I'm too proud,' she said. 'I've got some good friends, but I'm ashamed to be in such a fucking mess. Stupid, isn't it.'

'No, I can understand that.'

'I'm too proud to accept the sympathy that goes with the support they'd give. Things can change so quickly, and you go under.'

'Well, you know you've got my help,' said Theo.

'I know.'

'I really want to help.'

'I know,' she said.

'Tell me something about your life over there before you got married,' said Theo. 'What the hell were you doing there anyway?'

So they lay in the sun and Penny told him about being a ski instructor at Bear Valley and North Star at Tahoe, about meeting Erskine at a diner in the city of Truckee where she went with friends. She said most ski people in the States had money, and women were often into the scene because the right sort of guys were plentiful there. She told him about the professional instructors from Italy, Germany and Austria, and how many of them were talents broken by drugs, or booze. It all seemed a long way from Drybread and a custody case, and reminded Theo that there was so much of Penny's life of which he knew nothing.

He told her that he'd never been skiing in his life, but had visited Courchevel Le Praz in the summer season while he was backpacking around Europe, and worked for two weeks there for Grummande the undertaker, gluing mahogany laminate to cheap coffins. The younger Grummande told him that the corpses he liked best were those of climbers, or skiers, who died in avalanches. Penny accused Theo of making it up, but he assured her it was true, and why should Grummande lie to him? The undertaker also told him that the season before, a girl had fallen through the ice in the local river and not been found for two hours. He'd been called to collect the body, but just as he was about to put the drowned girl in a body bag, a Scottish doctor on a walking tour stopped and resuscitated her. Many thought it was a miracle, but the doctor said the intense cold had prevented brain deterioration.

'Maybe I should live in a cold climate then,' said Penny. 'My brain's going damn quick.'

'Central must be cold in winter.'

'Jesus, I've just got to be out of there by winter,' she said.

'Sometimes I think of you and Ben in my place: how we could organise the different rooms and stuff like that.' Theo hoped she'd say something, but Penny just smiled and gave his shoulder a small push.

'Ice cream,' said the little boy. His thighs were chubby, and his miniature penis and scrotum palely sculptured on the smooth flesh of his groin.

So Penny dusted the sand from his legs, dressed him and they set off as a threesome back to the cars, where they left the rug, and the pottle half full of ivory pipi shells. They took the piazza steps that spanned the railway line, and sat outside one of the Bay Hill restaurants. Penny was relaxed. She was in an unfamiliar town and with a partner: ordinary and anonymous. Away from Drybread, with all its present and past associations, they talked more casually, more openly, of their lives, allowing some basis for familiarity without assumption of it, or intrusion.

'What do you miss most?' asked Theo.

'Money mainly, to be honest. It sounds trivial and selfish, I suppose, but you get used to having stuff around you for comfort, and enough money to spend without worrying about it. It gives you confidence that you have independence and self-respect. If you're poor you're a failure. That's the guts of it, and I'd forgotten. You can put up all sorts of arguments to save yourself from acknowledging it, but you see it in people's faces, in the way they treat you. Poverty is failure made tangible. And it's so much easier to adjust to going up in the world.'

'I could lend you some money.'

'I hope it'll come right soon. Thanks, though,' said Penny. 'I think I could get something from Zack Heywood if I had to.'

'You had a pretty nice place in Sacramento, I suppose.'

'We built a new home in the style some wise-guy called Californian Tuscan. We've got a pool, a sauna and a water feature in the formal garden. We're even close to the river. Water's a big thing in California.'

'Sounds pretty flash,' said Theo. 'No wonder Drybread's a bit of a comedown.'

'I thought the other day of something they had in common – they both began as gold mining settlements. Sacramento kicked on from there, you might say, and Drybread didn't.' They both grinned. Theo liked the wryness she was capable of even when she was unhappy. For him the only significant link between Sacramento and Drybread was personal: Penny herself, leaving the Manuherikia, living in the fast lane of California's capital, then making a bolt back to Drybread when her marriage didn't work out. 'I can't seem to imagine myself over there now,' she said. 'It's like something I've watched on television, not my own life. It's still absolutely clear, but it doesn't seem to have any connection with me any longer.'

'It's the numbness of trauma, I suppose,' said Theo.

He and Ben had a short tug-of-war with a paper napkin, quite without words, but the boy smiled. Theo put his large hand over the small one, and was surprised by the warmth there. What is it that children take from the interaction with adults outside the family, and how accurate is their gauge of sincerity?

'How long is it since your divorce?' she asked. It was one of the few personal things she had asked of him, and her voice had an unaccustomed gentleness.

'We broke up a couple of years ago.'

'Do you still see her?'

'Oh, odd times,' said Theo. 'We don't stick pins into effigies – well, I don't anyway.'

'Are you glad there are no kids?'

Theo nodded. 'That's the best thing about it.'

'And maybe the worst thing too,' she said. 'With a child there's always something wonderful left of the love you had.' She was right. How could that time together have been wasted, how could marriage be futile, when a life had been created as a result? 'The best thing that ever happened to me was having a baby,' she said.

'Kids can suffer, though, can't they?'

'Sure they can, but mine won't.'

'Well, women have a natural love for children I suppose,' said Theo. 'Maybe men are different.'

'Bullshit,' said Penny. 'I know some men who are wonderful fathers. Some guys are better parents than their wives. You learn that your own family situation isn't the norm, thank God.'

'Well, what would I know?' said Theo. He was surprised by Penny's sudden vehemence, and assumed she was making a rare reference to her husband. He didn't want to destroy the easy mood of the day.

They chose to return to the bay by way of the footbridge that led over the cutting and onto the tiered concrete seating facing the soundshell. Theo carried Ben down, and when released on the lawn the boy ran ahead and into the narrow pedestrian tunnel under the loop road. The tunnel was dim, its tiled sides alive with the swooping, stylised graffiti of taggers. Theo and Penny quickened their pace so Ben wouldn't be too far ahead in the carpark, but when they came out they saw a woman in jeans hustling him towards one of the vehicles.

Instinctively realising the threat, Penny reacted more quickly than Theo: he was at first merely puzzled. How could a woman be a danger to a child? Penny started calling out. The woman didn't turn to face them, but pulled Ben on more urgently so that he began to cry. As both Theo and Penny ran to catch up, Theo recognised the car the woman was headed for: a maroon Civic in which a man sat who was surely the parson. Theo could see his round, balding head, his hands already on the wheel.

Perhaps the woman had time to reach the car with Ben before she could be stopped, but the boy stumbled and spun from her grip just before the open door. His face hit the dry ground with a force that made his dark hair fly forward, and he began a long, quavering cry. The woman clambered into the front passenger seat and locked the door just as Theo reached it. Penny knelt to her son. There was a moment of anger and helplessness as Theo beat on the window and the parson put the car into gear. Neither the parson nor the woman would make eye contact with Theo, or register his shouts. They stared ahead as if willing the car to be already some way in the distance. It was just a moment, but one stretched out by the intensity of what it contained. Theo could see the woman clearly: she was young and good-looking, and wore a gold chain at her throat. He wanted to get a grip of her blonde hair and force her to look out at Penny and the fallen Ben. He wanted something long and solid in his hand with which to strike the parson. But in seething anger and frustration all he managed was a painful kick into the side panel of the car as it accelerated away. 'That bastard,' he said.

'You know who it is?' said Penny sharply.

'It's a guy who's followed me before.'

'You stupid prick, Theo. You stupid, stupid prick.' Penny was yelling, down on her knees to comfort her son, who was still crying and had blood seeping from his nose. She carried him to her car and began to put him into his seat. Theo followed and stood close to her in the open door, tried to put his arms around her, told her how sorry he was, that there was no need to go right away, that the parson wouldn't hang around after that. 'You should've told me about him. You should've thought he might be following you. Christ,' she said. She was shaking, and resisted Theo's attempt to hold her around the shoulders. Ben stopped crying, and to placate him she began some lie about what had happened.

'How could a girl do something like that?' said Theo.

'Money, of course,' said Penny.

All that was left of the day was for them to part. Penny

no longer felt safe, and wanted to start back to Drybread. Despite everything she had said, it was a bolt-hole after all. Theo offered to follow her back to make sure the parson didn't do the same, but Penny refused. There was no kiss, no talk of the pleasures of the day, just a hurried goodbye, and some effort by Penny to mitigate her accusations. He watched them go; caught a second, brief glimpse of her car as it did the first loop of the angled road, and then was left alone in the carpark with the bright sun, a scented breeze from the sea and an elderly man in a hand-knitted cream cardigan with leather buttons who wished him good afternoon in passing.

Theo's anger was turbulent and slow to subside. His attitude towards the parson had always been tinged with disdain, but the afternoon revealed him as someone sinister and determined. Ben's fall, his anguish, the bloodied nose, remained clearly with Theo on his return drive to Christchurch, and he was pissed off with himself for not taking care on the morning trip to ensure he was unobserved.

He tried to express something of his feelings in an email to Penny the next morning, and a day later she rang from Alexandra when he was just home from work. 'It's been just the same here,' she said. 'Nobody's been poking around. The main thing is I've still got Ben and he's fine. Nothing else really matters.'

'He's okay then?' said Theo.

'He's been sleeping and eating fine. I told him the nice lady thought he was someone else.'

'I'm sorry how it turned out. You were absolutely right – I should have been more careful.'

'It's not your fault. I just had to let rip at someone.'

'I feel like complaining to the police,' said Theo, 'but of course they're after you too. Bizarre isn't it. There we were having a quiet time together, and someone tries to kidnap Ben, and all the time we're the ones going against the law – officially, I mean. Jesus, though.'

'Yeah, well, the whole thing's a mess until we can get some change in the court order.'

'You hang in there. Okay?' said Theo. Through his living-room window he could see his garage, and realised that he'd left the side door open again. What did it matter? He didn't want to be standing there by himself: he didn't want to be in his own house. Better by far to be in Alexandra, in a phone booth with Penny, and then the three of them could go back to Drybread together.

'There's no bloody choice any more, is there,' Penny said.

14

She seemed more hopeful when she rang again a few days later. Zack Heywood had been contacted by her husband with what the Virginian lawyer termed conciliatory approaches. Penny asked Theo if he could be a sort of go-between as well. 'You're the only one who knows anything about how I feel,' she said.

Theo was surprised by the pleasure the compliment gave him, but could only be prosaic in reply. 'What did your husband say about the parson trying to kidnap Ben?'

'Parson?'

'The guy with the woman,' said Theo.

'You know he's a parson?'

'It doesn't matter,' said Theo. 'You reckon your husband didn't know anything about it?'

'I haven't talked to him – Zack Heywood did. I haven't

said anything to anyone about Timaru, so how would they know?'

'That's right, of course. You're in Alex?'

'Yes, I'll take Ben to the park while I'm here and pick up groceries. I'll email Zack before I go back and tell him you're okay with being involved. I appreciate that.'

'I wish I was there with you,' said Theo.

'Me too,' she said. 'My language is reverting to that of a three-year-old. My talk's all about tip-trucks and engines with faces. Thank God for books and sometimes a newspaper.' Theo hoped there were reasons for them being together unrelated to her vocabulary, but didn't get into that.

Four days before the Easter break, Zack rang, wanting Theo to come in. When he asked him if it would cost money, Zack just gave his relaxed laugh, so Theo assumed that meant it wouldn't. The next afternoon he walked from his office to Zack's, and was kept waiting on the red buttoned leather of the foyer couch for less than twenty minutes. Not bad.

'I liked your last piece,' Zack said. 'The background stuff about the Californian judge and his conservative stance. And the way you implied that judges here shouldn't just be rubber-stamping decisions when at least one of the parties has New Zealand nationality. Good angle about the little boy too. All that confusion's bad enough for an adult, isn't it? And I think you're right that the television appearances back there are irrelevant really – nothing to do with Penny Maine-King now.'

Zack's suit coat was on a hanger in a neat alcove off his office. He wore a blue and white striped shirt with silver cufflinks. In the shops Theo knew, the shirts didn't have the holes for cufflinks any more. Zack must patronise exclusive boutiques that catered for guys who remained true to cufflinks and non-quartz watches.

'So what's up?' Theo asked.

'Erskine Maine-King has been in touch. He wants to work out a compromise that suits both of them and the boy. If that can be done, I think we could get a stay on the warrant, and a Family Court rehearing.'

It was what Penny wanted: some way of reopening the issue and so creating the chance of at least equal custody. It gave Theo considerable satisfaction to know he might have played some part in it.

'She won't meet him herself,' said Zack. 'She won't come out of hiding until the warrant's lifted. She wants you and me to talk to her husband on her behalf. God knows what she thinks he's going to do.'

Theo, with knowledge of the parson and Timaru, could have told him. 'Well, being hidden, being unable to be found, that's her top card, and she won't jeopardise that,' he said. 'Sure, I'll do anything I can, but this is all legal stuff, isn't it?'

'I know about the law,' said Zack, 'but she thinks you know what she wants from the situation. She's keen you be involved.'

Again Theo felt pleasure that Penny put some trust in him. When they'd been together she'd sometimes seemed offhand, but now there was this sign of preference, despite what had happened. And in accepting that preference he allowed for greater possibility in their relationship. He took care, of course, that Zack was aware of none of that. He said he didn't see that he could contribute much, that he'd need to talk to Penny before any meeting, that he didn't feel he knew what it was she wanted.

'You'll have time for all that before we leave,' Zack said.

'Leave?' said Theo.

'Erskine Maine-King wants to meet in Nice in a fortnight. He's got business in Europe.'

That was a crunch point right there. It wasn't so much the issue of getting agreement from the paper, or taking so much time on it, or whether Theo could handle it. He needed to understand why Penny wanted him as part of something so important to her, and if his acceptance would mark a final commitment to the whirlpool of her life.

When Theo said he needed to talk to Penny before making any decision, Zack said that was fine provided he had an answer soon after Easter. He offered Theo a mint from a lidded jar, tinted light blue, which sat on the client side of his desk. Maybe the sweets were for the infrequent children who accompanied their parents into Zack's office, but Theo took one anyway. So did the lawyer. They bulged their cheeks at each other because the mints were landmine size, but Zack didn't seem to feel incongruous even in his crisp, striped shirt with silver cufflinks. There's a lot said about the need for men to express their emotions, to talk more about how they feel, but the Virginian and Theo enjoyed the reassurance of reticence, and talked briefly about one of the paper's other stories before Theo left, the mint rattling against his teeth. Zack just nodded to him at the door.

It was a long time since any woman had asked something significant of Theo. He found it both affirming and yet unsettling.

15

Theo finished the fourth article on Penny during the morning that preceded Good Friday, with Nicholas complaining of a sore throat and coughing often to prove it. When he took his copy through to Anna, she said it was easily the best story of the year. Theo thought it was just that other journalists were shut out because Penny dealt only with him, but he was pleased with it because he considered he had kept the tone from being mawkish, and built sympathy by mentioning the attempted kidnapping of Ben without giving too much away. 'Take some credit, Theo,' Anna said. 'You've given good legs to this story. That stunt in Timaru reads as bloody good drama. So much publicity in Penny Maine-King's favour must be putting pressure on the court.' Normally he wouldn't take his pieces to Anna, but she'd been supportive of the story all along, and he was preparing the way for his request to go to Nice with Zack Heywood.

He didn't feel like turning to any other writing that afternoon, wanting to let his mind lie fallow for a time, so after lunch he went to visit his parents, who lived in a retirement village in New Brighton. It was a two bedroomed brick home of strict conformity sanctioned by the village ordinances, but they seemed quite happy with all the strictures of the place and the various service charges and community levies. Theo's recollection of his mother and father when they lived in small towns was that they were independent, with strong sources of individuality, but in retirement they had morphed into city lemmings, seeking security and the company of their own age group. Bridge and bowls were the two poles of their world, and television filled most of the space in between. His mother had the slightly greater enthusiasm for bridge; the order was reversed in regard to bowls.

Sometimes Theo thought that his infrequent visits were an inconvenient interruption to their complacent routines, though they never said so. He called out of filial duty, and they received him with similar convention. He talked of sport and his outward life, asked after their health; they dutifully asked him about his work, and told anecdotes about Mandy and Tom, their grandchildren by Theo's sister, their only other child. The stories of infancy arose in Sydney, but fed into the life of Theo's parents by email, cards, phone calls, texts and small but uninhibited artistic favours from Mandy and Tom. It was one of the few aspects of a visit to the retirement compound that Theo enjoyed: the tales made loving and humorous by kinship, the unsteady kindergarten lions and hippos in thick crayon on the door of the fridge, the reassuring victories over croup and nappy rash.

Stella was rarely a topic of conversation, nor was anything else from the time of Theo's marriage. His parents didn't have the experience, or language, to grapple with divorce at such close quarters. They would no more enquire about his emotional life than they would question his religious beliefs: probably thought both unnecessary, if they existed within their son at all.

'Been reading your stuff about the Californian woman who's hiding out with her little boy,' said Theo's mother. 'It's just so sad for everyone. Why can't they leave her alone? Surely they couldn't send her to prison with a child to look after.'

'She could be imprisoned for contempt of court, though,' said Theo. 'She's actually a New Zealander who married in California.'

Iris Esler was a spare woman with a long face. In the photographs of her youth it was softened by the skin's bloom and a frame of dark hair, but with age the heavy, slightly mulish bone structure was coming through. It gave her a disputatious appearance that was entirely false. 'Oh, poor thing,' she said. 'I'm sure it will all work out. The little boy must be about the age of our Tom.'

She had turned down the television, but it still flickered across from the three of them in the small lounge, so that it was difficult not to observe the silent action while talking of other things. For Christ's sake, why couldn't people turn the set off and give attention to each other. It became an unacknowledged filler when conversation lapsed, sometimes even a substitute. When talk lagged, his parents' attention would be drawn back to the screen: sometimes his father would give a little grunt of inappropriate amusement during a conversation, because of some pratfall on the television. Bridge and bowls weren't so bad, all things considered. Direct experience at least, instead of hunched obeisance before the screen.

Theo looked at his father carefully. Recently he'd had some difficulty in recalling his appearance when they weren't together. In memory Don Esler was small and strong, like a lightweight boxer, springing in and out of truck cabs, working twenty bales high on the haystack or urging steers up the inclined race into the stock crates. He had become even smaller, with a Punch face of oversized features and a waist so slender that his trousers were bunched there by the belt. Time exaggerated a certain unpromising individuality of looks in Theo's mother, but had worn his father to generic old age. In the street, or the supermarket, Theo might well pass his father without recognition. And if former appearance was lost, what else was there to act as link between father and son except memories to which the older man laid no claim.

Theo made an effort when his mother was in the kitchen. 'So how are things?' he said.

'Not so bad. Not so bad,' said his father.

'How have the bowls been treating you?'

'We've been doing okay actually. We played yesterday and it was that hot on the greens. There's this great bloody hedge all round and the place gets like an oven.'

'Do you miss the business, the trucks and all that? You know, the farms you used to go to and the people you knew?'

'Eh?' his father said. Was he glancing at the television?

'I mean do you miss all the stuff you did before you retired?'

'Never miss it. It wasn't any picnic, you know, keeping trucks on the road, and trying to find steady guys and enough business.'

'It was lovely country, though, Dad,' said Theo.

'Never miss it,' said his father emphatically. He sat like a goblin Abe Lincoln, with both arms resting on the chair. His hair was a grey stubble, his face slightly scaly from constant exposure to the glaring, antipodean sun.

'One day I'd like to take you and Mum back to some of those places for a day or two. Some of those lovely, quiet beaches out from Cheviot perhaps.'

'Yeah, well, we're pretty busy until Christmas,' his father said. 'And we're hoping to get over to Sydney to see Lee and the kids.'

It's not uncommon for children, adult or otherwise, to find the company of their parents an imposition, but Theo hadn't thought much about the reverse being true. The visits to his parents were dutiful on everyone's part. He brought nothing that engaged their existing priorities: nothing of bridge, or bowls, nothing of common ailments of decline, above all no absorbing and spontaneous children with handicrafts of love. He came with the shadow of a failed relationship. His gift was a supermarket cardboard basket of Easter eggs, their gaudy foil wrappings catching light from the television when his mother placed them on the tray table.

'Thanks for that,' she said matter-of-factly. If his personality lacked sufficient charisma to enthuse even his own mother and father, what chance did he have with Penny Maine-King?

Theo tried again when his mother returned with three buttered halves of apricot muffin, the exact number a warning of individual allocation. 'I was saying to Dad that you might like to have a trip back to some of the old places.'

'It's just we seem to be so busy,' she said. 'Goodness knows where the time goes.'

It went on assembling a losing hand of playing cards, on bowling biased balls up towards the kitty, on finding a Thomas the Tank Engine T-shirt for Tom, and a pink plastic tiara and fairy wand for Mandy. It ticked by during the chatter of teacups and vapid voices in cream-painted clubrooms, and it advanced remorselessly as they watched repeats that filled their small lounge with canned laughter and stock imitations of life.

Theo told himself that his mother and father had a more essential existence than was ever on view, or revealed in their conversation. What was presented could not be all they possessed of life. Such a belief was presumptuous and judgemental, but he held to it. Surely when they talked privately, his parents had topics and understandings that were enriched by personal philosophies and subtle epiphanies which arose from their own experience. That they chose not to reveal themselves to him was a lesser blow than the possibility that the banal drift of their lives was really as it appeared.

'What do you hope for these days?' Theo enquired recklessly.

'Hope for?' His father's tone was almost of derision, and his mother gave a slight laugh as though to cover inappropriateness.

'I mean your ambitions for yourselves – what you're aiming for. Hopeful, special things.' Even as he spoke, Theo winced at his own words. The television images jiggled; the heavy, yellow sunlight of afternoon through the Venetians tiger-striped the small lounge.

'Winning Lotto and not getting sick. That's what we bloody hope for,' said Theo's father.

'And for the family,' added his mother piously. 'It's all family, isn't it.'

When Theo had turned fifteen his father taught him to drive. It was the one time that Theo felt Don had an urgency to pass on something to him. Maybe behind the value his father attached to the ability to drive well, was the expectation that Theo would end up continuing the family trucking business; perhaps he felt contributing to such a practical skill absolved him of the need to offer any emotional inheritance. There were four trucks, and the biggest and best was an articulated Mack that his father rarely let anyone else drive.

Theo didn't learn on the Mack, or any of the trucks, of course, although he later drove them to earn money in school and university holidays. In the end he could back a stock crate to match a loading race within an inch or two. No, he learnt in the family Ford, and even then was surprised by the patience his father showed, and his concern for the welfare of machinery. 'Listen to the engine,' his father would say. 'The engine talks to you. Its tone of voice tells you everything: when you need to change up or down, when it's at ease and when it's straining.'

The driving sessions Theo had with Don were the best times they shared when he was a boy. They started just sitting in the car with the motor off, and his father talking of how an engine worked, how all the controls and instruments enabled the driver to get the best out of it. They ended many weeks later driving over downland

and hill roads, with Theo behind the wheel, and his father making brief comment sometimes beside him of trucks, and farms, and stock, and the people concerned with that life. Theo hadn't realised then that he was experiencing the greatest closeness he and Don would ever have.

They came to the door to farewell him, his mother glancing to the houses on either side to see if they were observed, his father working his Punch features comically in lieu of anything to say. His mother tall, with her long, equine face angled to regard Theo; his father reduced, like a jockey, at her side.

Theo felt a mixture of dissociation and baffled tenderness as he gave a wave of farewell. He was conscious of the soft movement of the air on his face as he walked to his car, of the warmth of the sun, of the fragrance of cut grass, and the hovering white butterflies in the garden strip. In the grassed centre of the cul-de-sac turning circle was a large kowhai tree, with contorted seed pods spread at its feet like a swarm of dead bees. It was his time to be alive, he reminded himself, and he shouldn't waste any of it. It was the very short time when green life was allowed him in the endless shuffle of people past, present and future. He would run in the evening when the sun had slipped below the horizon. He would admit to himself and Penny that he wanted to be with her as a complete partner, and resolve to attain a life that had something in it which was valiant and purposeful in terms of the spirit. He would drink less in the evenings, and give greater support to his colleagues during the day. He would seek something of significant value outside himself to acknowledge.

16

'My neighbour's gone mad,' said Nicholas. He and Theo were standing in the night on the stark, concrete top of the building in which they worked. There was a small fortress in the centre that housed the narrow stairwell and the vitals of the central heating and air conditioning, a broad strip on all sides and then a concrete wall to waist height. There were grilles in the flat concrete to take rain, and a few straggling pipes and antennae reaching up like the enfeebled shoots on a vast stump.

It was an unauthorised place, but people came up anyway seeking some respite from the offices and machine rooms below. There were cigarette butts and small, flattened juice packets on the north side, which gave a view towards the river, the old law courts and grassed spaces. Even though it was night, much of that was still visible because of the city lights.

'Completely mad, I'd say,' said Nicholas.

'How's that?'

'He has these discussions with his dog, a runt of a fox terrier so highly strung that it's in a constant state of quivering agitation. He has discussions about politics, bowel movements and diet, leaving pauses for the foxie to reply, and then carrying on as if it has. Sometimes he laughs at something the dog says that I can't hear. Spooky really. He'll go on for ages, but whenever I meet him he's not interested in neighbourly conversation. I'm no substitute for the dog.'

'What's his name?'

'Rossiter,' said Nicholas.

The streetlights were on, and many rooms in the office blocks were lit up, maybe for security, or for the cleaners who came into the lost empires when everyone else had gone home. There was always some traffic, especially taxis, and some walkers also, loud and skittish in twos and threes, or quietly making a solitary way.

'I'm not sure what to do,' said Theo.

'This is about Penny Maine-King?'

'I'm not sure what's the best thing,' said Theo. 'Her husband wants a meeting to sort things out, and Penny won't come out of hiding yet. She wants Zack Heywood and me to go and talk to him in France.'

'France. Jesus.'

'He has some sort of business there. I really want to help if I can, and this might be the way to do it. I'm just worried about stepping into the life of a family where there's so much pain, so much at stake. I don't know what she expects.'

'She expects you to want to sleep with her.'

'But it's not just her and me involved, is it?'

'Women see sex as the start of something,' said Nicholas, 'and men see it as an end.'

'But it's not really about that. If you want to be with someone you have to take on what's important to them – the accumulation of their lives. Their grievances and achievements become your own. I don't seem to be very good at that.'

'Don't get gun-shy because of what happened with Stella,' said Nicholas softly. Flippancy and cynicism put aside for a moment, he leant forward over the concrete wall in pretence of observing some activity in the street below. 'I wish to God some woman was interested in me,' he said.

Theo had no reply to that. The sincerity struck home though, and a sense of the loneliness Nicholas lived with. Theo realised that his companion had deliberately let that show, and that such brief vulnerability was his display of friendship.

They were quiet for a time, looking from the darkened platform of the building across the city with its lines of streetlights, lit chequerboard windows, coloured neons and the fireflies of the moving cars. 'When I'm up here,' said Nicholas finally, 'I always feel I want to smoke. I don't know what it is.' Theo felt just the same. It wasn't just the butts scattered at their feet. Something more than that: something to do with being at a height, temporarily cut off from the stress and bustle as the paper was put to bed below. Something to do with night and an almost schoolboy delight in truancy. 'Well,' said Nicholas, 'I'd better head back down, I suppose. I'm supposed to help one of the subs go through some stuff on American politics.'

'Is your neighbour really that weird?' said Theo. 'A lot of people talk to cats and dogs. Maybe it's healthy even – a form of catharsis.' He'd read of ponies, goats, pigs and white rats being taken into rest homes and kindergartens, where the inmates lined up to pat them and be told they shared almost all their DNA.

'This Rossiter is something else, though,' said Nicholas. 'It's not just the interminable conversations with the dog, and the cultivation of Peruvian cacti and succulents in a glasshouse he can only crawl into. I've seen him standing naked in the heavy rain and soaping himself.'

'Is this the guy who complains when you play classical music?'

'Yeah. He set the council noise abatement officer on me. Didn't have the guts to come round himself. As it happens I know Ray Mortensen from the council anyway. He said Rossiter was in tears when he made the complaint.'

As a journalist, Theo often dealt with people who were emotional about their views. Unlike most of the public, however, he realised that conviction and anger aren't guarantees of justifiable grievance. Vehemence is often confused with truth. The world can't believe that a weeping and distraught mother can be in the wrong, or an impassioned witness be false. What about Penny then, and the view he'd espoused?

In the cool night air Theo and Nicholas walked back to the stairwell. The final access to the roof was just a steel ladder bolted to the wall, which flexed slightly when you climbed it. Nicholas went first. He paused when he was halfway down, his face upturned to where Theo waited his turn. 'If I were you, Theo, I'd give this chance with Penny Maine-King my best bloody shot.'

'Yes,' said Theo. 'It's easily the best thing that's happened to me in a long time.'

Nicholas was out of sight, but his voice came up to the roof. 'Just don't start screwing her until you're sure of what you're prepared to take on. I mean the boy and everything.'

17

Theo had sent an email to Penny in paradise, saying they needed to talk, and that he'd drive down to Drybread on Easter Monday unless he heard back from her. There was no answer before then, so early that morning he walked the considerable distance to his work carpark where he'd deliberately left the Audi. The parson was on his mind, although he'd seen no sign of him since Timaru. Theo didn't take the main carpark exit, but drove down the narrow alley between the paper and the backs of the beauty parlour and the pet shop, and out to the other side of the block. Once clear of the city he relaxed.

Solitary, long-distance driving was an exercise in containment: just him, just the vehicle, transient in the passing landscape. Other people's lives were also turning, but they seemed at considerable remove. Penny and her son may have been already on the autumnal hillside; Nicholas putting his feet up to watch CNN news on television; Anna tying on her netball bib to take her place in a workmanlike seniors team in the Easter tournament; Zack entertaining his daughters with tales of his Virginian boyhood; Erskine Maine-King already on his way to Nice perhaps, thinking of his son rather than business. The parson may have been entering Theo's study, morning light catching the buttermilk complexion of his bald head. Maybe Stella was meeting a friend she and Theo used to visit together: Stella would be bright, wouldn't she, bright with that sort of brittle determination to make the best of her talent and opportunities, and because Theo had proved dispensable.

Theo occupied himself by making a considerable list of Stella's virtues, and a shorter list of his own. Both were as honest as he could make them, but they didn't mesh well together – that was the rub. It's not virtues that marriage needs, but compatibility. Stella was particularly adept at identifying his selfishness. 'Not everything is about you,' she had said, but somehow for Theo it always was. He had to learn that always you carry a spear in the drama that is other people's lives.

Stillness and open heat had been his experience of Drybread on the first visit, stillness and high cloud on the second trip, but as he drove through the Maniototo towards the Manuherikia and Penny's gully that third time, a full and persistent wind blew from the west. It groomed the gullies of gorse and broom, fluffed the dry grasses and the tussock on higher country, swept high birds through the sky without a wing beat. On the last stretch into the hills on the gravel road there was no hanging plume behind Theo, for the dust was gusted away from the wheels, and the wind whistled at the exterior mirrors.

He parked by the macrocarpa hedge, but not in its lee, so the wind almost wrenched the car door from his hand when he got out. Penny was looking out of the window as he approached the house, and let him in before he needed to knock. 'It's a shit of day,' she said. They were too familiar to shake hands, not familiar enough to kiss: she rested her hand for a moment on his arm as he came past her in the doorway. On the floor of the all-purpose room, Ben was kneeling on newspaper and rolling Play-doh into unpromising cigar shapes. He wore a Bob the Builder sweatshirt and had a large Band-aid in the centre of his forehead. 'No, it's nothing,' Penny said, 'He just saw them in the drawer and wanted one. He knows they're supposed to make you feel better. He's bored.'

Sometimes it's so easy to make a little kid's day. Theo had remembered to get something for Ben at the service station: a couple of chocolate eggs half price because Easter was almost over. Penny didn't allow the boy more than one. She helped Ben take off the rosetted foil, smoothing it out for him to play with later. The child gave Theo a roll of dough in exchange, and insisted he have a pink Band-aid on his face also. Theo moulded the dough as he sat on the sofa and told Penny about the visit to Zack Heywood and asked her why she wanted him to go to France. 'I haven't got anyone else to ask,' she said. The doors were rattling in the wind, which made the cottage resonate.

Theo didn't think she said it to get sympathy, but Jesus, how isolated she was. At a time in her life when she expected to have the greatest sense of family and community, she was fighting her husband and a court order, and had to ask Theo for help. No brother or sister to support her, her mother ga-ga in a retirement home, her friends thousands of miles away. 'What I know of Zack I like,' she said, 'but I want someone else there to ask things a lawyer mightn't want to. Someone I know better. A real person to stand in for me.'

'So Zack's not real?'

'You know what I mean,' she said. 'It's just a job, isn't it, even for the best lawyer.'

'I need to know what's essential,' Theo said. 'I don't know much about your life, your husband or what the hell you expect to happen. A cock-up over there could be pretty disastrous for you. You know that.'

Penny didn't answer. Bending over, she encouraged her son to put four legs on one of the dough lumps, then raised her head and looked at Theo levelly for a moment. 'But are you willing to help if you can?' she said.

He said yes, because how could he not when she and the kid were stuck the way they were? He said yes because he'd like to fuck her, but it was more than that. He said yes because he felt best when he was with her, and that was the strongest and least explicable reason of all. When he was with her he felt somehow at the centre, instead of at the edge.

'You haven't had any lunch yet have you?' she said. 'Ben hasn't either. Let's have something, and them maybe he'll sleep and we can talk.' It was a scratch meal, with nothing heated. Ben and Theo shared peanut butter sandwiches, apples and bought fruit cake but diverged when it came to drinks: diluted juice for the boy, and a can of Speight's for Theo. Penny had eaten but drank a beer. Ben seemed cheerful enough, and told Theo it was too windy to play outside. Theo was about to say something to him about the parson and Caroline Bay, but thought better of it. That experience was better left dormant in the boy's mind. As long as he had his mother, maybe he didn't care much, and he was too young to realise that they'd come down in the world. Little kids are emotionally resilient, we tell ourselves, because we don't want to consider otherwise, and we don't want to think too much about our own childhoods.

Wind isolated the bach as motion had isolated the car. Theo had a sense of everything outside being fleeting and disturbed, and the three of them inside the bach close-knit, fixed, with just the juddering doors between one state and the other.

When Theo asked Penny if Erskine was an unreasonable man she said it was difficult to be reasonable when your kids were involved. He then asked for her bottom-line requirements, and she said shared custody and fair distribution of what they owned.

'You mean half of everything?' he asked.

'Less than a quarter of what he's worth would do me.'

'Zack said he's got plenty.'

'He's rich enough, and I don't want to live over there any more. The point is the money thing for him is just a bargaining chip in the real issue of custody. That's the guts of the thing you have to realise. The judgement there gave him custody and me only visiting rights.' Theo had wondered about the reason for that, and as if to explain it, Penny went on. 'That judge had a thing against psychiatry as well, and I was having counselling.' There it was, for the first time, the fuse of something important in everything that was happening, but Theo let it lie.

The little guy became sleepy as Penny and Theo talked, so she took him through to the one bedroom, while Theo picked up the newspaper from the floor, folded it, took it to the back door and jammed it underneath to stop the noise. As he came back down the short passage, Penny was at the bedroom door. 'He's out to it already,' she said, and stepped back for him to see Ben on the double bed which filled most of the low-ceilinged room. She'd slipped off his shoes. He lay in his light clothes totally relaxed with his small arms spread on the faded patchwork quilt, and his breathing so easy no movement could be seen. The walls were rough tongue and groove, a worn marmalade lino covered the floor, stacked on the far side were four matching blue travel cases, incongruous in their obvious quality and fashion. All of it spoke of things gone awry; of a time of painful and uncertain transition. Maybe Penny was as aware of that impression as Theo himself, but neither of them referred to it as they went back to the main room.

Without Ben's presence and distraction, without Play-Doh being thrust at them for improvement, Theo and Penny were at one of those cusps of possibility in their friendship. She was asking something significant of him, and when a woman asks more, a man is entitled to seek some return. He imagined how good the sex would be with her; it was many weeks since he had last been with Melanie on the Christmas tree bed in her flat by the Heathcote. One voice told him just to reach out to Penny, kiss her and discover the reaction; another, with greater regard to experience, advised thinking with more than his cock. In the cliché parlance of the magazines, Penny was vulnerable, so it wasn't the time to ask for involvement. And sex involved some degree of commitment. Half an hour on that old couch while Ben napped, and he would be drawn into their lives, inescapably implicated in an unhappiness that had nothing to do with him, except professionally.

And Penny didn't seem set on seduction. She'd taken

no extra care with her appearance, and talked on about Zack and Nice and how her husband would meet all expenses. She'd taken no extra care, but nevertheless Theo lost his last reservations about her attractiveness. He had become accustomed to the startling whiteness of her capped teeth, her careless hair, her sometimes wary expression and assertive language. He liked the fullness of her hips and her long arms, and was drawn to her smooth, muscular neck. And her breasts weren't that small.

'Fixing something up with Erskine in Nice is the best chance,' she was saying. 'Probably the only chance, because we can't stay here much longer. It's not fair on Ben, and the money's running out, and Zack reckons if we don't have a compromise to take to the Family Court very soon that'll be it.'

'Did you play a lot of squash, or something?' he said.

'What's that got to do with anything?' Penny said.

'You look fit, that's all. Stronger than a lot of women.'

'A lot of women in the States work out,' she said. Then she paused and looked directly at him, and her expression gave a little wry twist that was almost a grimace: unattractive in itself, yet so typical of her that Theo found it quite moving. She was sitting on a kitchen chair and he was on the sofa. The wind still buffeted the building, although the thudding back door had been muted.

'Theo,' she said, 'I'm not looking to get into anything right now, okay.' It was a rebuff, but she leaned forward to deliver it. 'I'm only just holding things together as it is. I'm close to tears half the bloody day, and I can't sleep at night. I can only just keep myself together for Ben's sake, okay?'

'I can understand that,' he said. 'It's a rocky time for you. I just hope it all pans out, and you know I'll do what I can.'

'I like you,' she continued, 'but I'm a wreck right now. I can't take on anything else. You wouldn't want to know what's inside my head sometimes.'

'Maybe I would,' said Theo quietly.

'Fuck, no. Believe me you wouldn't.'

And that was the end of thinking with his cock for that day. He was glad he hadn't made a bigger fool of himself, that she had intervened before that happened. The surface of the conversation showed little of the stir beneath, but there was change. She knew Theo wished to be confidant and lover, and as she chose to continue a friendship he took it optimistically – assumed she was deferring opportunity rather than refusing it. And it suited his pride to think that, rather than seeing himself as the only help at hand.

'How old are you?' she asked. Non sequiturs had begun with him, so she felt justified.

'Thirty-eight.'

'So am I,' Penny said. 'You look a bit older.'

'Thanks,' said Theo.

'Anyway, let's get back to the Nice trip. I don't want you to feel you have to, but I see it as the best shot of finishing the business for everybody, and you'd get a good final exclusive out of it.'

They talked more openly than before about her marriage. 'You'll probably like Erskine,' she said. 'He gets on well with guys.'

'But not women?'

'Other women he gets on well enough with.'

'So you're splitting because he played around.'

'No,' said Penny. 'It's because we don't love each other enough any more and that's quite different. That bit's simple, but we both love Ben a great deal and that makes it hard.'

The wind continued to buffet the house around them, which made it seem even smaller, but no rain came. Rain would be both a novelty and a blessing at Drybread, just as it had been in the North Canterbury hills. Theo remembered how his father would leave the table to go and stand beneath the carport and watch the rain falling. 'Send her down, Hughie,' he would say, and the longer it rained the happier he became. In the winter, perhaps, rain came to Drybread as well as snow.

Theo faced the long drive back to Christchurch, and needed to get going. Also, for some reason not clear even to himself, he wanted to be gone when the boy woke up. Penny said he could spend the night on the sofa, and meant exactly that. 'Don't come out,' he said. 'It's a bastard of a wind. I'll talk again with Zack Heywood and send you an email.'

'I like you a lot,' she said. 'I don't think I can get through all this without your help. It means a hell of a lot to have someone on my side at the moment.' She reached out towards his face, and for a moment Theo thought she was about to stroke his cheek, but she gripped the Band-aid strip and removed it without comment.

She stood briefly at the window as he left, and gave a quick wave. Even the solid macrocarpa hedge was swaying slightly and the clear hill facings higher up were an undulation of tussock. The wind pressure made Theo's hair uncomfortable on his scalp and he was glad to close himself in the car. Was he going to get out of his depth in the whole thing about Penny and the boy? Who could say how much selfish calculation, how much selfless concern, lay in their attitudes? What passes between a man and a woman is a fluctuating charge, and never fully decipherable.

18

At the back door was a hard rubber and metal-studded doormat on a folded sack. The dirt from her father's boots would fall to the sack, and her mother would shake it out on the lawn every other day. On the concrete beneath the overhang he'd leave his boots when he came inside. She would glance there when she came home from school, up the unsealed track from the road gate where the bus dropped her. The road, too, was unsealed, the gravel ploughed into furrows and mounds by occasional traffic. The back window of the bus was always dusty, and Dylan Churcher would write 'Fuck Me', or 'Okker Sucks Pussy', and make sure the others noticed. Okker was their headmaster. He came from Dubbo in Australia. By the time the bus reached her place there weren't many kids left. Dylan Churcher always went further than any of the others.

The kitchen window of the farmhouse had been enlarged. She could remember when it was done. Her father had taken out the old sash windows by sawing around the frames, but his skills weren't up to fitting the replacement window, and a young carpenter who was working on McFedrons' new house came over and spent a Saturday doing the job. Her mother liked to say it was a conservatory window, but didn't explain the term.

It was her third form year, and she liked the smooth, brown skin of the carpenter's face, and the way that sawdust caught in the fair hairs of his forearms. She liked the agility with which he could squat down to measure, or cut, and then bob up again like a cork, even if he had something heavy in his hands, and his breathing didn't alter. He talked to her while he worked, facing the window. He asked her if old Okker was still the same, and told her the only thing he'd enjoyed about school was playing in the first fifteen. He was planning to go to Australia where builders' wages were just about double what he was getting. 'Nothing much happens around here, does it?' he said. From the back he was pretty ordinary, with ears that weren't quite level, and a double crown that made his hair stick up.

The enlarged window gave an even better view of the yards and the woolshed. That's probably why she took no pleasure in the renovation. When she did the dishes she looked at the yards and the old concrete dip, or the disused pigpen, the pine shelter belt on the hill behind, or her mother's lavenders and climbing roses so much closer. She didn't need sight to evoke the woolshed: the smell of dags and sweat and new wool, the heat from the exposed tin of the roof, the mixture of awkward shame and abrupt determination with which her father would push her face down in the soft, open bale. He was never so unnaturally far away as when he was so unnaturally close. In the year of the kitchen renovations he never penetrated her. He would push between her thighs from behind and say, 'Okay, okay, it's all right, okay', over and over until he spurted. He'd wipe her thighs with the slightly yellow skin end of fleece wool and say, 'It's nothing, is it, nothing, okay. You know I'd never do anything to hurt you,' he'd say – and the thing was she knew they both believed it then.

19

As it happened, Zack and Theo flew into Nice on Anzac Day, though that meant nothing to Europeans. They didn't need any historical instance of bonding to confuse Kiwis and Aussies. Nice has a large, busy airport, but there was no direct connection from New Zealand. Theo and the Virginian flew through Singapore to Paris, and then down to the Côte d'Azur. Theo had been to the place once before: as a twenty-two-year-old following the completion of his degree. As Zack and he came into central Nice by taxi, he recognised the long sweep of the beach on which he'd sat for two days because he didn't have enough money to do much else. The fountains he recognised too, and the old quarter rising up the hill beyond the bus station. He told Zack about the ancient fortress on the summit, and the maritime curio shops close to the sea with brass navigational instruments, slave chains, ships in bottles and authentic scrimshaw. 'I think you'd find that anything bone, or ivory, would be prohibited by Customs,' Zack said.

Zack wasn't intrigued by Nice as a repository of history or art. He just wanted to do the business and go home. He was more interested in assessing the comforts of their hotel in Rue Gioffredo than the Chagall gallery, or the desperate zoo of the Algerian quarter. He didn't relax until he'd made contact with Erskine Maine-King and confirmed a meeting for the next day. 'Let me assure you we're committed to finding a way through,' Theo heard him say. 'I know, I know, but she didn't feel she could, and that's not a sign she doesn't want a solution. It's just that she doesn't feel up to a face-to-face meeting right now.' With his free hand Zack checked the quality of the linen on the bed on which he sat. 'We look forward to meeting you too,' he said. 'It's on for ten o'clock tomorrow at his hotel,' he told Theo. 'I thought he sounded a regular enough guy. I never could get Mrs Maine-King to say much about him, so it's not easy to know what line to take. Did she say much to you?'

'Not a lot. She's afraid of the way he uses his money I think.'

'We'll have to play it by ear,' said Zack. Money didn't frighten him. He'd found it a useful partner and companion.

In the dusk Zack and Theo walked from Rue Gioffredo to a couscous restaurant in the old town which had been recommended by the woman at hotel reception. The place was in a steep, cobbled street, and quite unpretentious: simple checked cloths on the wooden tables, and walls free of any decoration. The meal looked like something prepared in a musterers' hut, all meat chunks, and the gravy it was cooked in poured over the heaped couscous in a large bowl. It cost a musterer's weekly wage too, but that wasn't Theo's concern. He enjoyed it. He half expected Zack to be a wine bore, to go on about the vintages of some preferred Bordeaux *vin rouge*, or some local treasure he'd stumbled on while touring in Languedoc, but Zack drank what the Algerian waiter recommended without comment, and talked of family. In appearance Zack could have been that typical sort of Frenchman who is finely built and neat, yet masculine as well. Only when he spoke did he assume his nationality.

'Break-ups are so much more difficult if there's children,' said Zack. 'I see it again and again. You can separate out property, money, even citizenship, but children and memories always live on as the evidence of a relationship.'

'But you wouldn't put off having kids because you thought you might split up, would you?' said Theo. 'I mean you've got to have faith, surely?'

'Faith, yes I suppose so.' Zack sounded unconvinced, however, as if it were a point needing judicial scrutiny. 'I tell you what, the more marital and custody work I do, the more attention I pay to my own wife and family. Sad, unhappy people, Theo – I see plenty of those. Some of them achievers and bright as hell, some of them born losers, but sad, unhappy people because they're not right together. Some of the stories I hear, well, Jesus . . . as I say, I go home and feel like a lucky man.'

'I like stories,' said Theo. 'Stories are a journo's business.' But he didn't want to hear too many on that topic, or tell his own to the lawyer.

'Ah, professional confidentiality,' said Zack lightly, as if he had been pressed just a little.

'Of course.'

'There are times when things turn out well too,' the lawyer said, 'when common sense and respect provide a way through. It's the kids that matter most.'

Towards the end of the meal there was sudden, heavy rain. It surprised Theo because he hadn't been outside to see it building, and because he had no experience of rain in Nice. The weather you remember in a place is the weather it experiences forever. Through the open door of the small restaurant they could see the water gush down the narrow, sloping street, the uneven cobbles creating small turbulences. The proprietor took the opportunity to empty several ashtrays and a small container of rubbish into the stream. It was all over in twenty minutes, and Theo and Zack were able to walk back to the hotel. The market area at the edge of the old town, close to the bus station, full of food and flower stalls, soaps and hand-painted postcards during the day, was bare and glistening after the rain. There was a slight smell of engine oil, citrus soaps and vegetables, and an even fainter one of lavender.

It released in Theo a recollection of his time there years ago, when he'd met up with a South African boy at the railway station, and been best friends for a night during which neither of them could afford accommodation. There'd been nothing sexual whatsoever, just their common situation and the spontaneity of youth, and they'd walked and talked and drunk the night through before taking separate trains the next day. And in knowledge of the necessary transience of their friendship, they'd been quite candid with each other. Theo couldn't remember a name, but the guy told him he'd been attacked by two Algerians the night before and had stabbed one of them in the face. He showed Theo the knife he carried, which had a handle of bound cord, and stains on his clothes which he hadn't been able to wash out. They'd been sitting in the bus terminal, and as Theo passed there with Zack, he thought the dingy concrete bays, the litter, the few figures in dark corners, looked much the same.

20

Erskine Maine-King's hotel was more opulent than Theo's, and his room looked out towards the Promenade des Anglais and the sea. There was a low, glass-topped table surrounded by four black leather chairs. Close to the window was a large brass elephant, bearing a spidery plant instead of a howdah. Erskine introduced himself, and then his lawyer whose first name was Oliver. They were both tall men with similar and pronounced Californian accents. Zack's own nationality was a temporary point of interest, and Theo was aware of being the only non-American.

Theo had wondered often enough about the motivations and character of Penny's husband, but not his appearance, and found it oddly unsettling to have a physical presence finally before him: to notice that Erskine's thick hair was already greying at the sides of his head, that his visible teeth were almost as pristine yet unoriginal as his wife's, that he had no tan at all. Erskine bore no resemblance to any brash, beach-boy Californian stereotype. He looked like a man who, rather than playing sport, did some gym work to hold back incipient bulk, and on the pale bridge of his nose were two slightly pink indentations made by his glasses, which lay on the table. There he was, a complete stranger in appearance, yet Theo had been writing newspaper articles that concerned him, had attempted to make love to his wife, had bought sweets for his child. Erskine and Theo had no history, yet both knew Penny's body fragrance, the high arch of her blonde eyebrows, a certain brittleness beneath her assertive manner. Erskine had greater possession of her past, and Theo, surely, more understanding of her present. The future was a ground of contest.

'You've come a long way,' said Erskine, 'and I appreciate that. I would've come to New Zealand myself if Penny was willing to meet me, but we won't go over that again. The whole thing for me is wanting Ben back again. I don't hate Penny, and I hope she doesn't hate me, but I need my son and I think he needs me. I've never said Penny can't see him. It's what the court back home decided, that he live with me, and she have visiting rights.' He paused and took several regular breaths to ensure he was fully in control of his emotions, that he wasn't too partisan. 'I thought that was okay by both of us, and then wham, Penny took off.' He tipped his head back a little as he recalled it. 'I guess I wasn't paying enough attention to things,' he said.

'I think she was overwhelmed by a sense of the inequality in your situations,' said Zack. 'In a country not her own, not working, no financial security, her marriage disintegrating, her friends mainly yours . . . she must have felt powerless. So she went away with the child: the only really important thing she had left.'

'It's no long-term answer, though, is it?' said Erskine.

He was right. Even Penny had come to recognise that. Theo was surprised by the reasonableness of his manner and his views. He barely mentioned Penny's defiance of the Family Court order, her secrecy, her willingness to discredit him. He was obviously a man used to meetings and negotiation, to finding ground of agreement, yet his real concern for Ben was equally apparent. He must have wondered about Theo's connection with Penny, but it wasn't until almost half an hour of discussion had gone by, and coffee had been brought up, that he asked Theo to talk with him alone.

They left the two American lawyers in their chairs by the low, glass table, and went into Erskine's bedroom. A laptop computer was set up on the bed with the screensaver swirling and some papers alongside, but all else was tidy. Erskine and Theo stood at the window, looking out over the bustling street, the promenade, the long sweep of the glamorous beach and the Mediterranean beyond. Aircraft vapour trails formed and gradually dissipated in the blue, slightly hazy sky. It was all a long way from Drybread with its empty hills and sharp horizons, its gold tailings in the gully scabbed with broom and gorse, the old sod house with a church pew at the back door.

'I don't want to sound rude,' Erskine said, 'but I'm not sure where you fit into all this. I know you've written those newspaper articles. I've read them and I could say a hell of a lot from my point of view, but she wanted you here as well as her lawyer so you must be close?'

'She's afraid she's going to be squeezed out of Ben's life.'

'Well, Jesus, I know the feeling.' Erskine looked appraisingly at him, then, tall and solid, watched the people beneath the hotel window. Theo thought perhaps he was going to ask directly if Penny and he were lovers. Maybe he was going to say something that would be appropriate for such a situation in a television drama, like, are you getting laid by my wife? But maybe Theo was imposing his own priority, and Penny's husband was worried that he was after money in some way.

'You see her? They're okay?' Erskine said.

'Not really. Penny's beside herself with worry a good deal of the time.'

'She should've come herself. We're still a family,' Erskine said. 'She must really trust you. It's almost like a death, you know, when your child's taken away from you.' His voice was steady, but one hand gave a brief flutter at his side.

'Did you think of that when your private detective or whatever tried to grab Ben back?' said Theo. He remembered the boy falling, the blood from his nose, and the parson and the young woman in the car refusing to face what had happened. 'Do you blame Penny for not coming or saying where she is?'

'I don't know anything about any snatch. Nothing at all. Ben wasn't hurt, or upset?' Erskine's concern was evident: he came a step closer to Theo as if to be certain of gauging his answer.

'Not too badly,' said Theo.

'You're sure of that? And Penny's okay?'

'They've coped pretty well from what little I've seen. You've got someone there looking for them, though, haven't you?'

'Of course I have, but I wouldn't do anything to hurt either of them. You think I'm not just as worried? I'll ring the guy and see what the hell's going on. He's supposed to find them, that's all. I'm entitled to know where my son is. Your police seem useless.'

Erskine wasn't someone who aroused immediate dislike. Theo could understand his situation rather more than he wished. 'You need to ease up,' he told him. 'Both of you need to ease up and get things sorted out. It's too important to leave to lawyers.'

'Does she talk to you much about her father, or mother, about when she was a kid?' Erskine said. That came out of the blue.

'Hardly anything at all. Her mother's in care and I think her father's dead.'

'Dead, but not gone,' said Erskine. He still wore his wedding ring, and Theo, quite close beside him at the window, was aware of the fragrance of aftershave. He also noticed that Erskine had no lobes to his ears. The laptop screensaver showed characters from the Simpsons surfing – waves tumbling, boards bobbing, comic mouths open – but no noise at all. Maybe California was determined to have some presence on the Côte d'Azur, however marginal.

'I'm not with you,' Theo said.

'Penny's got a whole bunch of issues from when she was a kid on the farm. Some of it pretty screwed up stuff, which makes things difficult for her at times.' Erskine seemed relieved Theo wasn't familiar with her childhood, as if that were evidence enough that he wasn't Penny's confidant, hadn't been given the intimacy of mind which would follow nakedness together. 'I suppose I seem the bastard in all of this, but all I want is to be a part of Ben's life, and for him to be happy. I think Penny knows that. I'm not saying we all have to live together, for Christ's sake. You know? The marriage is gone, I guess, but we need some way to carry on as parents. Maybe you can help explain to Penny.'

'I don't think she wants to leave New Zealand again,' Theo said. 'Not permanently anyway.'

'Okay, sure, but I need to know where they are, and be able to have time with Ben. We can get the lawyers to sort out all the Family Court stuff, as long as Penny stops messing around. She'll have to come back to the Californian court for a while to get any change anyway. You know that: you know how the Hague Convention works.'

'She needs money too, a fair settlement, if she's to have a life for them both until she can go back to work.'

'There's no problem there, Theo, as long as she – as long as I'm able to be part of my son's life. That's what it's all about for me. There's no one to punish here. It's all gotten somehow out of hand. Zack tells me you're divorced, so you understand that a marriage is too complex and personal for the law. The law gives no redress for the things that matter. And it's not just mothers who love their kids, you know. If you can get Penny to talk to me tonight, I reckon the legal eagles will have something your courts will be happy with by the end of tomorrow. Okay?'

Theo said he would do what he could, despite having no telephone link, and they shook hands. Erskine asked how Ben was looking and stood in a slight stoop of concentration to listen. As Theo talked about the boy, a faint, quite unselfconscious smile appeared on Erskine's face, as if the image of his son were coming up more clearly before him. 'I hear your country is an ideal place to bring up kids,' he said.

Erskine's laptop was the easiest and quickest way to get in touch with Penny, but Theo thought it better, even after what Erskine had said, that he leave no record of her email address, so he sought out an internet café from which he could send Penny his hotel phone number. It would be late at night over there, but he knew she was expecting something from him and would go into Alexandra when she could.

Two or three blocks from Erskine's hotel, chance presented one of those glimpses of the life of others that seems to cry out for relevance. A blue Renault backed up to get enough space to swing forward and drive away from the kerb, and in backing nudged the bumper of the campervan behind. The van barely moved, but as if a switch was activated, the blind on the window close to Theo went up with a flurry, and revealed a naked couple lying on their blankets. Both were on their backs, the man with his head on her stomach, and her thighs on each side of his face, as if he had been carrying her on his shoulders and just fallen back onto the bed. The woman was olive-skinned. Her short hair was cast back from her face and her full breasts angled away on each side of her lover's head. The man was pale, round faced, the greying hair at the centre of his chest like the smudge from a cigar in a white ceramic ashtray. Theo and the couple looked at each other steadily for a second, the surprise and candour too complete for any reaction, then he stepped on again down the street with fully clothed and fully closed people as usual about him. It was a long time since he had been party to such relaxed nakedness, and the close, personal satisfaction of two ordinary people emphasised his exclusion.

A Scottish backpacker with a dirty collar sat at the computer next to him in the email café, his legs over his pack for security and taking some of Theo's space. He wanted help with access to hotmail, and Theo felt resentment rather than sympathy: convinced that nothing in the young guy's life was of any significance at all in comparison with his own priorities. Theo didn't give a bugger for his ferrety girlfriend in Aberdeen, if he had one, or his dying ex-merchant-navy father in a Glasgow tenement. He was at once close enough for Theo to see the ginger glint of his eyelashes, and so far away that he signified nothing at all. What Theo thought about was Penny and the boy, waiting on the other side of the world to find out what was going to happen to them. And the couple in the van.

Penny rang late that night, and Theo was glad Zack had his own room. 'What time is it?' she said, and apologised when he told her. As they talked about the morning's meeting with her husband, Theo was surprised by the emotion in his voice, and sensed warmth in hers. Maybe it was just relief that at last there was a good chance she could be released from limbo, and have some sort of life. She wanted to talk with Theo before contacting Erskine, and that reliance on his opinion was gratifying too. He asked her if she wanted him to wake Zack, but she said all the legal stuff could wait until she spoke to her husband. She was ringing from a public phone booth in Alexandra. The call was costing an arm and a leg she said, and laughed when Theo told her to add it to her expenses claim. 'It's so sunny here,' she said, and then she was interrupted by Ben wanting to talk.

'I got new shoes,' he said clearly, then lost interest. He didn't use Theo's name, no doubt had no idea to whom he was talking, no idea how important the day was in his life, but Theo could picture him clearly, and his mother too, in the open sunlight of the Central Otago town. Blonde Penny, who moved with a sort of grace that mastered desperate agitation, and dark-haired Ben, always looking up at the world.

'Okay then, I'd better ring Erskine,' she said. 'Anyway, I think you're right. We can't go on in this sort of stand-off.'

'No.'

'I'm looking forward to you coming back,' she said.

'So am I.'

Theo didn't go back to bed for while. He wanted to be awake during the time Penny would be talking to her husband. Theo had the mean-spirited, but very satisfying, thought that she wouldn't be telling Erskine she was looking forward to him coming back. He thought also of what Erskine had said about Penny's problems, and wondered if he had created, or exaggerated, them to lessen any responsibility he felt for the failure of their marriage. The marriage is gone, I guess, he'd said to Theo at the window of his bedroom that morning. There was a half-hidden bewilderment in his tone that found an echo in Theo: marriages are there, and then they're gone, although the people remain. You paddle one side of the canoe for a straight line, then you find you have to paddle both sides to get ahead. You have to find within yourself a fellow conversationalist.

The traffic noise was surprisingly loud so early in the day, and Theo lay in the warm darkness of the hotel room for some time before falling asleep. He dreamt not of Penny and Erskine, or of himself and Stella, but of the middle-aged lovers in the campervan, both on their backs and entwined. There was about them the indolent ease of mutual satisfaction. More even – the accomplishment of having for a moment wrested happiness from the tight fist of everyday life.

In the morning Theo talked to Zack about Penny's call, and her willingness to co-operate with Erskine as long as Ben was able to live mainly with her. As they came away from the thin French breakfast, the desk clerk gave them a message from Erskine, asking them to come to his hotel again at ten. 'Their talk must have gone okay then,' said Zack. 'Rather odd, don't you think. You and I come all this way and it's effectively settled by the Maine-Kings with a late night phone call.'

'Being hidden and having the boy with her were what gave her security I suppose. Will Ben have to become a ward of the court, or something, for a while?'

'I don't imagine so,' said Zack. 'As long as the parents have an amicable agreement our Family Court will want to assist a settlement. It just has to be done with the Californian court in mind, so that the judge there doesn't feel his jurisdiction has been disrespected. That particular judge is very sensitive as to his dignity and that of the law. It's really all about that central provision of the convention that children should be returned to their country of origin for disputes to be resolved. Penny Maine-King will almost certainly have to go back there and eat humble pie.'

At Erskine's hotel the four of them sat again in the dark, comfortable chairs around the see-through tabletop, and with a view of the promenade and the shifting blue glitter on the sea as if from broken glass. It had all been decided, really: the two lawyers remained to work through the legalities of the application for a stay of the warrant, a rehearing and a separate financial settlement confidential to the Maine-Kings, while Erskine and Theo left the hotel and dodged through the traffic to the beachfront.

Even the road noise was different in Nice, with a high-pitched component from the scooter traffic so typical of France and Italy. They sat on seats above a fresh water sluice point for swimmers on the long, postcard beach, and Erskine flinched in the glare of the sun. 'Damn,' he said. 'I've left my sunglasses in the room. I've inherited a reduced tolerance to direct sunlight.' He faced away from the sun, yet still frequently put his hand above his eyes as they talked.

'You'll have to be careful when you come to New Zealand then,' Theo said. 'It's supposed to be at its most dangerous there.'

'I hear it's a beautiful country,' he said. The mantra of the foreigner to Kiwis abroad.

'When do you think you'll come out?'

'As soon as the legal stuff's sorted, and as soon as Penny's comfortable with it. It breaks me up, you know, not to be able to see Ben.'

'You need to rein in that private detective guy then,' said Theo.

'I'll get that done today too.'

Why should Theo dislike such a reasonable man, who said things Theo imagined he would say in the same circumstances? He had come to Nice prepared to face a nasty bastard, and found someone trying to do the best he could in painful and bewildering circumstances. There weren't many swimmers in April, but the bright day brought out a variety of people to sit on the sand. Close below were a middle-aged couple with their arms companionably about each other, and a backpacker with 'Argentina' on the back of his jacket. He had the good looks of youth, and sorted carefully through his limited possessions, almost as if he were taking inventory. A grubby bandage swathed his left hand. The isolation of proximity seems more evident when you travel. The compatible couple, the young guy, and Erskine and Theo: all with their paths in life and their own imperatives, randomly sitting quite close in Nice, with absolutely no connection.

'Penny never talked much about her own country,' said Erskine. 'I had no idea she wanted to go home, yet from what she said last night I think you're right – a place in New Zealand as well as California might be the way to go.'

'When things are tough you think of home,' said Theo.

'They tell me it's a good place to bring up kids,' said Erskine again. 'The space, the education system and all.'

'But you said she was unhappy growing up.'

'I'd better not say anything more about that – I never really got a handle on it all. Another thing she told me last night was that I wasn't to gossip to you.' It was perhaps an admonition, but Theo rather liked it. He took it as a sign that she cared what he thought about her, what people might tell him. 'She's a very private person,' her husband said. 'There's a bunch of stuff there she holds in and hasn't come to terms with.'

They took refuge in discussing Erskine's work – his firm made special fibre items, mainly strapping. The sort of stuff used for seatbelts, alpine gear, haulage restraints. His father began the business in California and there was a factory in Nice as well. He asked a bit about Theo's journalism, and then both felt they'd done all they needed to part on terms that wouldn't cause awkwardness if they met again. 'Maybe I'll see you in New Zealand, Theo,' he said. He squinted past the couple and the backpacker on the beach, put out his hand. 'You tell Penny,' he said, 'I sure as hell want everything to work out.'

Theo watched Erskine walk away, fully the large, successful American he was, but not arrogant, not loud. The couple on the beach strolled away soon after, and Theo followed on the promenade above. The backpacker remained, with no one close, but paid no heed to that. He reminded Theo of his own visit years before. Maybe he was deciding if he could afford the cheapest *plat de jour* in a backstreet café, or must join the French teenagers at McDonald's. Maybe he would become a notable politician in his own country, or a criminal of equal distinction. In either case the small piece of his life on the beach in Nice would be some part of that progress.

When Zack and Theo left from the Nice airport four hours later, the beach lay like a bright scimitar far below, pale outcrops on the Alpes-Maritimes caught the low sun. Erskine and Oliver were at the strapping factory perhaps, concentrating once again on making money.

21

At the end of her fifth form year she went to a school dance in Alexandra. She wore the first full-length dress of her life, apart from the bridesmaid's one she had worn at her cousin Sandra's wedding in Dunedin earlier in the same year. She hardly knew Sandra, and couldn't work out why she'd been asked. Her mother said weddings were all about family, and bridesmaids were better to be younger than the bride. The ball dress was blue and had the bra cups sewn into the bodice. A shimmer of blue from her bust to the floor, and her shoulders quite bare. Her mother said blue suited her eyes and hair, but Penny thought that her arms were too brown for the white of her exposed shoulders.

Like a good many of her classmates she didn't go with a special boy, but she danced with Shane Taylor several times, who everybody said was going to be head boy next year, and she twice told Dylan Churcher that she'd rather not thanks. Dylan had a pudding face and still smelled considerably of himself, while

Shane knew something of toiletries, perhaps because his father was a doctor. Shane's clean hair lapped over his collar a little, and she would have liked to touch it. He had a habit of raising his eyebrows and pulling a face when people said something that was supposed to be funny. His Adam's apple stuck out in his smooth neck, but even that was somehow attractive.

She went in on a special bus that came all the way through from Ranfurly, bringing some seniors she didn't know, and it left again at eleven thirty, dropping people singly, or in small groups, all the way back. Her father was waiting for her at the turn-off to Drybread. She recognised the Holden even in the dark. 'Don't be a stranger round school,' said Shane. Suave – was he ever.

'See ya, Penny. Grow those tits,' called Dylan, as she went down the steps. A creep – as ever.

She didn't talk much about the dance on the drive home, and her father didn't seem that interested. 'I suppose there was a good turnout?' he said. He didn't repeat the question after her silence. After a whole hall full of young, tight-skinned people he seemed old, even in the dimness of the car. His hands on the wheel were old, his hair had no gloss and the slope of his shoulders was old. In two months she would give him a photo frame for his forty-ninth birthday: eleven different indigenous woods represented.

Her mother was in bed, and they talked in the bedroom briefly while her father locked up. Her mother was always interested in the suppers at any formal occasion. Whether there were hot savouries as well as club sandwiches, and furthermore were they home-made, or bought; whether there were chocolate éclairs with real whipped cream, or just lemon and pineapple cheesecakes; whether the punch was alcoholic maybe. Was there a white cloth on the trestle tables, or just taped paper? And she asked if the blue dress had become sweat stained. Her mother was three years older than her father: it seemed a lot more. Both of them were older than the parents of her friends.

Her father came through to her room when she was putting on her pyjamas. 'Everything okay then?' he said. She put her hands between her legs to stop him going there. She stood close to the bed, facing it, but he put arms around her and pressed himself to her side. 'You know how much I care about you,' he said. He was always a loud breather, even when at rest.

When she had sessions with the therapist years later in Sacramento, that was one of the things she talked about: the heavy insistent breathing. She continued to hear it for years after leaving home. She would hear it during a pause at a dinner party, hear it emanating from the poor reception of a television set, or as a background to the change in the weather as she drove. Most of all she heard it when she slept.

'Don't,' she said. 'Don't do it, or I'll call out to Mum.'

She could never bear to call him Dad in those moments of greatest and most unnatural intimacy. 'I will. I'll yell.'

'Don't be silly. It's just play. You know I love you.'

'Mum,' she said loudly.

'What is it?'

Her father moved away, leaving her with what he intended as a paternal pat on the shoulder.

'Should I sponge the sweat stains?'

Her father left the room.

'Good idea,' her mother said sleepily. It was an undramatic, but final, victory.

Frottage with my father, she joked to the counsellor. She had the terminology by then to discuss sexual relationships and practices. The counsellor laughed on professional grounds – laughter is a healthy, cathartic response – but both were aware there was little humour in it. Even the account of Penny's final undramatic assumption of the power of refusal didn't assuage the damage much, or mitigate the enduring contradiction between natural love and natural hate – for the same person.

For some reason she told the counsellor that as her father had stood clasping her, she'd seen a bird flapping soundlessly at the darkened window, palest light through the splayed feathers of the wings, but there'd been no bird. The curtains had been drawn in her bedroom, the blue dress empty and spread on the bed. There'd been no bird, and she had no idea why she'd created it. Did she crave symbolism for the occasion? She never talked about it again, and the counsellor showed no curiosity concerning it, yet on the rare, unpleasant occasions the scene returned, at the window, outlined against a luminous sky, was a bird with wings outstretched.

All seen in the intense, coruscating glare of past emotion.

22

Theo didn't see Penny during the first week back. Anna and the editor seemed to regard Nice as something of a junket, despite Erskine Maine-King paying for the trip, and the value of the exclusive article Theo would be able to write when Zack Heywood had made his submission to the Family Court. There was a good deal for Theo to catch up on, Anna said. Her strongly developed team ethic made her suspicious of too much individual play. Theo couldn't drive down to Drybread, and Penny still didn't feel secure enough to leave the place until she knew the court's response. She left a message on his answerphone saying she hoped to see him soon and thanking him for making the trip to France.

Before going south, Theo called Zack, who said Penny had been in touch, but it was way too soon to expect anything from the court. 'Come on, Zack,' Theo said, 'you must be getting some insider vibes.' Theo imagined Zack's easy smile as he sat with a freshly laundered, quality shirt in his well-ordered office, the light catching the blue peppermint jar perhaps and the metal burnish of the frame that held the photograph of his family. Zack was accustomed to dealing with importunate people.

'Well, I think we made a good case for a rehearing, and it doesn't do the court any good to have an outstanding order either. This new willingness of the Maine-Kings to compromise and work together is positive stuff, but a judge will make the decision, and then of course there's the response of the Californian court. Whatever happens here, that original decision can only be addressed at source. We're dealing with a lot of variables in all this you know. Maybe it would be better if you didn't write much in the meantime – the judiciary's very sensitive about media pressure. Is that possible?'

'I can talk to the editor.'

'Are you planning to see Mrs Maine-King soon?' asked Zack.

'Probably.'

'If the warrant's withdrawn, Penny and the boy can have a more normal life. And her husband wants to come out almost immediately if that happens. It'll strengthen their case if both parents are in the country and willing to appear before the court.'

'Sure.'

'I've told her most of this,' said Zack.

'Is Penny okay for money now?'

'A financial settlement is going through. I don't really think I can be more specific than that, Theo.'

'No, that's fine,' Theo said.

'You look after yourself now,' the lawyer said. 'You've made a considerable contribution. Erskine Maine-King told me he had no complaints about you being in Nice, and that could've been tricky considering the stuff you wrote here in New Zealand.' Did Zack really feel there was no more ambiguity than that in the meeting, or was he exercising professional discretion? There could be fireworks there if things go wrong, he might say to his wife. Someone's going to be hurt pretty badly, he might say.

Theo thought about the Nice visit as he drove to Drybread, and about why Penny and Erskine, who seemed so competent as individuals, should have failed as a couple. If she were asked, maybe Penny would say marriage restricted her growth as a person, or her opportunity to have a career. She might say she wasn't valued sufficiently, or that her husband demanded an open relationship, which was contrary to her beliefs. She might say she had left too many friends and memories behind in New Zealand, or that she had a vision of the risen Lord while doing pilates in a mirrored former ballet training studio above a whiteware showroom in downtown Sacramento. She might say that only when she had a son did she understand the meaning of love. She might talk about her father.

Penny's bach in the gully slumped under a strong sun, even though it was May. The pale yellow-grey sod of the original walls by the front door was warm to the touch, and she had both doors open to air the place. She and Ben had been waiting, and for a brief time she and Theo stood there talking, with brightness at two ends of the short hall through the house. It made the bach seem like one of those false fronts of a movie set, lacking the dimension of depth. Penny was in a mood new to Theo: less guarded, infused with relief. She thanked him again. Relaxation suited her, gave her an added attractiveness. For the first time he had a true sense of the fearsome pressure she had been under, and the willpower and stubbornness she had needed to withstand it. He hoped she hadn't assumed too much, and reminded her that the court hadn't made any ruling, but she was convinced the agreement with Erskine was the key. 'Everywhere the law recognises the good of the child is the main thing,' she said.

'Come in to the cake,' said the little boy beside them, impatient with adult talk. He took hold of the pocket of Theo's trousers and pulled him into the main room. On the small wooden table was a rectangle of chocolate cake, still sitting on its supermarket wrapper. 'Cake,' Ben said, looking up for Theo's affirmation of the treat.

'Great,' he said. 'I like cake.'

'We can eat it.' He still held on with a small hand. Theo noticed how much he had tanned since he first saw him through the window, asleep. He was an attractive kid, endearing even, but Theo felt a slight uneasiness, as if he were in some way an imposter. Maybe it was just the feelings he had for Penny, his recent conviction of Erskine's love for the boy.

'I told him he had to wait until you came,' said Penny. 'I knew you wouldn't have had anything to eat.' She had three filled rolls on a plate as well.

'Until Theo,' said Ben loudly.

'And now he's here,' said Penny. She and Ben had a brief contest of wills over the sequence in which the food was to be eaten, but she was firm, and Ben sat up at the table, his head not much above it, and ate half a roll while eyeing the cake as if he feared it might disappear.

Penny said they should be able to move from the place soon. 'Erskine accepts that the marriage is over and that Ben's first home should be with me. I've phoned him twice since you've come back. We've sorted a lot of things. Sorted stuff that I should have talked with him about instead of just taking off. It seems so obvious now, and so impossible then. But then you see things differently after a few months like I've had here. I feel at last I'm climbing out of the pit.'

Drybread was the sort of place in which it was difficult to maintain self-deceit. There was a basic, stripped quality to the landscape and existence that made evident lessons which were elsewhere able to be evaded because of the press of people with varied, plausible opinions, and the deliberately false and noisy march of trivial entertainment, received values and distraction. People complained that they couldn't hear themselves think, and were intent on maintaining just that protection.

Theo was determined to reflect Penny's optimism and not bring her down. 'So hopefully I'll have one last exclusive article for the paper, with a happy ending to it all,' he said. 'I had a talk with the editor about not printing any more until the court's made a decision, and he agreed. Zack thought it would be advisable not to be seen to be putting any pressure on.'

'A scoop,' said Penny. 'Christ, you'll have a genuine scoop, and your editor and everyone will be chuffed. Doesn't everyone love a happy ending, next to heartbreak and tragedy of course. And I hope this isn't just any old story for you, is it?'

'A story of immense personal significance,' said Theo. He meant it, but used a tone which disguised sincerity.

'You must have to disengage from stories, though, in your job, I mean. You spend time working to get close to people and what's going on, and then it's over and you move on.'

'You do, but you take something with you. If you're half a journalist you learn as you go.'

'And you must meet some real weirdos,' said Penny.

Ben, permitted at last, was concentrating on his cake, so Theo told Penny of a story he did while on his London fellowship.

There was a one-armed man living in King's Cross who claimed to be a descendant of Philip Stanhope, fourth Earl of Chesterfield. He had a three-rung, wooden library ladder and would mount it outside hotels and tube stations, read from Lord Chesterfield's published letters and seek donations with a green, fabric-covered hatbox. He was adamant in protestation, but had no evidence of aristocratic origins whatsoever. And no proof, either, of having lost his arm in the service of Queen and country.

He was happy to harangue Theo, and delighted with any publicity, but refused to give an address, or be interviewed at his home. After three attempts as sleuth, Theo tracked him to a forgotten orange portaloo behind a builder's yard, and saw him creep in at nightfall, as a border collie would to its kennel. He must have hung his one neat, grey suit above him, the useless left sleeve folded with a large stainless steel safety pin, and then slept curled on the floor. Theo had said nothing of that discovery in the published story. The guy could be dismissed as mad, Theo told Penny, but maybe it was profitable delusion. The conviction of noble lineage sustained him when he had nothing else on which to base esteem: it even gave some sort of living, and a role to distinguish him. 'I am of this blue blood,' he'd say at every pause in his readings, swaying on the ladder stool and as testimony holding high with his one arm the book of the Earl of Chesterfield's letters.

'It's sad and funny at the same time,' said Penny.

'The best stories always are,' said Theo. 'My friend Nick reckons people love to read about what they fear most for themselves happening to someone else.'

Theo, Ben and Penny took their pieces of cake to the back door, all three sitting on the Randall and Elizabeth Nottage church pew. The day was very still, and the faint smell of sheep and warm ground was in the air just as it had been on Theo's first visit several months before, though the oppressive heat of summer was gone. It was almost as if they had never left the gully, and yet all the subsequent developments had happened nevertheless. Back then Penny had seemed to him selfishly absorbed in her own problems, but he had come to realise something of the isolation, the sense of disintegration, she had fought against. Let nothing go wrong, Theo thought: just let nothing go wrong for her.

They had some of Penny's beer, and Ben drank water with a little juice added. Penny said that undiluted juice rotted kids' teeth: good teeth were obviously something of a priority for her. They talked about Nice, for Penny had been there several times with Erskine to visit the business, and knew the hotel in which he always stayed. 'I like the antique shops close to that big monument by the sea,' Penny said, and Theo felt a throb of identification with her recollection. He thought of the Argentinean backpacker by himself on the sand, making an inventory of his limited possessions. 'I like the way it's both a very modern city and an ancient one at the same time,' she said. 'The old doesn't inhibit the new, and today's Nice hasn't obliterated the past.' Theo thought of the dingy railway station, and the people he had seen years ago from the train dossing down under the bridge ends. He had an image of the South African showing him his knife and the bloodstains, and being his best friend for one night of their lives. 'Erskine just spent his time at the factory whenever we were there,' she said. 'Nothing about the city, or its history, interests him at all.' Theo attempted to visualise Erskine seated with them on the pew at Drybread with the sod wall behind them and a view of the stubborn plum tree and the long-drop dunny, but the incongruity was too great.

In the middle of the afternoon Penny took Ben into the one bedroom, hoping he'd sleep. For a while he talked to himself, but didn't come out, and then he was quiet. Penny sat on the pew with Theo, and he began again with something Zack had said about the American judge, but she stopped him. 'We're always talking about me and the awful crap that's happened,' she said. 'I realise that. Always on about me and Ben and custody as if there's nothing else in the world. You get like that when you're in trouble. That's something I found out years ago. You get into a sort of spiral of selfish preoccupation and misery. I bet you've had a gutsful of listening to my problems.'

'Doesn't trouble make you more sympathetic to others, though?' Theo asked.

'Did you find that? Did you find the failure of your marriage made you more sympathetic – or more bitter? When you're in the shit your emotions contract, it seems to me.'

'Maybe at the time,' Theo said, 'but later, yes, I think

you can understand better what people go through. Not everything of course, but understand better. You have a sense of people hurting when they're talking about quite harmless things. You know? Maybe they're on about something that sounds stupid, or trivial, but there's a certain suppressed agony in their voice which you recognise, a hollowness which mocks what they say.'

This was going to be the time they talked about his marriage, his feelings, he thought. Penny had shown little curiosity before. Theo, she might say, we've been through a lot of the same testing experience, and can understand what it's like for each other. But Penny didn't have that in mind. 'Sometime we should get into all the serious stuff,' she said, 'but not today. I hope we'll still see each other when things are sorted?'

'Me too.'

'What I'd like right now is for us to be able to take a walk in the hills. There's great walks round here, even an old gold sluicing pond at the top of the gully. With Ben I haven't been able to do any of that, but I remember it all from when I used to come here as a kid myself.'

'We could walk the section boundary, though,' Theo said.

That's what they did. Up the rough grass slope to the plum tree and behind the wooden dunny, down a fenceline of rusted out wire and a few remaining, tipsy waratahs to the great macrocarpa hedge by the gravel road and their two cars, back along the other side boundary marked by three gnarled apple trees, and a return to the church pew by the back door again. She was almost as tall as him, and they walked quite close together, side by side. Without intention they found themselves talking of the Californian television programme again, perhaps because they wanted to avoid the whole custody thing, and weren't quite ready to talk about their feelings for each other. Penny stood in the spikes of the brown grass in old sneakers and jeans: any gloss of an American television programme seemed a world away, a world in which exposure was the measure of significance, and recognition more important than achievement.

'The set is so bloody crowded,' Penny continued. 'That's one thing I do remember. You've no idea when you're just watching a programme how many people there are hovering, mouthing, jabbing gear about, just out of shot. And it's hard not to sweat because there are lights everywhere, hard not to look at people off camera.'

They ended up in the patch of shade by the back door, and that's where Theo kissed her. Neither of them said anything immediately before or after it. They just had that long kiss with their bodies close together, then sat on the church pew. Penny rested partly on his shoulder and partly on the seat back. He tried to remember if he had condoms in the car, what he had done with the packet after the last time at Melanie's. For a long time he had looked forward to sex with Penny, and now in the most obvious place at the most predictable time maybe he wasn't prepared. He put his hand beneath her shirt and cupped a breast in its soft fabric bra. 'Shall we go in to the sofa?' he asked lightly. She stood up without reply and led the way inside.

The sofa wasn't large: they ended half curled, half lying there. Theo undid her bra and the dark metal top button of her jeans. They kissed and she put the flat of her hand on his stomach. 'You're not fat at all,' she said.

'No one to cook for me,' he said. The remaining chocolate cake sat on the wooden table, and beyond it the black stove. He thought of Ben asleep a few paces away, Erskine wanting to keep some sort of family and Penny at a vulnerable time. None of those things diminished his eagerness to make love. He could feel the slight roughness of her nipples beneath his fingers, catch the faint womanly smell from the skin of her shoulder. One of the bewildering things about sex is that it seems to promise something else: an accomplishment of the spirit quite unrelated to the act itself.

'You don't have to do anything out of obligation, you know,' he said, fumbling for the zip on her jeans.

'I'm not the sort of girl who fucks from gratitude.' Her voice had a matter-of-factness that surprised him. 'You got the necessary?'

'Not on me.'

'Then it's no go,' she said. 'But you can give me a rub and I'll jerk you off.'

He hadn't heard a woman use that expression, and it seemed dated anyway. Maybe it had come back in America. Their first lovemaking wasn't developing in the way he had imagined it, but the more he thought of the car glove compartment, the less he could visualise a packet of sheaths there. So they had a rather busy and manipulative encounter: he with one hand ranging her breasts and the other between her legs; she giving head then a vigorous hand job. Plenty of localised pleasure and release which left Theo damp and out of breath. 'I'd better check on Ben,' was the first thing she said. The separation was something of a relief to both of them.

Penny came back and sat close again, however, a sheen of light sweat on her face and collar bones. 'You can't take chances without a rubber,' she said. Such an American term – rubber.

'Of course.'

'It was what you wanted, though, wasn't it?' she said.

'Great,' he said, 'maybe just a bit mechanical.' Why did he say it? A bad mistake. He could see her face stiffen.

'Mechanical. Jesus, Theo, I never thought I'd hear a guy complain about sex being mechanical. Fuck you then. I'm sorry I wasn't loving enough for you.' She started to cry, and went from the sofa to sit at the table.

Theo knew you could never really recover in the short term from that sort of blunder, but he said, and meant, all the things which laid blame on him and not her. To be in the midst of mutual masturbation one minute and arguing the next, is superficially inexplicable, but both exchanges are based on intimacy.

'You think it's easy here, with my son in the next room, no proper bathroom. And everything that's happened to me in this place. Christ, Theo, try to think with something besides your prick for a change.'

His name again. Penny rarely used it when she talked, but now seemed to find it both appropriate and a satisfaction. And the accusation of thinking with his cock. Such an easy score against men, and so customary that no rebuttal is permitted, or expected. And so often true. But the important thing that Penny said was quite apart from any of that. 'Everything that's happened to me in this place', that was the phrase, and she meant more than the unhappiness of the last months. Theo could see Erskine at the hotel window in Nice, hear him saying that Penny had a whole bunch of issues from her childhood. And that reference to her father – dead, but not gone, he'd said.

But it wasn't a time to be asking Penny anything of that: it was a time for apologies and then hitting the road. In their talk they worked their way rather awkwardly back to the shelter of friendship. 'Well, maybe it's me too,' Penny said. 'I'm an emotional wreck at the moment. Thank God soon I should be able to leave here, and Ben and I can have a proper home.'

'Surely you'll hear from Zack soon.'

They went down to the hedge and the cars, the sun still warm, and they still aware of the sweat of sex, but with that awareness kept below the surface of their conversation. 'I'd better get back,' she said. 'He'll wake up any time now.'

'I'm sorry about, you know –'

'Yeah, well, it's not easy. It doesn't matter.'

'We'll keep in touch, though?' Theo said, hopefully. 'Things will be better, won't they, when you aren't cooped up here. I spend a lot of time thinking about you. Often I think about nobody else. There are things we need to talk about, but it'll be better when all this stuff is sorted. Okay?'

'I know. We'll get to it. There's just so much going on.'

Would that always be the way of it: so much going on, so much having gone on in their lives, that they couldn't have something special between them? The heat was more concentrated in the car even though the window was open. They didn't kiss, but Penny leant down and said goodbye, put a hand lightly, briefly, on the side of his neck and then his shoulder. Her lips were pale, but one ear was pink; her capped teeth were in perfect marching order. 'Email me if you want,' she said. 'I'll catch it in Alex sooner or later. And thanks for coming, thanks for everything.'

Theo swore softly as he drove down the snaky, gravel

road. He turned the driver's mirror to catch glimpses of his face: a grey tinge already in the hair above the ears, a touch of something white at the corner of his eye that he wished he'd wiped away sooner, a flush beneath the beginning of stubble. Who was he kidding? Even his breath was heavy with chocolate cake. What had Ben said – until Theo? But what about after Theo?

23

Erskine tried to talk to her about it several times. The physical side of the marriage, he called it. She imagined it a section heading in a library book promoting matrimonial harmony. The Physical Side of the Marriage: among chapters on the Importance of Maintaining Dialogue, the Significance of Children to the Marriage Bond and the Concept of Intellectual Partnership. She never felt any confidence that generalisations about human relationships had a useful connection with her own experience.

Erskine said she should see someone about it, that he was willing to go with her, that maybe the responsibility was his as well. He thought it was her, though. She could tell from his impatience, and the occasional glimpse of suppressed and dismissive disappointment. Once in a ski chalet in Colorado, with conifers far down the white slope, he said the women he'd known before he met her had liked it well enough. Lovemaking should be a trip for two, shouldn't it? he asked her. That evening they went down to one of the restaurants and had flapjacks, which she never much liked anyway, and tried to pretend there was something besides a sad familiarity between them.

She did go to a counsellor. The guy in Sacramento not much older than herself, and still able to be slightly embarrassed by intimate disclosure. At most sessions he mentioned something about his wife and daughter, as if this establishment of involvement elsewhere made a discussion of sexuality less personal. He was large, fair-haired, subject to persistent, subdued coughing and didn't take many notes. She took the last characteristic as a reassurance that the things she told him were humdrum in his work. She went alone to these sessions, for which Erskine paid. How could she talk about sex with him there? How could she talk about the tight, deep things even to the happily married psychiatrist? She wasn't a Californian woman so emancipated in sexual matters that vibrators, multiple orgasm and cunnilingus were coffee topics.

She talked about her father in the way she thought women would discuss such abuse but found little relief in it. She said what she thought the psychiatrist expected to hear, and wished he'd give more of a lead. But she was unable to put into words the things which came most powerfully between her and men at the very time that obstacles should be non-existent. That moment, for example, when a lover ceased to be an attractive guy, and metamorphosed into the generalised male insistence of panting spasms, fierce grip, self-absorbed rhythm, eyes narrowed in sexual gluttony. Fight against it as she might, how often she felt possessed again by her father at just that time: heard his harsh breathing in the throats of other men.

Penny could just remember a minor accident her father had while fencing. A strand of number eight under tension had whipped back from the strainer and cut the bridge of his nose and the soft skin beneath his left eye. He had come mid-morning into the kitchen, and Penny, not yet at school, remembered the blood and her mother saying it really needed stitches. Even without sutures it had healed well and was not normally noticeable. When he was aroused, however, when the map of his face was closest and alien, when she wanted some point of concentration other than herself, she saw how pale the scar was, how finely grained, distinct against the weathered suffusion of his face.

How could she talk about such things with the counsellor, or with Erskine after they had made love as best they could? And after a couple of years Erskine didn't bother to try to talk about it – didn't bother to do it that much either, especially after the boy was born. That was the point, wasn't it? How Erskine spent his spare time on his many business trips, how close his relationship to women colleagues, were questions never raised between them.

When Penny finished therapy, she gave the psychiatrist a present for his daughter, who was five years old – a charm bracelet, and he gave her a present for Ben who was two – a truck with non-toxic paint. 'I'm sorry,' he said, and, after coughing, 'I don't really think there's anything more I can offer, but I'm always ready to talk if that's a help.' Their children were what they had in common, safe territory to explore. There was no gift, though, that she could bring back to her husband when the sessions were over: no transformation, and any greater understanding wasn't gain enough. It helped to understand, of course, but there is a form of damage done to the emotions that is irreversible.

24

'Why don't you come round tomorrow evening?' said Melanie. 'Come round as a friend. You know what I mean.'

'Yes,' said Theo. 'It means we don't visit the Christmas trees.' He was at his office desk, working on a story about some big cat sighted in Mount Cook National Park. Some people said it was a mountain lion; some said it was a lynx. A tourist from Calgary claimed to have seen it at dusk on the Hooker Glacier moraine; an ironman athlete from Nelson glimpsed something he couldn't account for at Bush Creek; a pub owner in Greymouth said he'd been told by a casual drinker that a yachtie from Singapore had liberated something very strange. Journalists rely on a world of stories.

'We're still friends, though. We can still talk,' said Melanie.

'Of course we can,' agreed Theo.

He liked that about Melanie. She and Nicholas were the two people he could talk to without running into a growing incomprehension which required lengthy explanation to dispel. He might resent her tendency to direct him as to the best course of action, but her understanding was rarely suspect.

Theo saw her head and shoulders at the kitchen window as he came around the side of her house: the undulating corona of brown hair about her small face as she concentrated on preparing food. She came to the door to meet him, then went back to the kitchen and Theo followed. They had a beer there: Theo sitting on a wooden chair, Melanie drinking as she worked at the bench. She was preparing cannelloni, and he watched her spooning the mince and sauce mixture into the pasta tubes, her lips funnelled with concentration in unwitting correlation. What a good colleague, friend and occasional lover she was; how sympathetic, and yet equable and rational in her responses; how much larger in intelligence than appearance. Yet he'd never considered marrying her, before or after Stella. Was that some natural conviction of his, or a response to Melanie's strong independence?

'It's quite fiddly, this,' she said, 'but I usually make enough in one go for three or four meals, and have it in the freezer. An Italian mama wouldn't approve, would she? I'm going to run a series in the paper about how our attitudes to food are changing. It used to be a sort of pit stop, don't you think: pack in what you need and then have a breather, or get right back to work.'

'Eat to live rather than live to eat. You're right.' Theo remembered how his father had taken his meals, sometimes even standing at the bench, or in the cab of the truck.

He'd liked to read as he ate, and treated it as the necessary refuelling Melanie referred to: his eyes on the newspaper, or magazine, so that he was hardly aware of what he handed into his mouth. He ate steadily until he'd had his fill, and rarely made any comment afterwards on the quality of the food or expressed any preference beforehand.

Theo's mother had been under no pressure to vary the menu; in fact she'd had a not dissimilar attitude to food herself. Boiled vegetables and roast, or fried meat, were the staples, not so much favourites as dependables. 'We never had pasta, never had rice,' Theo told Melanie. 'We never had blue vein cheese, olives, pâté or nachos. I bet even now my parents wouldn't know what sushi is. My father had chops and fried tomatoes for breakfast, or bacon and eggs, and hardly distinguished one from the other.'

'Your mum and dad okay?' asked Melanie.

'Happy with their bowls and bridge.'

'Stella's father's not so good again.'

'Poor old Norman.'

'You did ring him?'

'Yes,' said Theo. 'He never complains much – just makes the best of things. He still does field research and writes up his findings for the university. He's got a rotating drum polisher in his workshop and works up pieces of greenstone, obsidian, agate and so on.'

'Well, he used to polish teeth, didn't he,' said Melanie.

'You're right. I never thought of the connection before, but you're quite right.'

As he finished the sentence, Theo experienced a little lurch of sadness within. It seemed to be directed at himself rather than Stella's father. He had noticed during the last two years such sudden changes of mood, and resisted them. They were self-pitying, self-gratifying emotions, and so to be repressed. They were the small aftershocks of his divorce, he told himself: explicable and of no significance. Some small gland somewhere was prompted to puff its chemical into the system, as those creatures of the soft sea floor become distinct for a moment and, with protuberant mouth, puff into the brine around them. Theo deliberately opposed himself to the sudden disposition by becoming more animated and passing on one of Nicholas's jokes to Melanie. 'What do you call a man who doesn't want sex?'

'Pass.'

'Dead,' said Theo.

'How are things with Penny Maine-King?' asked Melanie after giving the joke its due.

'Good news, actually.' And he explained what had happened.

'I mean between you and her,' said Melanie.

It was the question bound to be raised during the evening, yet Theo was taken aback by the difficulty he had in answering. He had no wish to be evasive: he valued her opinions and her concern. The inhibition arose not so much from a fear of intrusive revelation about Penny's life as from Theo's inability to judge just what had developed between them, and whether it had any real grip apart from the special circumstances that had brought them together. The turmoil Penny was involved in, the fluctuation of fear, resolution and disorientation, must mean any relationship with Theo was uncertain, however contained she usually appeared. Some of all that he endeavoured to convey to Melanie. He said nothing, of course, concerning his unfortunate sex with Penny at Drybread, or Erskine's references to her father; nothing of his own growing concern for her, and his affection for the boy. 'Until the whole custody mess is settled,' he said, 'until she's had time to feel part of regular life again, I don't really know where the hell we are.' He said nothing about the pleasure he felt in being able to help Penny by going to Nice, and how much more lasting that feeling was than the encounter on the sofa at the bach.

'It's good you want to give support,' said Melanie. 'You're not used to being relied on. You tend to drift along your own way.' She had an impressive confidence in her assessment of other people. 'What about the little boy?'

'What about him?' replied Theo.

'Is he a nice kid? Can you see him with you for years and years when he has a dad of his own? I imagine it's not an easy situation.'

'I quite like him. Not that I've talked to him much.'

'What's his name again?'

'Ben.'

'I thought some of the best bits in your articles were about him – about his need to have other kids to play with, and other adults despite Penny's devotion. She'd be aware of that too: the effects on him if they stayed hidden away for long.'

Melanie and Theo had moved into the small lounge to talk, and the fragrance of cannelloni drifted through to them from the oven. Theo neither resisted, nor resented, the talk of Penny and himself. In some ways it was a relief to discuss it, yet it made him sad again. There were so many checks and balances against happiness, and so many opportunities for hurt and disappointment from every decision.

'I may be heading for a rather similar situation,' said Melanie. 'Becoming involved with someone with kids, I mean.'

'Really? Do I know him?' But Melanie had gone off into the kitchen to get their meals, and called back that she'd tell him about it in a minute. It's easy to think that your own existence is the only one which progresses, and that other people in your absence become stationary, awaiting the return which activates their lives again. Such selfishness Theo recognised in himself, even without Melanie's cheerful mention of it.

'Robin Sellus,' she said, when they were eating. 'He's an architect with rooms at Papanui. The daughters are aged three and five. His wife died two years ago of a stroke.'

'How did you meet him?'

'He bought the place next door.'

'Here?' said Theo, surprised. The oddity of having Melanie's newly disclosed boyfriend so close inclined him to lower his voice.

'Of course here,' said Melanie. 'He's a nice guy and the kids are really good most of the time. They have a sort of housekeeper-cum-nanny.'

'I really hope it works out,' said Theo.

He meant it, but couldn't help but be struck by the element of convenient coincidence. The architect moving house and finding love, a wife and mother, next door. But that was the way in life. The myth of there being only one person for you in all the world, and the reality that you end up with someone close at hand. It was the same with Penny and him – that he should be attracted to her in the course of his work, and she at Drybread with no other contact with men. How unpropitious for stability the circumstances were.

Theo had come to Melanie's as a friend. She had clearly signalled that there would be no sex, yet despite that, despite his wish that she find satisfaction in marrying the architect and caring for his daughters, Theo felt a slight awkwardness. It wasn't that he was wrong in his understanding of Melanie's independence, but that, illogically, the presence of Robin Sellus in the next property seemed inhibiting. Perhaps he was watching from a darkened room to see when Theo left; perhaps he was showing a determined trust and reading storybooks to his young daughters; perhaps he hadn't been told that Melanie was serving cannelloni to an old boyfriend.

'You mentioned I'd be here?' he asked her.

'I did, yes. No big deal. We'll still be friends, won't we, Theo?'

'Of course we will,' Theo said.

'I believe you're entitled to keep the best of past relationships when you move on. Not the shagging, of course, but the friendship, the support, the shared experiences. Why should what's happened with one person be buried by being with another, when there's no guilt involved?'

'Absolutely,' Theo said.

'If there's a wedding, and it won't be any big deal, you'll get an invitation. I hope you'll like him.' Melanie pressed the abundance of her hair down with a small hand and leant back in the chair to rest her head and settle in for a good chat. Theo wondered what it was like to go through life so physically diminutive, and with so resolute a character. He had no clear recollection of the first time he'd met her. Odd, for the advents of Stella and

Penny were clear in his mind. Penny with her head back in sleep, and her graceful throat, as he first looked through the window at Drybread. Stella he saw first on the ramp of a parking building, after an exhibition opening at the new gallery that he'd reluctantly covered. She was wearing high heels, and was holding her arms out from her sides a little as a precaution on the damp concrete slope. She was laughing with a woman friend, and as she glanced at Theo in passing, the amusement was still there, like the flash of a colourful bird in flight.

'Maybe that's one of the things with you and Stella,' Melanie was saying. 'Because of the outcome you don't allow yourself to remember all the good things, the strengths she had, what you accomplished together. She doesn't criticise you all the time, you know.'

'I don't criticise her at all,' said Theo.

'The point is you hardly talk about it. The two of you managed the split bloody well, but I think you've got into the habit of always being sad about it.'

'It is sad, and talking doesn't help.'

'Have it your own way,' said Melanie. 'I reckon you spend too much time with Nick, and he's so bloody cynical. All those anecdotes when in fact he doesn't do much any more. You don't want to become part of some sort of club for divorced guys.'

It was ten twenty when Theo left. Not late, but he glanced at the architect's house as they said goodbye at the door. Melanie gave him a hug in which the significant pressure was all in the upper body. 'You make sure you keep in touch now,' she said. There was a cool breeze, a horned moon and many stars. He thought how wonderful a late night run would be in Hagley Park – the play of tree shadows in the mild wind and dim light, the ducks in headless clusters, the sharded sheen on dark water, the night sky's sense of vast hollowness, the freedom to bear a relaxed, nocturnal face through it all, rather than maintaining the conventional expressions of the day.

25

'I want to go running,' said Nicholas, two evenings later. 'I need that adrenalin rush, or endorphin high, or whatever. I'm stale and overworked, I've eaten too much – I'm bored fucking silly.' He'd been drinking, of course. His voice wasn't slurred on the phone: Nicholas never became falling-down drunk. He was contemptuous of people who took refuge in drink, who lost self-control, who couldn't face whatever was handed out to them. But he had drunk enough to make it natural to ring Theo at nightfall and want to go running.

'You're too old, and too unfit,' said Theo.

'You don't know what old is. I gave a talk to a Probus club today, and the experience terrified me. Row after row of geriatrics with necks like cabbage stalks, bright, nylon hair, and denture-swollen grins. I think they were all on medication. Really old people will applaud anything: have you noticed that? I gave them of my worst and they were spellbound. I think what they're really celebrating when they clap is the confirmation of their own existence as an audience, that they're still alive, that the address has come from someone other than the grim reaper.'

'You couldn't keep up on a run, but if you like I'll come round in half an hour and we'll have a walk.'

'Thanks,' said Nicholas with false humbleness. 'Will it be a brisk walk? There's something very English and bracing about a brisk walk.'

Theo almost reset his desk layout trap for the parson, before recalling his talk with Erskine in Nice. The search for Penny and Ben was no longer a priority for anyone.

Nicholas had a ground-floor apartment and a small enclosed courtyard close to the town hall. He'd made preparations for the walk by rooting out a pair of cheap, barely worn sneakers with such garish colours that they glowed in the dusk. Apart from these he seemed exactly as he would appear at his desk in the reporters' room. 'I'm going to start an exercise regime,' he told Theo as they headed past the floral clock and towards the river.

'Do Probus pay well?' asked Theo.

'No. Wine and flowers seem to be the thing. It's not lucrative at all. I've had to say no to a swag of other Probus clubs, Rotary, drop-in centres, even Grey Power. It's those stories I did on the third age that started it all. There's a whole world out there of people past their use-by date; and a different language of joint operations, protheses, magnetic underblankets, reverse mortgages, memory aids, and risk-free minor activities for physical and mental prolongation.'

Nicholas wasn't a great walker, and his speed was in

inverse proportion to the amount of talking he did and its significance. While dismissing old people he maintained a reasonably steady pace, but when he came to discuss women he was reduced to a stroll. He wanted to know how things were between Penny and Theo. Theo was quite open, and told him of his hopes once the custody thing was out of the way. There was one thing he didn't mention: he said nothing about Penny's father and her childhood. He didn't know enough, but more than that, he felt a strong repugnance for what might lie there.

'Do you think about her a lot?' asked Nicholas.

'I do,' said Theo. 'I think about being with her, and I wish I could do more to help. I grizzle about my life, and here's Penny's going through some sort of hell.'

'It's important you think about her so much. It's a sign when someone inhabits you even when absent.'

'Sometimes I dream about her,' said Theo.

'Oh, yes.'

'No, not sex usually. More about being with her when she's happy again. Most of the time I've had this feeling that everything I talk about is unimportant compared with the devastation of her own life.'

'I dream about my boys,' said Nicholas. 'And they still have the same voices, they're the same size, as when we were a family. Trish is never there – I suppose there's some Freudian explanation for that.'

Theo remembered Trish as being just as intelligent as Nicholas, and with greater warmth. They'd seemed compatible. Maybe some issue of principle had driven them apart; maybe just a trivial trait of character, grown rampant and insupportable. Nicholas always spoke of their split as if it had been an act of God, like an avalanche, or a meteor strike. Theo wasn't surprised that Nicholas often thought of his family past: nostalgia is a harmless form of depression.

They turned into one of the lesser streets, which was still well lit, but much quieter, with spaced young rowan trees along the grass strip where they walked. The line of streetlights played tricks with their shadows, and when they were half way between two poles, Theo and Nicholas had multiplied, with equal-density shadows both behind them and before.

'So you quite liked Nice?' enquired Nicholas.

'I did. Mainly I suppose because things worked out okay.'

'And the Maine-King husband coughed up for all expenses?'

'Yep.'

'Lucky bastard,' said Nicholas. He meant Theo, not Erskine Maine-King, though wealth impresses most of us. 'I've never been to Nice,' he said, 'but I spent a week in Arles years ago. An interesting river, Roman ruins and all that exploitation of the Van Gogh connection, although they despised the poor bastard when he lived there. There were begging dogs there, I remember, and when we were waiting to leave at the small railway station, a taxi driver was discovered dead in his cab. I had a glimpse of his face and it was very restful. You must be getting pretty close to Penny Maine-King in all of this support you're giving. You're not screwing her, are you?'

'No,' said Theo. From anyone else the remark would have angered him, but it was just his friend's way.

'I have a good feeling about it, about it all working out the way you and Penny deserve,' said Nicholas.

They walked along the river, then into Bealey Avenue with its central divide of large, dark trees, and traffic lights gleaming ahead. Nicholas said his two sons were coming to stay with him during the term holidays. He saw them only once or twice a year, when he paid for them to fly over. Charles was seventeen and Morgan two years younger. 'They just go gadding when they're here,' said Nicholas. 'They never say anything personal, so neither do I. It's as if the set-up is the most normal in the world, or too fucked up to talk about.'

'It's the same for a lot of kids now.'

'They'd never tell me anything about themselves if I didn't ask. I've been paying maintenance all these years, and Trish never even sends me a copy of their school reports. I know nothing about them. Two strangers come and call me dad. They eat a lot and go to movies and the beach, watch crap television. The little buggers never say thank you for anything, and they never seem to wash. They're like a war party of two: arriving, laying waste, then shooting through.'

'Well, you're not part of their real lives, are you? You're the holiday man.'

'Exactly,' said Nicholas morosely. They had turned into Colombo Street, back towards the central city. His cheap, firefly sneakers glinted as they passed under the spreading trees, and he peered into the darkness.

'You're just an old bugger of no account to them,' said Theo. He was determined to be realistic in the appraisal of his own life, so why shouldn't such pragmatism extend to his friends.

'Mind you,' said Nicholas, 'it would have happened anyway, even if Trish and I hadn't split. Boys cast off their parents, and resist parenthood themselves for as long as they can.'

Theo didn't answer, but he thought about his own move from home, the sense of expansion, the lack of homesickness and the disregard of subsequent communication. If he'd had children he would be in the same situation as Nicholas. Maybe daughters were different, but then their natural sympathy in a separation would be with their mother.

'You know what was just about the worst part of it all for me,' said Nicholas. He didn't expect a response, didn't wait for one. 'It was clearing out the bloody house where we'd lived as a family. All the junk that nevertheless meant something and was so painful to jettison. Especially the kids' stuff.' Theo could understand that. He'd experienced it, except that it must be worse with children's things. He sensed Nicholas's fear as all the trivial, physical totems of his family life were scattered and lost their potency. The trike hanging in the basement recess with small blisters of rust showing through the dusty red paint, and on the same hook a pair of ice-skates, the white leather of the boots brittle and contorted. The board games in the bottom drawer, with ludo counters, play money, pencil stubs and small dice in a chocolate box on which one of the boys had written 'Crap' in black felt pen in the pique of defeat. The battery men with shiny, carapace torsos and macho expressions, but with their source of power gone and an arm or leg missing. Discarded cellphones with which the boys had mimicked their parents, and the favourite books worn almost to disintegration. Theo imagined Nicholas in the desperate disposal of a haphazard accumulation which was the archaeology of his family life.

They had almost done a circuit, and were heading

towards the town hall and the river from a different direction, through the mainly one-storey shops and premises of modest commercial firms. Only the restaurants were open, their light spilling weakly onto the footpath, and the few diners glimpsed hunched over their food as if they feared dispossession. Nicholas had finished with his trials as a separated father, and was becoming almost cheerful in detailing the vicissitudes that had beset the university journalism department since his resignation. No one is indispensable, but to have your replacements suffer misfortune, or the consequences of their inadequacies, is heartening. 'I could see it coming all along,' said Nicholas. 'Too many pointy heads, too much ideology and wankerism.'

His perspicacity did not extend to random physical threat, however, and he was unlucky enough to laugh while passing one of the few parked cars, and the only one that was occupied. 'Who are you laughing at, fuckface?' and Theo and Nicholas were abruptly aware of the elbows jutting from the car's open windows, and behind them a bobbing agitation of faces like pantomime masks on sticks. Without thinking, Nicholas and Theo paused, when they should have carried on.

'What?' said Nicholas.

'Don't fucking what me, you shithead.' The car seemed to erupt bodies: young guys with shaved hair and big boots, all suddenly in violent movement within the poor light and shadows. They weren't tall, or bulky, but seemed to burn with the necessity to oppose – not anything specific, just what was there. And Theo and Nicholas were there. They were on P or something, surely, or they were so bored they were going to pound their way out of it.

'Steady on, mate,' said Theo, though there were four of them, their faces pushing into his personal space.

'Not so funny now, is it.'

'You gutless old cunts.'

'Yeah, not so funny now, you useless old fuckers.'

It was the accusation of being old that Theo resented most. He was thirty-eight after all, though admittedly Nicholas was forty-six. He had a momentary macho flare in which he thought of challenging one of the four to have a go, but he knew it didn't work like that, and what might they have as well as their fists and boots: short, straight knives, probably, and their thick foreheads full into your face. Besides, his last physical response, to the parson, had been a signal failure. He and Nicholas began backing towards the nearest open door, which was the entrance of a Chinese restaurant bold with rampant dragons in red and gold, but humble in internal dimensions.

Theo was aware that both he and Nicholas were placatory, even abject, in what they said. Sentences about no need for this, about no offence meant, remonstrances about the wrong end of the stick and cooling down, and taking it easy. Nicholas had the palm of one hand up like a traffic controller as the guys pushed closer. They closed in as a sudden, violent flurry when Theo and Nicholas were pushing open the restaurant door. The most painful blow Theo got was below his ear on the left side. It felt as if it had been delivered by an elbow rather than a fist. Theo was surprised a slight man could hit so hard. He and Nicholas were injected into the restaurant, stumbling upon a girl coming to see what the ruckus was. 'Call the police,' said Theo. He glanced at the three diners; a couple at one table, a older man in a bush shirt at another. He wasn't so much checking the level of protection, as ensuring that there was no one who would recognise him, no one to carry forth a description of his indignity.

'I'm dialling,' said the waitress, and she picked up a mobile phone from beside the till, waved it in admonition. She wasn't Chinese, and she wasn't distraught. She was thin and contourless, perhaps still a schoolgirl. A shorter, bland-faced Chinese man appeared at her side from the kitchen curtain, anxiety widening his smile.

The four young buggers gathered in the doorway briefly, shouting and swearing in a fury of triumph, but they didn't enter. It was as if they recognised that their habitat was after-hours streets and gathered cars, garage piss-ups or a sand dune fracas. They withdrew with self-congratulatory shrieks, and then their car laboured into the night.

It took time for the thudding of the words at the wall and window to die away, for the small restaurant to empty of such virulent, ugly language, and while it did no one moved. Then the three customers began again to eat, the schoolgirl put down the phone, and the proprietor waggled his fingers and smiled to minimise what had happened. Nicholas was bleeding from the nose. There were drops of surprising vividness on his jacket, his striped shirt and the pale gloss of the floor. The Chinese man offered wet paper napkins, and Theo and Nicholas stood between the counter and the curtain – not quite within the private domain of the kitchen, but territorially removed from the dining area though still in view.

'Young bastards,' said Theo.

'You can't reason with pricks like that,' said Nicholas. He made as if to wipe his blood from the floor, but the owner said he'd fix it.

'Do you still want me to call the cops?' the girl asked.

'No, what's the use?' said Theo.

They thanked her and the boss, then left, not pausing at the door in case that be seen as fear. The couple, and the older man, gave them a quick glance as they passed: a look not so much of sympathy as embarrassment, and satisfaction that they themselves had not been abased.

The two friends said little during the short walk to Nicholas's flat. As Theo helped his friend to clean up, soak his shirt and sponge his jacket, Nicholas quickly began to fashion the night's experience into one of his stories. Theo realised, however, that he was shaken nevertheless. Theo was upset himself; not because they had featured so unheroically, but because Nicholas's intelligence and worth had been so easily overcome by intimidation and stupidity. He was reminded that beyond their own circle of acquaintance and experience, their accepted codes and expectations, whirled incomprehensible worlds. Maybe Penny was in one of them and it, too, was beyond him.

'You and your damn exercise,' said Nicholas, reclaiming his wry humour. 'Don't ever bother me about it again.'

'You rang me, remember.'

'You have this thing about running – about fitness. I'd rather have the exercise at that Cargoe Street massage parlour. What's the name of the girl you had there again?'

'Becky,' said Theo. He was surprised by his own ease of recall, though he'd never been back. Her nakedness remained quite clear in his mind, but without lust, as you might recollect a well-executed painting of a nude.

Nicholas sat with just a V-necked jersey over his singlet. Greying hair showed at the base of his throat, and, though he had thoroughly washed, his nostrils were faintly pink with blood. The left side of Theo's face was sore to the touch, but the skin was unbroken. Both of them realised that what had happened was an aberration, unrelated to the rest of their lives. There was no sense to be found in it, no action regarding it to be taken. They began to talk of themselves again, as a form of comfort and normality.

'At any given time, the place I want to be in my life, and where I find myself to be, never seem to quite coincide,' Nicholas said.

'That's because you're an old, divorced bugger with too much time to think,' said Theo. 'Your sons will ginger you up a bit, and don't you drink much more tonight, or you'll be hopeless at work tomorrow. Take some Panadol and sleep everything off.' He wanted to go home and close off a night that had become meaningless and futile: exactly the outcomes he most feared for his life in general.

But Nicholas wanted Theo to stay, so reached into his grab-bag of recollections for something to hold him. 'I had an odd experience the other day. I was coming out of the chemist's, and I saw this woman walking away who must have been Cynthia Jenkins, one of my old girlfriends. It gave me a real jolt. I walked after her, and then she turned to look in a shop window and it wasn't her after all. From the back I could have sworn, though.'

'She'd have changed a hell of a lot by now. I bet she dumped you anyway, didn't she?'

'No, she terrified me with her possessiveness. It was my first experience of that in a woman. She was like one of those pilot fish who swim into the gills of sharks, or those African birds who pick the teeth of yawning hippos. She was always squeezing the pores on my face, hanging on my neck, combing dandruff from the back of my head. She wanted to know everything. What are you really thinking, she used to say, tell me what you really think. Even when we made love I felt this strange suction, as if she was determined to empty me out, to absorb me completely.'

'You've certainly struck some weird ones,' said Theo. 'Damn lucky it wasn't her, then. Anyway I'd best be off.'

'Did I tell you that Trish was a great one for talking in her sleep?' Nicholas began quickly to tell of being woken in the small hours and lying there as his wife unwittingly confided to the darkness long monologues which revealed her fears of humiliation, divorce and ageing, her extravagant hopes for her sons and her own material wealth, soft-voiced and precise descriptions of items in her mother's wardrobe recalled as by a child. 'In dreams even the closest of partners go their own way,' Nicholas said. 'I knew things about her life that were beyond her own conscious reach.'

'Was she interested in it all when you told her?'

'I never did. I never took advantage of it either, and I'd only say to you, Theo, but I take a small pride in that. Even in the bad times I never used it for ammunition.'

'Good on you,' said Theo. 'Maybe it wasn't all true anyway.'

'The subconscious makes nothing up – it just stores and selects,' said Nicholas. The interest of the subject had animated his face again, though his pinkish nose gave just a suggestion of clownish absurdity. Theo wished that expression to be the last he saw as he left Nicholas at the door.

'See you then, Nick,' he said.

When Theo reached home he sent an email to Penny, although it was almost midnight and she wouldn't retrieve it until she next went to Alexandra. 'Hi Penny, I hope all is well and that your spell at Drybread is almost over. I think of you often, no, all the time, and look forward to seeing you soon. Theo.'

Sending it made Theo feel closer to her, took his mind from his sore face and the dispiriting meeting with the hoons outside the Chinese restaurant. He dreamed that night of the three of them, Penny, the boy and himself, at a picnic: not in the open sweep of Central, or its small valleys, but some bush area with ferns, and fungi with bold, sematic colours. They were sitting on a yellow railway tarpaulin which Theo knew, with the unsubstantiated certitude of dreams, to be stolen, and Ben was singing a childish song about a spider and a waterspout. His small voice was threatened by foul, multi-toned mutterings from somewhere in the bush behind them. In the dream Theo was convinced that if he kept looking at the boy, kept a countenance of encouragement and attention, then those responsible for the growing chorus couldn't materialise. To maintain the focus wasn't easy; the tarpaulin became ever more steeply angled beneath him, and he wasn't able to see the expression on Penny's face. A silly dream, and obvious in its connection to the night's experience, yet the sense of sad dismay and powerlessness persisted long after he was awake and had begun his day.

26

Stella's father died after a fall from a ladder while attempting to clear the leaves from the guttering of his house. Stella was angry because he'd promised he would get a handyman in. The doctor wasn't sure whether the fall had caused the stroke, or the stroke had caused the fall, but either way it was very quick, he said. Stella found Norman, with slippers on, lying among the lavender bushes, with a child's yellow plastic spade by his head. She'd tried twice to ring him earlier in the day. All this she told Theo on the phone, so he wouldn't see the death notice in the paper without knowing about it.

'I'm terribly sorry,' Theo said. 'I talked to him not so long ago. I liked your dad.'

'I know you did. He quite liked you. He was slipping noticeably though. He got anxious over little things that once would never have bothered him, and he worried that he might be forced to go into a home. I suppose that's why he was so bloody stubborn about doing things himself.'

'Do you want me to come round?' asked Theo.

'It's okay. I've got a friend with me. I'm actually not too bad. I guess it hasn't hit me yet.'

'When's the funeral?'

'Wednesday. Dad wanted to be cremated. Do you want to say something?'

'At the service?'

'Yes,' said Stella.

It was probably the lawyer friend who was comforting her: the guy Theo had met at the Darfield pub on his way back from the Coast that hot day. He couldn't remember much about him except that he had thick, floppy hair, heavy wrists and a legal complacency of manner. How long ago was that? Stella had now lost her father and her mother, and she'd been close to them both. Theo wondered whether his parents' death would arouse in him more love than he felt for them while alive.

'I remember the spade,' Stella was saying.

'The spade?'

'He must have been using it to clean the guttering. It was part of a set I had as a kid, and we'd go down to New Brighton by the surf club building. There was a bucket and a little rake and shovel, and a flag, all yellow, and they'd watch me play where the sand was just right for building – between the dry dunes and the stuff at the water's edge that's too wet. It's sad, isn't it.' Stella was trying to keep her voice matter of fact.

'Bloody sad,' said Theo.

'You don't have to come at all if you don't want to.'

'If it's not awkward for you I'd like to come,' Theo said.

'Well, it's not really about us, is it. That's the way I look at it. It's for people who knew Dad and want to say goodbye.'

'I see it that way too,' said Theo. 'You let me know if there's anything I can do.'

'You and Dad got on well, Theo. I suppose you're alike in some ways,' said Stella. He put that observation aside to ponder later, for the moment assuming it a compliment.

Should funerals be wet and blustery as nature pays homage in its way? Wednesday was still and cool, with high, pale cloud like an eyelid. There was no inexplicable eclipse for Norman, no sudden rush of wind as some spiritual departure. He wouldn't have wanted anything like that. The chapel and crematorium were set in lawns and gardens, and only when you were close did you see the numerous plaques amid the roses, on artfully placed boulders, or set into the low walls of the terraces. Some were of brass, some of dark, polished granite, and some of a noticeably cheaper material that looked like Formica. So the demonstration of means follows people even after death.

Before the service began, Theo wandered among the long flower plots and the silver birch trees on which the leaves had turned to yellow. The lawn was closely cut, and the dew that remained in the afternoon was barely enough to gather on the glossed toes of his best shoes. By walking he avoided any prolonged talk with mutual friends from the time of his marriage, and any awkwardness he might cause Stella. He wondered how many dentists would attend the funeral, and how many geologists, and whether he would be able to identify members of each group without knowing them individually. The dentists would surely have a short-sighted appearance, and be better dressed than the geologists.

Norman's cremation provided the occasion for Theo's first meeting with Melanie's boyfriend, and his formal introduction to Stella's. He was made more aware of being on his own, and wondered if he was pitied by the people gathered at the chapel door. 'Theo had no one with him, did he?' they might say, and speculate as to his mode of living and state of mind. 'I've not heard of anyone, have you?' they might say.

By a round bed of camellia bushes, Theo met Linda from work, and an accompanying woman who was introduced to him as a fellow photographic artist. 'Theo used to be married to Stella,' Linda said frankly. Neither did she pretend any particular grief, but spoke about an exhibition of monoprints that she had seen the night before, and then was curious as to Norman's age.

'I'm not sure,' said Theo. 'Early seventies anyway.'

'Women live longer than men,' said Linda. 'They have a stronger immune system.'

'Something like that, I gather,' said Theo.

'Exactly like that.' She bent down and pulled chickweed from the base of one of the camellias, then walked on, leaving her friend standing for a moment with Theo. They exchanged wry, slightly awkward smiles. 'Coming?' said Linda. Theo was reminded, as he watched the two of them move away, that her urge for trivial dominance was not entirely sexist.

Melanie and Robin Sellus came from the grouping around the chapel entrance to meet him as he walked back.

The architect was a bulky man with heavy crease lines on his forehead and neck. He was talkative concerning his own interests, but distracted when others had a chance to speak, glancing obviously about him as if in search of more distinguished company. Theo was disappointed in Melanie's choice, and thought her kindness and intelligence wasted on Sellus. She looked even smaller beside such a heavy man. Her halo of hair trembled as she kept a conversation going among the three of them. Theo had never intended to marry Melanie, or live with her, but felt an immediate vindictiveness towards her choice of partner. What could he be except an egotist and a thuggish lover?' Theo accepted that this conviction might be proprietal envy, but was surprised by the concern, the affection, he felt for her.

Entering the crematorium chapel for the service, he took Stella's hand briefly, and she introduced him to a second man that day who had supplanted him. There was an irony to it that he appreciated, and he filed it for mention to Nicholas. 'This is James Rowlands,' Stella said, and the two men shook hands.

It was an unequal situation in so many ways, not just who stood with whom. James had a great deal of information about Theo from a privileged, but not unbiased source, and Theo knew next to nothing of him. Would the lawyer recall having met him that hot day at the Darfield hotel?

'Good to see you again,' said James.

'Maybe we'll have a chance to talk after the service,' said Stella.

'Sure,' said Theo, and passed on to allow others to express their sympathy.

Theo took a back seat. He had declined Stella's offer

to say something about his ex father-in-law. His role was to be respectful and, yes, take a back seat. Gillian and Thor Aargard came and sat beside him. Thor taught at the university with Stella. Theo had met the couple socially, but not since his divorce. Social acquaintances are like waiters: you know when you go to certain places they'll be there, but they have no essential place in your life. 'Quite a blow, quite a blow,' said Thor quietly, and proffered his hand.

'Nice to see you, Theo,' said Gillian. Theo was aware of her unabashed and intent scrutiny. She was looking for evidence of his life since splitting with Stella: the stains of takeaway meals perhaps, unchecked nasal hair, the false ebullience of incipient alcoholism and the scorch of indulgence on his breath.

'How have you been in yourself, Theo?' she said.

'Not so bad,' he said.

'We've been meaning to have you for a meal. The time just flies, doesn't it. We see your pieces in the paper, of course.'

'It's quite a blow for Stella,' said Thor. 'I didn't meet him myself, but I gather they were very close.'

'It's nice she does have personal support though isn't it,' said Gillian. 'You've met James?'

'Gillian,' chided her husband.

'A few times,' said Theo. 'Seems a nice guy.' Truth wasn't the aim in such a reply, but to deny her the satisfaction that any glimpse of pain, or a falling away in life, would give.

'I gather her father was well known as an amateur geologist?' said Thor.

'He was a specialist on the volcanic origins of Banks Peninsula. He did a great deal of fieldwork there over the years,' said Theo.

'And things have been going okay for you?' asked Gillian. She was adept at the verbal angler's art.

'I'm pretty busy,' said Theo. 'The journalism's always demanding, but the sex is great. You know what it's like for single guys.' It came out unplanned, but intended. Gillian wasn't put out, but her smile contained a grimness that showed a realisation she was baulked.

'Ah, memories, memories,' said Thor lightly. There was no more conversation among the three of them.

Nor was there an opportunity to talk to Stella following the service, after the burnished coffin had passed through the cosmetic entrance and presumably into the maw of the furnace. The invitation hadn't been a serious one for either of them. Theo slipped away through the birches and the rosebeds studded with plaques. He resolved that he would think of Norman over a drink that night, for he had paid little attention to the service. Most of the time he had been thinking of Penny, and Ben too. Penny long-limbed and wry at the sod bach at Drybread, with the heat and the openness and the bare hills – perhaps the heat no longer visiting, and frost warning of later snow. Penny Boomerang: all the way to America and marriage, and back again. Penny and her son, feeling the world was against her. Norman had been a decent guy, he had been significant in Theo's life for a while, but he was dead, and Theo was concerned with the living. It's harder for the living.

Stella phoned him at the paper on the following Monday morning. She wasn't back at work yet. Theo wondered if there was any message in that, conscious or subliminal. An evening call from one home to the other might be expected to be longer, and more personal. 'I just wanted to thank you for coming to Dad's funeral,' she said.

'I've thought about him quite a bit since then. How he always used to give me a book voucher for my birthday – an old-fashioned gift, in a way. And how very proud he was that you ended up at the university. He had an amateur love of scholarship, and that's old-fashioned too, I guess.' They talked of the service briefly, though Theo remembered the grounds more clearly.

'What sort of plaque are you getting?' he asked.

'The wording you mean?' said Stella.

'No, the actual plaque. There were some cheap and nasty ones. Brass and marble last well and they look so much better.'

'I think I chose granite,' she said. 'Not the cheap stuff anyway.'

'What's the difference between granite and marble?'

'I've no idea,' she said.

'Odd, isn't it. That's exactly the sort of thing Norman knew all about.'

'Anyway,' said Stella, 'I just wanted to thank you.'

'Sure.'

'Melanie tells me that you've met someone through work – that woman in the custody case you've been writing about. She seems to have had a real time of it. No doubt appreciates your support. I hope it works out for you, Theo.' It was distancing, the use of his name. Close people rarely use names.

'Likewise,' he said. 'I thought James seemed an all right guy, but I'm not so sure about Melanie's architect.' Better not to have said that. Stella told him things he didn't know about Sellus: how he came home from his office to find his wife dead on the kitchen floor and his two infant daughters with all the cupboard doors open and stuff everywhere. She became quite animated while recounting the tragedy, but then had not much more to say.

'Well, I'd better let you get back to the job. All busy in the madhouse as usual I suppose.'

'Pretty much,' said Theo.

'Okay then, bye.'

Theo knew that, with the phone replaced, Stella would still be standing by it. She always did. No matter that he'd never seen the inside of the house she now lived in, had no vision of the physical detail around her. She would be standing there, with one hand to her hair, as if fixing in her mind what was important from the conversation. That was Melanie, she used to say, or that was Dad, or Nicholas, Diane, or whoever, and go on to give a synopsis of what had been said. It didn't matter if Theo had been in sight, even in earshot. He might hear her from the kitchen, or his study down the hall, or turned in his chair from the television. It was always the same, and such habits aren't cast off when a partner is changed. She would be standing there with the phone, her hand to her short hair, and lawyer James would perhaps be hearing the summation of her conversation with Theo. Theo had become one of the them, not the us. The removal of familiarity bears so close a resemblance to the removal of love, that the feelings are sometimes indistinguishable.

27

The Family Court granted a stay in execution of the warrant in the second week of June, pending a rehearing, and Penny's exile at Drybread was over. She rang from Alexandra to give Theo the news after talking to Zack Heywood. 'That's bloody great, Penny,' he said. 'Jesus, what a relief it must be. What happens now?'

'The hearing's set down for the eighteenth of next month in Christchurch, and Erskine's coming out. We'll make a joint submission stating we've come to agreement regarding custody, access, the whole works.'

'Will you still have to go back to the States?'

'Probably. Just for the court there. It all starts and ends with the Californian court. But hey, I'm not the mad bitch on the run any more, and a favourable review here might help over there. I can visit Mum, I'm not tied to this place, I can give Ben some sort of decent life.'

'Are you coming up? Can I see you?' Theo asked. Penny said she was going to wait a few more days at the bach, finish there and travel up closer to the court date. There was a lot of media interest and she didn't want to have to cope with all that until she had to. 'It's my big story, isn't it,' Theo said. 'I can be in court, though Zack reckons you can only name parties at the judge's discretion.'

It should be the right ending, and the pay-off for the paper, but Penny, Zack and Theo all knew it was best that both his private and professional connection be played down. No extra guy to complicate matters for the judge; no triangle to give the story even more newsworthy angles; no obvious embarrassment for Erskine that might threaten his co-operation. And what was their relationship anyway? What was the basis of their somewhat uneasy move towards each other, apart from a mutual feeling of isolation and need, and the urge of Theo's cock.

'Zack can keep you up with everything,' Penny said. 'I'm really looking forward to seeing you of course, but everything's pretty hectic. As soon as Erskine arrives, we'll have a final talk through things before the court appearance.' Theo found it hard to imagine Erskine at Drybread: a well-dressed, well-fleshed Yank on the old church pew at the back door, looking up to the long-drop, or awkward on the worn sofa in the combined kitchen and sitting room.

'He'll come down there?'

'No,' said Penny. 'We'll come up to Christchurch closer to the hearing.'

Ben would see his parents together for the first time in a long while. Despite everything, Theo found that thought surprisingly positive. The boy was the one most at risk, and not aware of it, least able to influence an outcome. His image came up in Theo's mind with surprising ease: the dark hair with the gloss of childhood, the smooth, trusting face unmarked by life, the utter relaxation of limbs when in repose.

And the parson had been called off. No need for domestic espionage now. He would have submitted a hefty fees claim to his American client. Maybe one of the items was for recompense because of a line of duty scuffle in a darkened Christchurch carpark. Another may have been for damage to his shoes in the coal shaft at Mount Somers. The parson would close a file on Penny and Theo, and take a professional interest in the less high-profile troubles of some other poor bastards.

Theo heard nothing from Penny, or Zack, before the eighteenth, but he made the necessary application to the court to attend as an accredited journalist.

The morning of the hearing was a brooding one of low, rolling cloud and occasional drifts of fine rain. The city was nondescript and hunkered down. At the entrance to the court Theo saw a television crew that had been denied permission to film inside, and was waiting for shots of the Maine-Kings and comments as well. The frontperson was a young woman wearing an ankle-length blue coat embroidered with flowers; the two others were males in jeans and jackets. The lawyers they stalked were uniform in dark, well-cut suits. Such antithesis between media and the law is a conscious assertion on both sides.

Theo had to sign in, show photo ID, and was given a lapel sticker that had 'Media' written on it in green felt pen. The surroundings and proceedings were less formal than other courts he'd experienced, but still subdued, and rather solemn. Zack was there to represent Penny, a second lawyer for Erskine, and a third specifically to act in Ben's best interests. Theo couldn't see the boy anywhere in court: some caregiver must have been entertaining him while his happiness was in the balance.

It was all over in not much more than half an hour. The judge had decided from the documents filed that he would order a discharge of the warrant, and support the Maine-Kings' application for a rehearing of custody matters in the Californian court. He wanted just to have them before him, to have the surety of their own statements and obvious agreement to reach a compromise. Penny, Erskine and the lawyers sat only a short distance from Theo, but they gave no sign of recognition, even when the judge commented on the high publicity caused by Penny's flight. It seemed to Theo that Erskine was sensitive to the American stereotype, and made special efforts to be attentive and obliging, yet without obsequiousness. Even his voice was consciously subdued, and he sat quite still for most of the time. It wasn't that he lacked confidence, but rather that he was resolved to do everything he could that would restore his son to him.

Theo had a strong sense of exclusion, and it arose from more than the formal grouping, or the judicious concealment of his involvement with Penny. The causes of the estrangement between Penny and Erskine had nothing to do with Theo, yet sitting there in a public forum he felt both pity for their son, and an odd guilt for his own intention to supplant Ben's father. Who could know what it meant to a child to lose a parent from the family?

And Penny had rejoined the free population: she was no longer alone, no longer reliant on Theo as her only visitor and champion. Outside the courtroom, Theo watched the small group of journalists and television people gather round Penny, her husband and Zack, heard her answer clearly that she regretted the flight from California, heard Erskine tactfully admitting to some insensitivity, heard the three of them agree that Ben's welfare was the central issue. Yes, it was all a long way from Drybread and what had begun for Theo and Penny there. Back in society, she was open to the persuasion of convention once again.

28

Over the following two days, Theo heard nothing from Penny, so in the second evening he rang Zack at home. 'Do you know where Penny's staying here?' he said casually after some general chat. Zack thought he had a number in his briefcase, and excused himself to go in search of it. Theo could hear Zack's progress through the house, and the voice of one of his daughters asking how long he was going to be on the line.

'Not long, sweetheart,' he said, then, 'Okay, Theo, I've got it now.' His daughter was amused at something, and the warmth of her laughter made Theo aware of the silence in his own house.

When he rang Penny, she said she'd been going to call, that the hearing had gone well enough, though there were new developments. She said she wanted to see him, but her voice was subdued. 'I'd like that,' Theo said. 'Where are you staying?'

'We're in a hotel.'

'Why don't you bring Ben round here tomorrow, and I'll take some time off work?'

'Maybe it would be better if you and I meet somewhere in town,' she said.

He knew right then that something important had changed, some process of withdrawal had begun, although he didn't admit it to himself. He felt that slight constriction of breathing, that sense of colour leaching from the world, which come as premonitions of disappointment. 'Sure,' he said, 'sure, okay. You name a place.' The thing is to soak up punishment, isn't it, and stay standing.

The café was quite close to the Bridge of Remembrance. They sat outside with glass baffles between them and the traffic, coats between them and the cool breeze, and awkwardness between them as individuals. It was city Penny who met him, not easy Penny of the sod house at Drybread. She wore make-up, medium-heel black shoes, her hair was loose almost to her shoulders. Her teeth were as white and perfect as ever, and for the first time in his experience she wore jewellery: a heavy gold chain, a large diamond solitaire, and beside it a plain gold band. It was city and winter Penny, but she still had the brown, country skin of Central Otago.

'I've decided to go back to California almost straight away,' she said. 'Judge Weallans says it's the best thing to do in terms of showing respect for the court there and a final outcome. He's going write a letter to the judge and give a summary of what happened here.'

The sense of intimacy can be lost so quickly and absolutely. It wasn't so much that they had kissed at

Drybread, stroked each other, that she had smoothed sweat from Theo's face, taken his cock in her mouth, and he had tongued her nipples. It was more that each of them had been allowed to feel valued in the life of the other: slipped beneath the barrier with which individuals hold back the world. And here she was, telling him of her new plans, and in a way she hoped wouldn't be unduly ungrateful, or hurtful. No, she told him, it wasn't really a reconciliation, and she and Erskine would probably live apart. But Ben had to be safeguarded, have the opportunities he deserved.

'But Erskine agreed to give you money, plenty of money,' Theo said.

She said a child needed more than money, and that Erskine and she had to take greater responsibility. 'I can't just please myself, Theo,' she said.

'You worked all this out at Drybread?'

'Pretty much,' she said.

'I thought you were going to stay here, that we'd keep on seeing each other. Jesus, have you moved on.'

'I'm sorry. My life's been such a mess. I shouldn't have gone back to Drybread with Ben, but I had nowhere else. I went mad there, thinking about what I'd done, being cooped up and worrying about Ben, worrying about the court order. Raving mad some days. Sometimes you make a decision that tips you into a headlong slide which you can't seem to recover from. You just keep going down, down, past people, without making contact.'

'I thought we were making contact. I took it all seriously: took it to heart you could say.' The air was thinning, yielding less oxygen. Subtle changes in everything he could see gave a semblance of indifference.

'You were the only one I had. You were the only one

I trusted. The only one who really helped.'

A Chinese girl at the next table was talking to her Chinese boyfriend about buying a present: evidently it was important that the gift be exchangeable. Her accent was completely New Zealand. This is how it is at a crisis point in life. Something is collapsing, roads to travel are being closed off, expectation is revealed as absurdity, and around you the world presses on regardless with talk of footwear sizes, the groin injury of a sports star, and the formation of a tsunami watch organisation by Grey Power in coastal communities. Misfortune is the corrective that teaches you your place in the world.

What was the point of dragging it out with Penny, forcing her to give some explanation for deciding her own life, to make an apology that wouldn't assuage his own hurt? He'd been there before, talking with Stella as their marriage foundered, and found no relief in it. Those sudden changes others make in their lives, as if something has been stretched too far, then snaps, can never be reversed. 'Well, I hope it works out for you,' he said.

'Don't be like that,' Penny said. Her face screwed up a little, as if the traffic noise had suddenly intensified, or the wind had blown grit into her eyes.

'I really do hope so. I know it must have been terrible when the custody thing went against you, and you had to come back home and hide out without friends, or much money, or anything. I just had this feeling that perhaps there was something for us, you know. We met in the middle of all that grimness, and yet it felt special.'

'I did too, but all the uncertainty, the things that were going wrong. Christ, I don't know. Maybe if we hadn't been at Drybread it would've been different, but there wasn't anywhere else. I'm not good with men, Theo, for reasons that don't matter now. It's not as easy for me as it is for other women.'

Although Penny still sat there, full size, he had a sense of her receding, losing the lustre which made her so different from the people who talked and walked around them. Ben was with his father he assumed, and she'd go back to them after talking to Theo.

'Anyway,' said Penny, 'I wanted to tell you this now, as soon as I got it straight myself. And I want us to talk again before I go. I think that's really important, because everything's happening quickly, racing ahead. I've got to get back, but I promise I'll ring soon.' The promise relieved her, relieved them both, of any need to kiss, or touch each other: any need to cope with the occasion as the final time they'd see each other. So she didn't touch him, but passed so close that Theo felt the faint disturbance she caused in the air.

He was to pass that café by the Bridge of Remembrance quite often: recognise precisely where they'd been sitting, recall the Chinese New Zealand girl talking of gifts, and Penny still with the tan from Drybread and dressed up for the winter city. That's how it is when you live in the same place for much of your life. Tableaux from the past form in school assembly halls, hospital corridors, concrete block motels, bus shelters and restaurants. He'd pass a two-storeyed house inhabited by strangers, and have in his mind for an instant the view from the top, east bedroom in which a colleague lay dying. Spring, and his eyes would drift from the decline within, to the massed, red rhododendron flowers that bordered the unmown lawn, and the pulse of sunset beyond. He'd read of the desecration of a park monument, and be transported to a night tryst there so long ago that the girl's name was lost, and only the fragrance of her dark hair remained. In the backyard next to his own he saw always, when he glanced over, the sobbing and obscured figure of the fat woman who used to live there. She was struggling to peg a sheet up in the wind, and her rotund body was modelled loosely by the flapping fabric, just her gumboots visible beneath. He'd called out to ask if she was okay. She'd remained hidden, her rubber toes lifting, but after a pause to gain control of her voice she said, 'I'm at a loss, but thank you for your concern.' Such formality and such pain. The place you live in accumulates as a collage of experience, and the selection isn't always comforting.

When Theo got back to the office, Nicholas told him the editor wanted to see him. The editor wasn't a vain man, though he always took care to comb his thin hair evenly across his pate whenever he'd been outside. His office was large, but not impressive, strewn with books, folders and papers that he beat back from his desk with desperate energy. He told Theo that Anna was leaving to run a women's sports and fitness magazine, and that he wanted him to be chief reporter. The first piece of information wasn't a surprise. 'Don't pass it up this time, Theo,' the editor said. 'I promise you'll have time to do some feature stories that take your fancy. Okay? The work on the Maine-King custody thing – first rate. Absolutely first rate.'

It was a nice irony: a day earlier Theo would have accepted the job to provide additional security for Penny, Ben and himself. Maybe instead it would become a means of filling up his time.

'Take a day or two to think it over anyway, but keep it to yourself in the meantime,' said the editor. 'I think you're the man for the job. I really do. You've got a lot of support here, and I think you could pump up the administrative side of the position.'

'No, I wasn't asked,' said Nicholas when Theo went back out to the desks by the window. 'I'm too old, lack obsequious tact. You should take it though, if only to stop some useless fart here getting it, or worse, some useless fart from another paper.'

'I've had a bugger of a day, Nick.'

'Isn't life a bugger all round,' he said. 'Sometimes you eat the bear, sometimes the bear eats you.' He turned away from his screen and gave Theo more attention. 'It's Penny Maine-King, right?'

'Yeah. She won't come back after the Californian court hearing. They're going to patch up something for the boy's sake, so that's it for Penny and me, I reckon.'

'Jesus,' said Nicholas. 'It was something serious for you, I know. But so much was hanging, undecided. So much pressure and agony, and now she just wants some respite I suppose, and to know the kid's okay.'

'I suppose so, but what's good news for every other bugger is a real slap for me. No, no. I don't mean that about Penny. It wasn't just convenience and calculation. But Christ, she's just through the worst of it, and we could've spent a lot more time together. Just when things seem to be coming right is when old Murphy puts the boot in.'

'Why don't we go out tonight?' said Nicholas. 'It can either be a celebration for promotion, or a commiseration. I suppose one thing is that you got a bloody good story out of the whole business.' It wasn't a very convincing effort to staunch emotion, and he briefly gripped Theo's arm above the elbow.

'Yeah, great,' said Theo.

No matter how much you tidy things away in your mind, life continues to make its own links, mostly unwelcome, but sometimes surprisingly cathartic. Close to the Thai restaurant where Nicholas and Theo parked independently that night Theo recognised the parson's Honda Civic, its maroon gloss glittering under the streetlights, and the chrome tow-bar knob a luminous mushroom. He stood close to the Honda's flank and scarred it with his door key. He could feel the metal edge getting well into the paint, and coughed to cover the sound. He moved to the petrol flap and made a satisfactory gouge there. That's a place proud car owners check often, fearful of careless, or malicious, damage. The parson was just the man to ensure he always filled his own tank. Theo imagined him discovering the marks in the morning, even that night, and felt a tide of satisfaction. He imagined the parson's heavy face sag and the mouth turn down. Whatever job-related success he came from wouldn't be enough to sustain him, and if things hadn't gone well, Theo's actions would turn the screw. Yes, how petty it all was, and the pleasure of his vindictiveness was nothing to his general unhappiness. But there was satisfaction: some small retribution for the parson's attempt to abduct Ben, and his persistent appearance in a chapter of Theo's life that was rapidly losing appeal. A small pleasure, diminished by being fleeting and ignoble.

Later, at the table, Theo said that misfortune maybe turns you towards viciousness, and that he found spite more often in his own responses after any disappointment. Nicholas saw nothing unnatural in that at all, but claimed that rational people should curb the impulse, and that having murdered your aunt yesterday was no reason to cheat the butcher today. Each action should have its own moral justification. On another occasion Theo may have been interested in the point, but not with Penny's decision so raw. He ate and drank dutifully, rather than with enjoyment: he recognised the effort Nicholas was making to support him, but it wasn't enough. Maybe even within his friend's concern was the unacknowledged satisfaction that Theo's life wouldn't eclipse his own in an attainment of love.

'I interviewed a murderer once,' said Nicholas. 'I call him that because he admitted it and was convicted. Most insist they're innocent. He murdered a neighbour he'd been feuding with for forty-two years. It started when they were at school together and fought in the playground, continued when they drank and fought behind country dance halls, and played against each other in rural rugby teams, Catholic and Protestant. One seduced the other's wife in a musty committee room after a Scottish pipe band evening, and the other poisoned sheepdogs that strayed onto his property. The final argument was over a maimai possie – the guy I interviewed blew his neighbour's head to pieces with a twelve gauge Hollis.'

'I remember that. The guy went to the police straight afterwards.'

'Some reports made a good deal of such a violent end to such a trivial issue, but they missed the point: what happened was the culmination of forty-odd years of hatred. "That bastard always had it coming," that's what the murderer said to me. He said it was always going to end that way.'

'Nothing like a close-knit rural community,' said Theo.

'He told me it was something that had to be done, and he seemed a quiet enough, thoughtful guy. He had a damn good farm too.'

'Became obsessed, I suppose,' said Theo. He understood that Nicholas was trying to distract him but wondered what Penny would be doing; where she was; if Erskine was perhaps laying out a business plan for the future of their family. How absurd and flimsy Theo's hopes for Penny and himself had become.

'Exactly,' said Nicholas. 'Anyway, here's a toast to your promotion, and I'm really sorry it doesn't seem to be working out with Penny. Don't give up on it, though. Give it your best shot.'

29

Theo was watching a documentary on Bactrian camels when Melanie came round. The programme had a certain inconsequential fascination, and was pleasantly remote from his own life. He liked the sardonic droop nature had given to the camels' lips, and their worn, utilitarian tails.

The evening wasn't advanced, but at that time of year darkness had already come, and when he opened the door, Melanie's small, pale face, velveteen jacket and mass of hair caught the spilling light. 'Hi,' she said. 'Nick said I should check up on you, but bugger Nick, I'd made up my mind to call anyway. The phone's not the same, is it?'

They sat on the sofa. 'I was wondering if I preferred one hump or two,' said Theo.

'Funny,' said Melanie.

'So what do you know?' said Theo. He surprised himself with the pleasure her visit gave him, though he hadn't thought of her for days.

'I know you've been offered the chief reporter's job. Congratulations. I know things haven't worked out for you with Penny Maine-King, right? I'm sorry about that. We can talk about any of those things, we can sit and watch the camels, or we can have a drink, and bitch about the usual journo stuff.'

Theo switched off the camels. He said he'd decided to accept the job as long as Nicholas was willing to carry on as deputy chief reporter and actually accept some responsibility. He told Melanie he didn't feel like talking about Penny: it was all too fresh, too confused. 'In the morning I wake up feeling okay, but then I remember what's happened, and everything rolls in again.'

'You don't ever want to end up like Nick,' Melanie said. 'I know he's a good friend to you, but you realise that, don't you?'

They both knew that was something that needed to be said, but then set aside for elaboration at another time.

Melanie's romance with the architect neighbour hadn't worked out either. It was the daughters who were the sticking point – not that they weren't great kids in themselves, but that Robin put them first. It was understandable, even admirable, she said, but no basis for a marriage. His need was first a mother for them, rather than a wife for himself. No good, that, Melanie said: not the right motive for a marriage. He took her decision badly. The thing she'd noticed most since the split, wasn't the loss of his companionship, but the awkwardness created by their still being neighbours: mutual furtiveness in their respective sections, and the reluctance to speak, or acknowledge each other. 'It's so confusing for the girls, too. They still want to come over and tell me about their lives. They say they miss the treats I used to make for them. How do you explain these things to kids.'

'I'm sorry,' said Theo, but he wasn't. He could have said he'd never taken to Robin – thought him a self-satisfied prick in fact – but such honesty after the event would only highlight the earlier hypocrisy. He did wish that he could see Penny's loss with the same equanimity Melanie apparently felt about her break with the architect. There were obvious parallels: Penny with her son, and Robin Sellus with his daughters, and the outcomes for Melanie and Theo. No one else, of course, could feel as sharply and poignantly as he did himself; no one else could have so much at stake, or have lost a relationship with the possibility of such extraordinary and exemplary completeness. Stella had said one of his faults was selfishness, and for maybe the first time Theo admitted to himself the truth of the charge.

'Still, better that we made the decision now,' said Melanie. 'For us both. I think his pride's hurt as much as anything. I'm not expecting you to talk about Penny and what happened. Guys don't seem to find it helps much, right? And you've never been much of a one for crying on shoulders.'

'But it's really good of you to come round,' said Theo. Even with her own problems, Melanie had come to give some support. Empathy is perhaps a more natural and persistent quality in women.

'We've both taken a bit of a pounding. On the rebound and all that. Let's just keep in touch casually for a while. Phone when we can, meet with the others for a Friday drink. You know? There's no one I think of more as a friend than you. Nobody's more important to me.'

'Me too. Yeah, you're probably right.'

'You're an okay guy, Theo. You don't have to do things wrong for them not to work out. That's something we need to remember. Penny's had to make one of those hard choices, I suppose. Anyway, I'm going to leave you with the camels, if they're still on. I just wanted to come and make sure you were okay.'

Melanie sat forward on the sofa in preparation for leaving. She gave her springy hair several customary and ineffectual pats.

'I read your pieces on eating habits and on changing attitudes to debt,' said Theo, to show he was interested in what she did, and not overpowered by his experience with Penny. He didn't want to be pitied.

'I quite enjoyed doing it. Those appalling credit card figures – mind-boggling what some people said.'

'I did this story once about a Lyttelton woman who won several hundred thousand in the lottery,' said Theo. 'She was a radiologist and unmarried. She had her own house and had always been responsible with money, but the win seemed to set her off somehow. She decided to be a poet, and a whole bunch of pseudo literati and artistic wankers battened onto her until the money was gone on parties and vanity publishing. The house too. The friends moved on, of course, and she went back to radiology. About a year later she won an even bigger prize in an Australian lottery, bought a house in Merivale and invested the rest.'

'I remember that story,' said Melanie. 'What are the chances, eh?'

'Just sometimes life plays out a morality tale, doesn't it? She was a great person to interview – she really appreciated the humour of it all. She knew she'd fluked an almost impossible recovery, and made the most of it.'

'It's a good story, but I would have enjoyed it more if she'd squandered the second lot of money exactly as she did with the first.'

'That's been done too,' said Theo.

Even as he talked it occurred to him that, despite Melanie's warning, he was becoming more and more like Nicholas: packaging his life and experience into anecdotes which deflected his own attention and that of others. He didn't give a damn for the Lyttelton woman. He yearned to offer something sincere and revelatory to Melanie, something close and consoling concerning their disappointments, but all he found was banal and second-hand commentary. He wanted her to know that he admired her generosity and friendship, that he sympathised with her in an emotional setback, but instead he continued to talk of unlikely coincidences in life, and windfalls against the odds.

Melanie put on her black, velveteen jacket and gave him a brief kiss on the mouth. Theo walked out to the roadway with her, then watched until she reached her car. Three cats crouched close together on the grassed verge, waiting to regain their privacy. A cool breeze moved in the darkness. She was there for him, supportive, even though she and Robin Sellus didn't go to each other's homes any more, and only his daughters came, and would visit less and less as they realised that things had changed. Melanie was having a bad time of it, yet she was still concerned for Theo. Theo hadn't given a bugger for anyone except Penny, Ben and himself.

Melanie's visit didn't leave Theo content, or resigned.

He'd had several whiskies before she came, and he settled before the television with the bottle when she'd gone. Sustained and solitary drinking to the point of inebriation wasn't a habit with him, but then what was the point of being sensible when life was otherwise? The programmes continued upon the screen, but Theo paid little attention. His unhappiness inclined him to anger, and that was intensified by alcohol. He released the bitterness by directing it at someone whose responsibility was specious, but that's one of the conveniences of becoming drunk. What a bastard Robin Sellus was. How badly he'd treated Melanie. And nothing would happen, would it, because Melanie was too reasonable. A self-satisfied wanker of a guy who'd hurt someone so much his superior in every way. Action was needed on her behalf. That's what friends were for, weren't they? And Theo nodded at the screen in his own support, convincing himself that his concern for Melanie obliged him to be her champion. He found the phone book and the architect's number.

'Robin Sellus speaking.'

'What sort of a bastard treats a woman like Melanie in that way?' said Theo.

'Who is this?' The words were very clipped, deliberate.

'I say what sort of a bastard takes up with a woman just so she can look after his kids? It's not on, and she deserved better than you.' Theo was leaning down as he spoke, the mobile phone in one hand, with the other trying to reach the remote to turn off the television. Stooping in that way wasn't pleasant with so many drinks on board. His head seemed to enlarge painfully with each pulse of blood.

'Who the hell are you, and what business is it of yours?'

'I've been watching you,' said Theo. 'I've been watching you and I've got you sussed. A jumped up bloody draughtsman who's taken advantage of Melanie's sympathy for your kids.' Theo felt rather better when he was sitting on the sofa again.

'You're that guy on the other side, aren't you. I know you. The neighbour on the other side that Melanie's told me about, who can't keep his nose out. Mellhop, or Bellhop, or something. You need to mind your own business.'

'I've been watching you,' said Theo. He considered the possibilities created by Robin Sellus's mistaken identification. 'You haven't heard the last of this, you know. We're not going to let you get away with, ah, with treating Melanie like this.'

'You're drunk,' said Sellus triumphantly. 'I don't have to listen to your nonsense. I'll ring the police if you bother me any more.'

'I should come over right now and sort you out,' said Theo. 'I will – that's what I'll do. And you can bet you'll know all about it when I get there.' He took another swallow of whisky, but his stomach rebelled and his eyes hurt if he moved them. Abruptly the conversation no longer interested him: accusing Sellus and allowing a second neighbour of Melanie's to be falsely impugned weren't important. He wanted to rest. He interrupted the architect's angry reply to his threat by coming up with what seemed to him a very original and appropriate remark. 'I've been watching you,' he said slyly, and cut the call.

All he wanted to do was sit quietly back with his eyes closed. It would've been better if the light was out. Was the necessary movement beyond him? With an effort he reached the switch and returned heavily to the sofa. He wasn't aware of relaxing his grip, but he heard the whisky glass thump on the carpet and give a slight bounce. Each time Theo breathed out he made a small noise, something between a sigh and a groan, which was soothing and seemed to release the pain from his head. He fell asleep there finally, alone in the dim room with the flickering colours from the television screen playing on his face.

Did he dream? Perhaps a dream of sitting in the Mack while his father drove the unsealed country roads, the heat coming through from the engine, and his father's hand resting on the smooth, black top of the gear change with the fingers vibrating as some of the abundant torque came back through the lever. Did he dream? Perhaps a dream of first wearing his mid-calf, soft leather coat as he walked hand in hand with Stella into a London art gallery. Did he dream? Perhaps a dream of the Dunstan hills above Drybread and ascending there with a happy, loved woman who'd been able to escape the abuse of her girlhood. Did he dream? Perhaps a dream of being quite different from the man he was, with high purpose and some nobility of spirit. Did he dream? Does a sad drunk dream?

30

There was a farewell for Anna at the paper: Theo organised it, and gave a speech. He exaggerated one or two of the prevailing stories about her for effect, as is expected on such occasions. Anna took it well, and responded in kind when congratulating him on becoming her replacement. She said she'd been over him in more ways than one. There was a lot of laughter and goodwill during the night, and although Theo joined in, everything seemed somewhat reduced and at remove. In the midst of conversations with his colleagues, his mind slipped away to concern itself with the loss of Penny, and he found himself nonplussed when some response was required of him. Incompetent Michael kept coming up to tell him mediocre dirty jokes, and, under the guise of congratulation, insinuating that Anna was better gone. Theo was exasperated and also embarrassed, because one of his first jobs as chief reporter would be to recommend that Michael be sacked.

Late at night, when the celebration was winding down, when the editor and his broad-beamed wife had already left, when the grand swirl of the party was past its peak, and those people remaining had subsided into smaller, seated groups, Anna and Theo found an opportunity to talk together by the buffet slide. Three catering women washed dishes close at hand, but were engrossed with their own conversation. Michael, wearing a green smock donned during some nonsense earlier in the evening, came open mouthed towards Theo and Anna to distract them from friendship by yet another sexual cliché.

'Not now, Mike,' said Theo.

'Bugger off,' said Anna.

Michael tossed up his hands in mock horror and acquiescence, and wandered away across the reception room.

'I'm glad it's you taking over,' Anna said. 'You've got those gut instincts a journo needs.'

'Thanks.'

'Do you think I've made a silly move?'

'No, I admire you for having a go. You'll make a bloody good mag editor. You can build a team around you, and not everybody's got that sort of personality.' Theo meant what he said, and wished he'd shown his regard more before then. Anna was a Girl Guide a lot of the time, but she was professional and a good colleague.

'I know it's not working out with Penny Maine-King,' she said. 'Sorry about that.'

'Yeah, well, that's about par for the course for me, isn't it.'

Why should he be surprised that Anna knew? Everyone would. There was a process of osmosis by which your personal life became the mundane gossip of the workplace.

'I know it's trite to say it, Theo, but you'll find the right person. I hope it's Penny, but if not, things will work out in time.'

'You think I should pump it up?' said Theo to deflect concern.

'That's something you'll have to watch – making fun of him.' She laughed though, for she was no longer duty bound to be scrupulously loyal to the editor, and the freedom of it, and the relaxation and wine of the night, flushed her normally pale face just a little, and in an odd, asexual expression of intimacy she leaned her warm forehead on Theo's for a moment, then straightened.

'Yeah, I know. I've got to become a good boy, and let Nick have all the renegade fun,' said Theo.

'You'll do okay,' she said. 'You'll do just fine.'

Theo spent the next few work days arranging the chief reporter's office in the way he wanted, and drawing up a strategic plan which involved a professional development session with each of the reporting staff and the reallocation of rounds. Also he devised a role for Nicholas as deputy which was no longer nominal and took into consideration both his abilities and his idiosyncrasies. All of that kept the surface of his mind busy during working hours, and helped him to sleep at night.

It wasn't at all what he'd hoped for, however, and often he found himself suddenly wound down, quite still, staring at some object as if it had assumed the power of fetish – the outside tap and hose fitting perhaps, a donation envelope to combat dyslexia, the caps lock button on his keyboard, a small, pale stone embedded in the tread of a colleague's sneaker. He'd reached for too much: he'd allowed his prescription for happiness to outgrow what he deserved. He'd forgotten life's natural drive towards disappointment.

Penny rang to say they were returning to America very soon, and she wanted to talk to him before then. Maybe they could meet at the same place by the Bridge of Remembrance? But Theo didn't want to meet there, so they arranged to see each other at ten thirty the next morning at the coffee shop in the art gallery. There were so many other things he'd hoped to say to her: instead their conversation had retreated to appointment times. Her voice still had power to move him, although he knew every conversation was now part of the calculated retreat they were making from each other.

He was there before her, and sat looking through the ceiling to floor glass at the old university buildings on the opposite corner. He had marched from there in gown and hood to his graduation, years ago. Beverley Limm was in front of him and kept complaining that the pinned weight of the pink and grey academic hood was pulling up the top of her dress. The night of his graduation his mother and father had taken him to a hotel for a self-conscious family celebration, and Theo, rather than being grateful, had hurried through it so he could join his friends at a party in Spreydon, where he spiked his right foot on a hedgehog while running barefoot and drunk through a garden overgrown with twitch and rank asparagus.

Theo and Penny could see each other for some time before she joined him; both were aware of this, but choosing not to make acknowledgement until they were together. Theo watched her cross the road from the bluestone buildings of the Arts Centre and come into the gallery. She looked even less like Drybread Penny than at their last meeting. She wore a winter skirt and boots, a jacket with panels of coloured leather. Her pale hair was up and her lipstick on. She was almost beautiful, he realised with a jolt. She was almost beautiful, but she wasn't Drybread Penny, and that made the failure of his hopes the greater. She was Californian Penny, with the stability of Erskine's money and resources behind her again, and free to move about the city.

'I wanted to make a better effort to thank you,' she said after she sat down. 'I guess we were pretty wound up last time. I felt I didn't say the things I wanted to, and don't know if I can now. It all seems completely bloody selfish to you, I suppose.'

'I got caught on the hop. I thought something was happening that was good for us both, but there you go.'

'It wasn't natural down there at Drybread, though, Theo. I couldn't think how things might end. I'd taken off from Erskine in a panic, and finished up in a place that had some bloody awful memories. You were just about the one good thing for me – you and Ben.'

'I know it didn't go well that last time in the bach,' said Theo, 'but I thought that didn't matter. It had to do with Ben being there and stuff like that – you being under all that pressure.'

'It wouldn't be any different anywhere else. I can't think of you in the way you do me,' said Penny.

'Do men and women ever think of each other in the same way?'

'But I don't think of men in the way other women do either.'

'It wasn't the right time, I realise that now,' said Theo, 'but then we never seemed to have enough time together.'

'No, it's not that. Sex doesn't work for me the way it does for other people. I don't want to go on about it. My father fucked up that part of my life for me, you see. That's it really. He fucked me more completely than either of us could possibly realise at the time. It's ugly to say, ugly then and ugly still. It's no good when you hate the people you love, Theo. I'm not going to unload all my hang-ups on you, but I wanted you to know, even if you can never understand, that's all.' Penny's face had a slight agitation of pain as she forced herself to speak, but she continued to look directly at Theo.

'Christ, I'm sorry. What a bastard he must have been.'

'I owe it to you to talk about it I suppose, but I just can't. I've tried professionally, and even that didn't help. Stuff like that isn't fixed by sympathy or counselling or medication. Not for me, anyway. Nobody wants to know those things – even when you've experienced it you don't want to know. It's like some tumour, or excrescence, which you're ashamed of even though it's invisible. There's just part of your emotional response that doesn't work properly afterwards.'

'You know for me it isn't just about shagging. We've never even done it properly, for Christ's sake. There's more than that, and that's what I hoped for.' Love was the word Theo should have used, but he couldn't get it out. A word too much vaunted by puffery, and heavily taxed in everyday conversation. He'd never used it to Penny when there were hopes of the thing itself between them, and it wouldn't serve once love was unattainable.

'It's all in the bundle, though,' Penny said. 'What it comes down to for me, is Ben. I won't jeopardise his growing up for anything, and Erskine realises that too, now. He's the real thing left between us, and that's the most important tie I've got. The love you have for a child is completely untainted by whatever else has gone wrong.'

'Not much of a marriage,' said Theo, but he had no wish to argue against the rights of a little kid.

'But that's what I'm saying. I can't have much of a marriage, and that was decided years ago by my father.'

'Christ, what a mess.'

'So don't be too angry, okay?' She put out her hand tentatively, so that just the fingertip rested briefly on his wrist.

Where did you take a conversation after that? They didn't talk at all for a while, but fiddled with their coffee cups, and watched the people outside. And talk continued at tables around them, some laughter as well. Was there any reason however to think that Penny's and Theo's concerns were of more significance than those of others present? The suited man by himself may have just been made redundant, though he kept his hand steady; the thin woman behind may have been told she would never conceive a child, the student with shiny hair and small hands could be in possession of a letter offering her a place at Cambridge, and so the prospect of a marvellous career.

'I want you to have something,' said Penny. She took some sheets of paper from her bag, folded like an essay assignment, and put them in front of him. 'Zack drew them up for me. All you have to do is sign, and the bach in Central is yours. For all the help, and the newspaper articles especially. Well no, for the personal support especially. I want to forget that time, but not you.' Theo told her she didn't have to give him anything, didn't have to feel guilty. 'It's not that,' she said. 'I won't be going back there. It's not worth that much anyway. It's never been a good place for me, but I hope it'll be different for you. You like it there, I know. You like those places unpopular with most other people.' She put two identical and old-fashioned keys on the table. 'Maybe you can have a spell from your work there sometimes,' she said. 'Do some of the walks too.'

'I don't know. You don't owe me anything at all. What about Ben and Erskine?' Would he ever want to go to the place now she was leaving it?

'Erskine doesn't give a stuff. He's not interested in anything here. I think you'd get something from Drybread, and anyway it'll just go back and back if no one ever goes there. Even a place like that needs some basic care.'

'What's going to happen about your mother?' The lizards and frogs of the enclosed garden would be staring still, and old Mrs Bell equally static. On the broad paths and through the wide doors of the Malahide Home, the Zimmer frames and wheelchairs would be quietly circulating, the population migrating to the dining hall, then back to their beds and familiar chairs.

'We've talked a bit about that. Probably we'll bring her over to the States later. She'll never know the difference, and I'll be able to look after her more.'

'And you'll never be back, I suppose.'

'Who knows? But there's no reason we can't keep in touch if you want to. Erskine wouldn't see anything odd in that. If you want to we can be friends. I don't have any hang-ups about friends the way I do about lovers. Jesus, I'm almost normal in so many ways.' She laughed briefly to mitigate her tone of voice.

Theo wondered how he could ever have expected any other outcome. Drybread had been apart from the forces of the world and the logic which prevailed elsewhere. Despite the disappointment, and the anger that arose from disappointment and his powerlessness, he had never admired her more. 'Fuck,' he said softly.

'I wouldn't have got through it without you. I would've gone under. I know that now,' she said. Making a v of her thumb and forefinger, she pushed at one side of her heavy hair. 'I feel something's been tamed within me somehow because of all this.'

'Tamed?'

'Well, not tamed. I mean realising that you can do one impulsive thing, justifiable or not, and everything else starts to unravel. You know? You make one sudden shift and the world tilts. I don't want anything to tilt for Ben, and I don't think Erskine does either.'

Theo had no argument against her that wasn't entirely selfish, so he didn't try. He had for a moment the unfamiliar feeling that he was going to cry, but he drew his breath with deliberate regularity, and focused on the people in the foyer of the gallery not far away. 'I want the best for you and Ben despite what's happened,' he said.

'I know you do,' Penny said.

'It was absolutely bloody serious for me.'

'I know that too.'

They went out together, and parted without kissing at the lights on the busy corner. To suffer is part of growing up, but you become fully adult only when you have caused suffering in others. Theo watched her walk away: tall, blonde, small bosomed, in her skirt and boots, and the jacket with the bright leather panels of green, yellow and blue. There was nothing to show she was fucked up, and nothing to show of her resolution despite that.

31

Theo didn't see Penny again before she returned to the States with Erskine and Ben, and he wrote no more articles about her. It wasn't pique, just the feeling that for him the story had ended, and subsequent events were better told by others. Over a month later, however, he received an email from Penny in which she said the Californian court had withdrawn the custody orders because of formal reconciliation. Ben was settled and happy. She didn't say the same about herself and Erskine, but then she wouldn't, not to Theo, even if it were so. Drybread she did mention, hoping that he would go up there soon, in winter. 'It's even quieter in winter,' she wrote. 'I hope you have some good times, summer and winter. The bach is a bit of a dump, but the country around is fantastic. I like to think it'll be a happier place for you than me. One of the things I'll never forget is the calls of the parries flying up and down the gully.'

He did decide to go down in winter and asked Melanie to go with him, perhaps unconsciously seeking some shield from the memories that would be there. Dansey's Pass often had heavy snow at that time of the year, so Theo took the route through Oamaru and then up the Pigroot from Palmerston. It was a still, cold Sunday, with frost on the paddocks when they left Christchurch very early, and, hours later when they were heading for Ranfurly, still white in the strips protected by gorse hedges, shelter belts and inclines. There was snow on the tops of the Kakanuis and light skeins of mist draped in the steeper valleys. Melanie wasn't familiar with the landscape. 'Wait until we reach the Maniototo,' said Theo.

There the sky occupied more view than the land: an arc of cold blue, and the air not moving. There was hardly a car, and only occasional smoke ladders above the isolated farmhouses. The sun glinted on the ice of stock ponds close to the road, and the snow was splendid on the Dunstan Range and even heavier on the Hawkduns. Theo remembered Penny telling him that the Hawkduns lay across the prevailing weather. The horizon they made with the sky was as sharp edged as the fencepost shadows close at hand. 'You don't get the long view like this in Europe,' Theo said. 'The horizon fades out in a haze.'

'There's hardly any trees,' said Melanie.

'This was originally all tussock country, some of it up to the knees of men on horseback.' Theo imagined the sight it must have been: to break through into Central Otago and the Mackenzie Country, and find a sea of tussock stretching out swell after swell.

In the gully close to Drybread, the snow was on the ridge above the three old cottages, but not on the road itself. Theo parked by the great hedge, and they walked up to the sod house.

The long-shanked keys he'd been given by Penny were brown with a fine rust, but turned without difficulty. He still thought of it as Penny's house; perhaps he always would. Although he knew she was gone, there was just a moment when he went into the main room that he half expected to see her and Ben at the table, or the old sofa – her fair hair, and her son's dark hair and perfection of skin. How cold and still it was without them: the place quite different, inanimate, without the languid heat of summer and the presence of Penny and her boy.

Theo lit the open fire, and for a minute or so the smoke eddied out into the room because the chimney was cold and damp, but then the convection began and the flames leapt up. Melanie inspected the thickness of the original walls, then went into the single bedroom. 'It's tiny, isn't it,' she said, meaning the whole place. Beside the bed was a small, wooden locker with scratches, cigarette scorch marks and a candle stub in a crockery holder. The soft, buttoned mattress with a fading pattern of stripes sagged on the bed wire, and on the porous composite of the unpainted ceiling, water stains were outstretched like giant butterflies in brown outline. Theo remembered Ben sleeping there, and Penny's expensive travelling cases against the wall on the marmalade lino.

So that Melanie wouldn't ask anything of him, wouldn't see his face, he went back into the main room, and when she came through he mentioned the black, wood-burning oven, and they talked about the difficulties of cooking on it. He took her to the back door and pointed out the long-drop on the slope, emphasising with apparent zest how primitive it all was. And as he talked he noticed the leaves and beetle cases windswept and compacted into the corners of the church pew on which he'd sat on his summer visits while he talked with Penny, and Ben played beside them. How can things be the same and so different at the one time? How can someone be the essential focus of a place, and yet that place remain intact when they've gone? How can you reconcile urgent and intense hope with the flat outcomes of reality?

Melanie and Theo didn't light the range, but sat by the open fire and ate the picnic lunch she'd brought. The room grew warm quickly, and the noise of the fire was cheerful. The leather arms of the sofa were worn to the soft grey beneath the tanned outer skin, but the squabs were comfortable and Melanie and Theo sat close together there.

'How long was Penny here?' asked Melanie.

'Must have been over five months,' Theo said.

'Jesus. All that time without phone and power, no neighbours, and with a kid.'

'And cellphones don't work here,' he said.

'That reminds me. You didn't ring Robin and get stuck into him about me, did you? He reckoned it was Barry Mellhop on the other side, but that wouldn't be right.'

'Me?' said Theo. 'What was it all about?' And he had only a hazy recollection of being the culprit.

'Doesn't matter,' said Melanie. 'It must have been awful at times for Penny. But she's a strong person, isn't she. All of the stuff she's had going on, and yet look how she's left the place. It's pretty primitive, okay, but she hasn't left it grotty. I mean she's cleaned up, and not just shot through.'

It was a typical woman's observation. Theo hadn't thought of it, but Melanie was right. All that Penny had suffered there, and yet at the end she'd burnt rubbish, carted stuff away and left the bach in shabby and stark order. Maybe even then she'd decided to give it to Theo.

'When Mum died, I rented out her house for a while,' said Melanie. 'I didn't take to the landlord role much. There was one single mum with two kids. I felt sorry for her. She used to tell me the appalling story of her life, but then she took off owing me hundreds, and when I went into the house it just about made me sick. Her life was shit, and she was so self-obsessed and depressed that she didn't care about anybody or anything else. I reckon it even made her feel better to trash what she could of other people's things. There were maggots in the carpet, and tampons thrown into the long grass behind the garage. She'd sold off the curtains and most of Mum's appliances and cutlery. Mouldy pizza ends and chicken bones under the beds, scum in the shower, and a lot of the blue bench tiles were cracked. Poor Mum would've had a fit. No self-respect, no pride, you see.'

Theo did see. Penny had pride. He realised that, and admired it. So much more had been taken from her, demanded of her, than Melanie would ever realise, but she'd kept her pride, and her love for Ben. The world is opposed to pride, and equates it with vanity, yet pride is one of those trace elements needed for strength of character.

'Do you find it difficult to be here?' Melanie asked him, putting her hand on his near arm, and giving it a squeeze to show she meant the enquiry kindly.

'All the other times she was here. It just seems so bloody strange now she's not. This place and Penny are linked so closely in my mind, and yet now she's back in her flash home in Sacramento. Everything's just the same here, and yet utterly different.'

'But you understand why she's gone?' said Melanie.

'I suppose I do.'

'It's not you, you know.'

'She had a hell of a lot going on. It wasn't fair to expect anything really, but you do, don't you.'

'You don't have to tell me about that, Theo. But I think you've grown in a lot of ways through seeing what Penny went through, and by helping. You did damn well for her when she needed someone.'

'I like to think about the little boy, Ben. I like to think it's worked out in the best possible way for him.'

'That's the thing,' said Melanie, and her fingers closed on his arm again.

In the mid-afternoon they put the guard before the open fire and walked up the gully road. It was passable for cars for only a few hundred metres past the bach, and then became a runnelled, four-wheel-drive track which itself ended at a sluice pond at the top of the small valley. There the shingle mounds from the gold mining days were covered with gorse and broom, which had stock tracks like tunnels winding through. A walking track angled up the tussock ridge above, and when Theo and Melanie reached the ridgeline they could see thick snow lying not far above them, and below were the creek and gully, with the three small huts spaced down the road far away. As always when Theo had come, only Penny's had any sign of life, the smoke barely discernible, because the fire burned dry wood, and ascended almost vertically until it blurred and dissipated.

'It's lovely in its way,' said Melanie. 'Not touristy – no lakes or ski fields, no boutique wineries, no homestay farmhouses with horse treks thrown in. Maybe loneliness becomes a luxury in the end.' Theo said it was a pity the place was so far from Christchurch. 'You can get away from everything here, though,' said Melanie. 'You're bloody lucky.'

Penny hadn't been able to get away from everything here, however. For her the gully close to Drybread must have been a place she knew twice during her life, and at the very worst times. The ghosts would always be present for Penny, here and anywhere else she went. For Theo and Melanie it could be different. They were free to make their own emotional connection with the place.

'In the summer,' said Theo, 'we could climb some of these hills. Some view from there, eh? Next time we'll bring some stuff up and stay the night.'

'I'd like to do that. Everything's so clear, isn't it.' Her fuzzy hair undulated slightly in the cold air, and she was breathing through her mouth after the climb.

Theo understood that Drybread wasn't reliant on either Penny, or him, for its existence. Nature has its own sense of function and completion. Under high sun and full moon, in the ground haze of summer and the mantle of August snow, the three old baches would remain in the gully, paradise duck would fly the creek in pairs, and over that austere country the only sound would be the susurration of the wind, unencumbered by the experiences people may have had there.

How many times had he been there? How many times would he go there again? The visits seemed to coalesce with his recollection of them. The dry, gravel road, the sprawling macrocarpa hedge, the hut with a church pew at its back door, the plum tree and dunny on the slope behind. And the drift of faint background noise an unobstructed wind makes over a landscape. Little Ben looking upward with vulnerable appraisal, and Penny, almost Theo's own height, talking of that childhood place she had ended up in once more. Yes, it was the boy he found most pleasure in thinking about at the end. Ben with his natural mother and father, and having only a hazy recollection, or none at all, of Drybread and a stranger briefly in his mother's life.